MUSIC . . . AND MURDER

"Your kind of beauty, Eva, deserves far more recognition." The poet, having spoken, was all apologies for his tardy arrival, pointing to the bandage, and miming a fist fight.

"I was late, too," she told him. "You can imagine what we've been through."

"What's the matter? One of those famous tenors cancel the Gala?"

"Don't you know?"

"Know what?"

"Haven't you seen the papers?"

"No. I've been sitting in the goddamn VIP lounge on and off the flight, since seven this morning," he lied. "What's happening?"

"Get a drink first," she said, motioning for the waiter. Walter ordered a Löwenbräu. "The police found Petrov murdered in a cellar over near Ninth Avenue. And François Charron keeled over at a party at Mamma Guardino's."

"I'll be goddamned! It's a wonder you even showed up here. You didn't have to, Eva. I would have understood. I'll be double damned!" He tossed down what was left of the beer and ordered another round.

"I had to get away," Eva said. "The phones have been jammed. The police have been at me all day in my office, and I had to go to Mamma Guardino's, too. And Peter Camden asked me to represent the Gala committee at a press conference this afternoon. More like a wake! The whole thing is so sudden. So gruesome. They think it's a master plan. I think someone may be trying to sabotage our Gala."

GALA

Gala

William Lewis

PaperJacks LTD.

TORONTO   NEW YORK

PaperJacks

GALA

PaperJacks LTD.

330 STEELCASE RD. E., MARKHAM, ONT. L3R 2M1
210 FIFTH AVE., NEW YORK, N.Y. 10010

E. P. Dutton edition published 1987
PaperJacks edition published January 1989

10 9 8 7 6 5 4 3 2 1

ISBN 0-7701-0912-8
Printed in the USA

To the relative few, who genuinely honor a commitment to their art and who thank God for their gift, I dedicate this book.

The author would like to thank: Richard Marek, editor, mentor, and friend; Amy Mintzer; Richard Boehm, my literary agent; Alix Williamson, my publicity agent; and at the Met: Magda, Franco, Nina, Andy, Artie, Stanley, Arge, Florence, Victor, Charlie, Johnny, Bob, Shirley, Batyah, Doug, Rose, Winnie, Jim, Paul, Yvetta, and scores of singers and musicians; without whose help, support, and insights this book could not have been written.

CAST OF CHARACTERS

THE TENORS

The Frenchman	*François Charron*
The Italian	*Renato Corsini*
The German	*Horst Ludwig*
The Russian	*Sergei Petrov*
The American	*Walter Prince*

THE COMMITTEE

The Frenchwoman	*Mimi Charron*
The Hungarian Woman	*Katarina Tomassy-Conrad*
The Austrian Woman	*Eva Stein*
The Maestro	*Randolph Martinson*
The Oil Magnate	*Felix Conrad*
The General Manager	*Peter Camden*
His Wife	*Jill Camden*
The Inspector	*Lt. Theodore Pasing*
His Wife	*Lissette Pasing*
International Opera Divas	*Francesca Zandonai*
	Angelina Lombardini
The Physician	*Dr. Alberto Danieli*
The Music Publisher	*Boris Cherkassy*

Relatives, Friends, Government Officials, Townspeople, Good People, Bad People, Chorus, Orchestra, Stagehands, Supers, and Others

Act 1

Die Hölle Rache kocht in meinem herzen.
(Vengeance burns in my breast.)

—*Die Zauberflöte*
W. A. Mozart and
Emanuel Schikaneder

Scene 1

THE GENERAL MANAGER

Peter Camden waited patiently for one of the house phones to come available. He was tired, absorbed in thought, and in no particular rush to make his appointment. Moments earlier, after a long trip from John F. Kennedy airport, he had been discharged from a taxi at the Central Park South entrance of the Astor House. Even against the rush-hour traffic, the ride had been long and hot. Opera business had taken him to the West Coast and back in two days, and he still had a full agenda facing him this evening: the interview with Sir Rudolf Bing here at seven o'clock, and a meeting of his Gala committee in his office at the Metropolitan Opera scheduled for eight.

A portly, balding man in a peach-and-purple Hawaiian sports shirt backed away from the house phone he was holding and waddled his way across the lobby. Peter tried not to follow his progress, but he couldn't help thinking how out of place the man was. This was New York City, center of fashion and finance. And this was the Astor House, transient and sometimes permanent home of royalty, of celebrities, and of the rich. Peter always dressed in a suit—never sports coat and slacks—and four-in-hand tie when appearing for two minutes in public. He felt it was proper dress in New York City.

"Sir Rudolf Bing, please," he said to the anonymous voice on the house phone. "Ah, Sir Rudolf, I'm in the lobby."

Peter smiled at the familiar voice. That clipped Austrian accent of the former general manager of the Met was unmistakable. There had been three general managers in the interim between Sir Rudolf's retirement in 1972 and Peter's acceptance of the post in 1983: Goeran Gentele, Schuyler Chapin, and Anthony Bliss. But Peter considered Sir Rudolf the last word in operatic expertise.

Speaking of style, Sir Rudolf had set it for the esteemed house for twenty-two years. Peter Camden was beginning his fifth season—opening night was the twenty-first, in less than two weeks. There was much to learn from this vital octogenarian, who was descending by elevator from his lodgings of thirty-seven years.

Peter had requested a few minutes of Sir Rudolf's time before meeting with his committee, which was planning a fund-raising drive—one of his many projects to aid the Met's severe financial problems. The kick-off event was to be a Gala at the Met on the first of November. Often Peter had solicited advice from the former dean, a source of valuable information and insight into the machinery of opera, and always had been granted an enlightening interview. Peter hoped he was piloting the Metropolitan ship as well as Sir Rudolf had, knowing the two of them had a true knowledge of how intricate and time-consuming the position was.

"Mr. Camden," Sir Rudolf said, offering a hand without tensile strength, indicating to Peter the waning energies of

4

the once intensely vital administrator. "Will you walk me to my restaurant? It's on Fifty-seventh Street. Do you know it— the Fontana?"

"I do, Sir Rudolf." Peter hitched his arm in Bing's, and they set a slow pace toward the Fifty-eighth Street exit of the Astor House. Hotel staff and one or two guests greeted the knight, receiving a royal nod in return. Peter recognized the awe Sir Rudolf could still command. He had instilled not only respect but fear in the hearts of hundreds of singers, conductors, and stage directors who had been fortunate enough to have been chosen to perform at the hallowed house. Peter had no desire to emulate the man's philosophy, only his managerial techniques.

"You're planning a tenor Gala, Mr. Camden?" Always Mr. Camden, Peter thought; never Peter. The impersonal usage, keeping one at arm's length, was pure Germanic tradition, to which Sir Rudolf—even though a British subject and Knight of the Realm—unswervingly adhered.

"Yes, Sir Rudolf. We've contacted five of the world's most renowned tenors to participate in a fund-raising performance. We lost almost two million dollars last year, mostly on the spring tour. But I don't want to drop it. Opera belongs to the nation, not just New York. I mean to stir up interest again, get the ball rolling with this Gala. You know yourself what a service the Met does appearing live in the tour cities. But the Met is in grievous financial shape. We have to enlarge our audience, the interest across the country; and most importantly, we need contributors, sponsors, donors from everywhere in the land. This Gala must be the beginning of the snowball. Sir Rudolf, we have an emergency."

Peter had spoken in a rapid continuous flow, aware of Sir Rudolf's bright, observant eyes and crooked grin.

"Together? You're putting five tenors together? On the same stage on the same night?" The grin had grown to a wide smile, as Sir Rudolf preceded Peter into the Fontana di Trevi

5

restaurant, where a solicitous maître d' bowed a polite "*Buona sera, Signor Bing.*"

"Which tenors, Mr. Camden?" he asked.

Peter waited until they had been seated and a vodka gimlet had been placed before Sir Rudolf. "First, Sergei Petrov."

"I know him only from his marvelous recordings. I don't believe he's ever ventured out of Russia. How did you get him?"

"We have a committee member with entrée into exalted circles, especially in Washington. She managed to obtain a visa for Petrov from the State Department and a travel permit from the Ministry of Culture in Moscow."

"Congratulations," Sir Rudolf beamed. "That's truly a coup. I can't wait to hear him in person."

"François Charron will sing his Roméo," Peter continued.

"Which part?"

"The boudoir scene, followed by a segue into the tomb scene. The Juliette will be Angelina Lombardini—one of your favorites."

"Good! Go on."

"Horst Ludwig will sing Siegfried's death."

"*Götterdämmerung.*" Sir Rudolf's smile faded. "You have a problem there. Ludwig hates to sing in America. Only if the dollar is high against the deutsche mark will he come. And only if he is paid many dollars. He's anti everything American. A very bad boy!" Sir Rudolf was all seriousness now. He sipped his vodka gimlet.

"We have one American tenor, Sir Rudolf. Walter Prince."

"The cowboy! Is he any more reliable these days? I don't want to paint a somber picture, but you're dealing with volatile personalities."

Peter moved to the defense: "He seems to be most reliable, Sir Rudolf."

"You mean despite his ugly temper and personal over-indulgences—especially women." It was a statement, not a question.

6

"He's one hell of a tenor; and, yes, he's changed."

"That's what counts. The rest is up to us. We make the rules—you and me; and we set the style for the Met. One thing to never forget: the opera is a zoo, and the tenors are the King of Beasts. Expect the worst and you'll have it! Those singers wanted me on my knees. They almost succeeded." Sir Rudolf had smoked several cigarettes since they had been seated, as if to catch up on the years he had abstained, respecting the allergic sensitivities of his singers.

"I remember what Zinka Milanov said to me in our first years at the Met. 'Mr. Bing,' she said. 'I don't like tenors. They are very bad for your health.'" Sir Rudolf laughed at the remembrance. "Who else? You said five."

"Renato Corsini."

"*Mein Gott in Himmel!* Did I say trouble? I meant catastrophe." Sir Rudolf stubbed out his cigarette and fingered the Croix d'Honneur he wore in the left lapel of his black Charles Austen suit. "Do you want to ruin the Met? Renato Corsini has no human trace in him. He almost killed me. He will kill you. You must know how strongly politics affects the opera—not petty politics, but governments, factions of every country. Corsini's political. Why did he accept your invitation? He hasn't sung outside Italy in ten years. He's one of the richest, most powerful men in Italy. He's so immersed in the morass of political intrigue his father left him, he can hardly sing. I know him, Mr. Camden. Get rid of him."

"But he's the successor to Caruso!"

"Was, Mr. Camden. Was." Sir Rudolf pointed a finger straight at Peter's nose. "No matter how good your intentions, you've set a time bomb for yourself. If egos were TNT, Corsini and Ludwig could blow the opera house into the Hudson River. Cancel this idiotic Gala before it's too late."

The interview was over. Peter shook hands with Sir Rudolf, thanking him for his time and his advice. Then he fled, his expression a combination of determination and defiance. He thought, Maybe you couldn't handle it, Sir Rudolf; but I

7

can. I have no choice. The Met is in a lot worse straits than I can confide. And, if the Met ship continues to sink financially, I sink. I like my job, believe in it. I don't want to lose it. The public will pay to hear the tenors, so I'll put them on the same stage together and let the fireworks go off.

Scene 2

THE COMMITTEE

WEDNESDAY, SEPTEMBER 9, NEW YORK, NEW YORK

Peter's voice resonated through his spacious office. "The total cost to us will be one hundred thousand dollars for the house, maintenance, catering—meaning an open bar at intermissions—and all those menial, paltry necessities, which I'm certain needn't concern you unnecessarily.

"The good news is that I've just returned from San Francisco, where I met with H. Preston Hadley, always one of our most generous patrons, and he assured me our evening of tenor singing will have his full support. He will double the amount we raise, as his contribution, with the hope that one day the Met will tour as far west as San Francisco."

"It's perfect!" piped Mimi Charron, enjoying her first participation in mapping a Metropolitan Opera Gala. Her joy was delightful to the others. "I know the wife of Monsieur Hadley. She buys many originals from Juliette, my boutique. She has much money, no?"

"Yes, Madame Charron, the Hadleys have much money,

and they both love opera. We are fortunate to have them as donors. However, Mr. Hadley has grave misgivings about presenting so many superstars on one evening. He's evidently aware of the caprices of tenors and does not want his name linked to the project unless it is well planned and runs smoothly." For the moment, Peter omitted any reference to his interview with Sir Rudolf Bing and the misgivings inherent in that conversation. He poured himself another drink and acknowledged Eva Stein, who shyly raised her hand.

"Mr. Camden, Peter, we're deeply grateful to Mr. Hadley and all those interested in our project. Nothing bad will happen. We must work diligently to prevent errors or problems. Please assure Mr. Hadley we will protect his reputation as we sincerely promote ours."

Felix Conrad, the only Met board member on the committee, spoke with the manner of one well accustomed to such meetings. "I believe I speak for the entire board of directors when I say there is always the possibility of five last-minute cancellations when you're dealing with five tenors, which would leave us in a tremendous financial hole. But I myself realize what a potential success it could be, if we pull it off. I agree fully that the Met, as the principal operatic institution in this country, must continue to spread its influence throughout the land. The tour has always been successful in that respect; so let us reaffirm our commitment to it as soon as possible, and, as you suggest, make it pay. The ramifications are extensive: a Met without a tour seals the coffers, but a Met doing a service, bringing opera to the provinces, taps purses across the country, not only for the tour, but for the ongoing solvency of the mother house."

Caught up in the enthusiasm of the meeting, Felix had risen from one of the couches to voice his support. His tall, slim, Ivy League appearance—carefully tailored custom-made suit, button-down shirt collar, and understated tie—attested to his positions of leadership as chairman of the board and principal stockholder of Con Oil International and member of the board of the Metropolitan Opera, a definite asset to the Gala committee. Having spoken, Felix sat down again next to his wife, Katarina.

"Hadley's not the only one with reservations," Peter continued. "Rudolf Bing's against our plan. I met with him earlier this evening. He cites the tenor ego as the major problem."

"But aren't the positive factors enough to ignore the negative ones?" Katarina Tomassy-Conrad asked, her long blond hair twitching first one way and then the other as she embraced each committee member in turn with her flashing blue eyes.

"I'll tell you, my music-loving, tenor-loving friends, that this is the greatest moneymaking idea since Minsky got Sally Rand to drop her ostrich feathers." It was a shade bawdy coming from elegant Peter Camden, but the laughter generated reminded the committee what a sensational idea they had collectively birthed.

Peter rose from his high-backed maroon leather chair and walked to the bar inset in a niche on the wall opposite the windows that overlooked Damrosch Park. He poured from a decanter of sherry for the ladies seated: Mimi Charron, the former wife of the reigning French tenor, François Charron; Katarina Tomassy-Conrad, the talented translator of operas into English from any one of seven foreign languages and the wife of Felix Conrad; and the successful Broadway producer Eva Stein, a widow and ardent supporter of the opera. One year ago, Peter, after much deliberation, selected his committee from a long list of candidates known for their interest in the arts, and of widespread influence in the social community and outside the Metropolitan Opera's board of directors or administration. Peter wanted to incorporate new people with fresh ideas into his expansion program.

He handed out the sherry glasses. "Five of the world's greatest tenors on the same stage on the same evening doing a scene for which each is world-famous. To me, it seemed a surefire success, one year ago when we began. It still does. That's why I asked the four of you and Maestro Martinson to help me put the Gala together. Needless to say, it is a project dear to my heart—a dream, if you will—that's vital to the Metropolitan. I can't stress enough the importance of its success at this moment. And I thank you all for your dedication and your diligence this past year. Without your goodwill and your tireless effort, we could not have come this far."

Peter had grown attached to each member of this committee, and, ever the theater man, was thinking how he would cast the three ladies in the room if they were singers: Mimi Charron was most assuredly a pert, vivacious Zerbinetta, with her stylish short black hair, dark eyes, and perfectly proportioned figure, accentuated that day in a tight-fitting black dress, which at the moment rode somewhat above the knee. Katarina Conrad was Mimi's opposite. Mimi would probably hire someone like her to model her designer clothes from her boutique on Madison Avenue. Katarina looked every inch the high-fashion mannikin: at least five feet eight inches tall, with natural white-blond hair held back over her ears by clips and then allowed to cascade down her back to her belt line; her eyes, wide-set, above a Nefertiti nose, including the slight rise halfway between base and tip; and a full, winning smile. She would sing Norma if she were a dramatic soprano. She *was* the Casta Diva.

Conjuring up a role for Eva Stein was becoming more and more unsettling. For Peter thought of her day and night. He had never planned to let their relationship, which had begun with their first meeting to discuss the Gala, burgeon, nor interfere with his marriage; but it had. Peter had found in this woman, who was probably sixty years old, a warmth he had never known. He was drawn to her as surely as a river to the sea. If there was a role for her, it would be most decidedly the three heroines of the *Tales of Hoffmann*. The beautiful, auburn-haired, green-eyed Eva filled Peter's thoughts, causing him to fantasize himself as the poet Hoffmann in love with three women in one: courtesan, artist, and ingenue.

As if she might have read his thoughts, Eva spoke, jolting him back to the business at hand. "What better way to promote this worthy cause than by presenting opera buffs and opera lovers with a 'dream evening'? We know how little government support the opera gets in America. This isn't Europe, where everything musical is subsidized. Katarina, Mimi, and I are from Europe. We know about government aid, and we know the problems of funding the arts here. The audience will expect fireworks at the Night of the Tenors and will, doubtlessly, not be disappointed. No wonder we can charge twenty-five hundred dollars a seat."

"What a thrill! Oh, I love the tenors. I was married to one," Mimi trilled. "Now we have the very best ensemble."

"I guess we all get goosebumps when we hear a tenor," Peter said. "The Viennese psychiatrist Gustav Reich wrote that women are attracted most to men in military uniform and to the rare tenor voice. So that's why so many women swoon in the aisles when they hear a performance of *The Student Prince* or *The Merry Widow*. All those tenors parading around in uniform, launching high B-flats and C's. Pretty lethal!" He sighed contentedly. "So, the Gala is set for Sunday, the first of November. And I say again, I look forward to the evening, as much as or more than any of you."

Peter was standing directly in front of a full length, larger-than-life portrait of Enrico Caruso, which filled much of the wall next to the bar niche. Because of its overpowering size, it had been moved from the lower-lobby portrait gallery, where former Metropolitan Opera luminaries are represented by artists of varying talent, to Peter Camden's sanctorum. To many, Caruso *is* the Metropolitan. His ghost is thought to be very much in evidence, even in the Met's new home at Lincoln Center. Peter, standing there directly in front of the portrait, created an interesting *trompe l'oeil* effect.

"You probably don't know it," Peter continued, "but I'm jealous of these tenors. I once thought I could join their ranks, but after much dedicated study, I couldn't squeeze out any note higher than an A-flat; so I gave it up. Or should I say, opera gave up on me." There was real disappointment in Peter's tone. "I'm delighted our Gala exalts tenors. Their vagaries are much maligned, but without them there would be no opera, and it would be very dull indeed around here."

Katarina Tomassy-Conrad pressed Peter's arm. "Without *you*, tenors wouldn't have a place to sing. What you're doing for opera is unbelievable. You give too much time to your work. Felix and I have discussed this often. But I'm glad you're piloting this ship. We need you. The tenors and basses, sopranos and mezzos need you." Total sincerity from the lips of one of New York's most prominent, charming, educated, and influential society women. Katarina Tomassy-Conrad, born forty-three years earlier in Budapest, pulled Peter Camden down to her and kissed him on both cheeks.

"Are we agreed on the name for our evening?" Peter asked.

"Gala," said Eva Stein. "Short and to the point, with a subheading in half caps: NIGHT OF THE TENORS; and then for the sake of peace on earth, an alphabetical listing of the participants: François Charron as Roméo, Renato Corsini as Otello, Horst Ludwig as Siegfried, Sergei Petrov as Cavaradossi, and Walter Prince as Turiddu. With Maestro Randolph Martinson conducting the Metropolitan Opera Orchestra."

Offering cigarettes to all present, pouring sherry, mixing a martini for Felix Conrad and a Scotch and water for himself provided Peter with a moment free of conversation to examine the exigencies that could arise from the assemblage of five superstar tenors. The first problem, he was sure, would be to curb the egregious homosexual promiscuity of Horst Ludwig while he was in New York. Peter was more concerned with Ludwig's social image than with the anti-Americanism which

13

concerned Sir Rudolf. Perhaps his personal secretary and companion would help soft-pedal his activities. Heinrich Gerstmann, the former *Wehrmacht* captain, bald and over-poweringly tall, was always close by the fair-haired tenor. Peter made a mental note to keep an eye on the pair, even have a private discussion with Gerstmann on his arrival.

Another likely trouble spot lay in the proximity of François Charron to his former wife. Mimi had been an enthusiastic worker this past year, accepting Peter's invitation to join the committee at once. Also, she had contributed a sizable amount of money to the project. Peter would try to mitigate that encounter as best he could.

Walter Prince was not likely to cancel or to cause any trouble. He was building a solid career, seemingly trying to improve his reputation as a reliable performer. His only objection to the Gala was the choice of Randolph Martinson to conduct. He wanted James Levine, as did Ludwig and Charron; but all three accepted the committee's decision. To Peter's displeasure, Katarina Conrad had insisted on Maestro Martinson in place of the Met's music director, who graciously conceded the baton for the Gala to the newcomer. Peter felt James Levine was the best conductor in the opera business, and Martinson could make something akin to war with these tenors. It was not going to be easy.

As to Renato Corsini, Peter could only watch and wait. If Sir Rudolf's fears were well founded, he might wish he had never heard the name Corsini. "Those singers wanted me on my knees," the former general manager had said.

"My friends, thank you for a good meeting tonight," Peter said, shaking off his thoughts. "And please don't worry if one of our stars disappoints us. I venture to say that any one of them could fill the house by himself."

"Yes, but perhaps not at twenty-five hundred dollars a ticket. That will take all five," Eva Stein said.

"They'll pay that and more. And with extra contributions, television revenues, and Mr. Hadley's help . . ." Peter paused. "I don't have my calculator handy, but the Met stands to be millions of dollars richer on five sets of vocal cords. Perhaps one to five million per throat!"

All of the committee members—Mimi Charron, Katarina Tomassy-Conrad, Eva Stein, Felix Conrad, and Peter Camden—raised their glasses in a silent toast.

Scene 3

THE GENERAL MANAGER

WEDNESDAY, OCTOBER 28, NEW YORK, NEW YORK

The window above the kitchen sink was open as far as possible, allowing the early morning sun to stream through, bathing the room in cheery light. Peter Camden stood, as was his habit, with his face upturned to the warming rays. Peter was tall, but the window was placed high for light, not for viewing the traffic and pedestrians on Madison Avenue twelve stories below. Dressed for the office, Peter poured coffee into two mugs and made his way into the bedroom, where his wife, Jill, was sitting up in bed with pillows supporting her. The bedroom shades were drawn, shutting out most of the bright October sun. And Jill's firmly closed eyelids obscured the inner light from her crystal blue eyes, which Peter knew so well. Peter placed the steaming mug of coffee on the night table, pausing to admire her patrician face and the alabaster skin of her neck and shoulders before returning to his study, where he had spent the night. In fact, he had been sleeping on his Castro-Convertible for a long time.

I've got too damned much on my plate to worry about Jill's moods, he told himself. She heard me come in last night. It wasn't that late. Eleven o'clock, or thereabouts. She didn't make a sound, pretending sleep. Maybe, if we could talk, get things out in the open, we could sort out the problems in this marriage. She's closed off, and I don't know where to begin. Still, I'm afraid that if we do talk, it will be the end of almost twenty years of marriage. Do I want that? Does she? Hell, I don't know.

Jill was gone all last weekend. I wonder where she went. She didn't venture an explanation. Could she be seeing somebody? No, she probably drove up to New England. She loves to drive that MG of hers. She could have driven up to see Janet and Jackie at Bosford on the way to visit her parents in Proctorsville. Bosford is right on the way to Vermont, if you go through Hartford. Well, maybe a little extra drive. God, Janet has her sixteenth birthday on the first of November. That's next Sunday. Gala Sunday. I've got to get the girls down for the Gala. We can celebrate her birthday the same day we celebrate the tenors. I musn't forget this year. With all the preparation for the Gala, it could happen.

I wonder if Jill suspects I'm seeing Eva. She must know I'm with someone. She just can't be that naïve. But I've been as careful as I can.

Jill has never really understood the work I do. I think she resents it, the time I have to spend at the Met. But Eva understands. As a producer herself, she can empathize with me. We have much in common, besides sexual attraction. I like the way she thinks, direct and to the point; and she's been tremendously supportive. She thinks the gray in my hair is becoming. She says it's just my nerve ends showing. Every time she sees me looking harassed, she runs her hands ever so lightly over my shoulders, my chest, my back, seeking the tension spots, which she says generate more heat. God, she's so much a woman! How could I not have fallen in love with her?

Peter finished his coffee, refilled it in the kitchen, and reentered the bedroom.

"Don't you think it's about time we broke this silly silence?" he asked.

Holding her mug with both hands, her eyes closed, Jill answered: "Just what did you want to talk about?"—terse, cold.

"About us."

"I suppose you haven't had time to notice, I've been attempting communication with you for several months." Jill's eyes were open now, challenging.

"I hadn't noticed that, no."

"In point of fact, the span has been over the past four years, since you took the job at the Met. You're like the man who came to dinner but had to eat and run." She spoke without humor.

"Are you going to blame this estrangement between us on the Met? I've heard the accusations on the soaps, read the novels about the poor forsaken wife . . . the executive's widow."

"That's simplistic. You're married to the Met, Peter, like everyone else over there. Admit it and do something about it, because I've had it up to here." She thrust her thumb under her chin.

"I'm not going to dignify your attack," he said. "I've got a competitive job that will last only as long as I perform it well. Like the singers who work for me, I'm judged on my last performance."

"Well, I can't remember your last performance in my bed. How long has it been? Or do you care?" Her voice had risen in pitch and volume.

"That's a cheap shot!"

"How easy it's become for the high and mighty g.m. of

the Met to look down his nose at his cast-off hausfrau. To her, he scatters the crumbs of life. But I'm not ready for retirement, Peter. For God's sake! I'm only forty-three years old."

"How can you talk this way? We've had a wonderful life. Janet and Jackie are beautiful daughters. You talk like a spurned woman, not a wife and mother."

"Not a mother? Hah! What would you know about being a father, for God's sake? You haven't bothered to call the girls at Bosford since September. You hardly saw us at all last summer, shuttling around the festivals, auditioning singers, hearing some more opera—whatever. Did you notice that Jackie still has her braces at thirteen? I'm sure you didn't. Did you notice that your wife is approaching menopause and hasn't slept with her husband, or hugged her husband, or kissed her husband in months?" Jill's eyes were swollen with tears. "The only thing you know is where every last one of your singers is at every minute of the day or night. You're a cross between a Svengali and a voyeur, Peter. Did you ever think of that?"

Replacing her empty mug on the night stand, and taking Jill's hands, given reluctantly, in his own, Peter summoned his patience. "The Metropolitan is going under financially. It has been since I took over. Bing left a legacy of debt. Chapin and Bliss improved the situation, but our audiences have decreased. I've tried to be innovative, but the public is slow to educate. Whatever the reason, the fact is the till is emptying faster than ever before, and the blame is on me. I'm doing my damnedest to right my wrongs and the wrongs of others. The Gala is almost here. Its success could turn us around. I love my job, Jill. I don't want to lose it, and I'll kill to keep it."

"Do you love it more than your family?"

"That's a stupid question!"

"Not so stupid. Unless you rethink your schedule and your life to include us, you're going to lose us. We need more than we have at this moment. We need Peter Camden."

"After the Gala," he mumbled. "I'll come back to you then."

Carefully, Peter closed the apartment door, fighting down a mouthful of bile, escaping the truth in Jill's words. I can't dwell on Jill's problems, he thought. Not now. Today I will hear the first of our superstars. Sergei Petrov has arrived from Moscow.

Scene 4

THE RUSSIAN

SUNDAY, OCTOBER 18, KIEV, THE UKRAINE, USSR

Even as he sang, Sergei Petrov could not digest the idea that he was being allowed to leave the USSR. The document in his breast pocket was official, however. It stated that he could travel from Moscow to Amsterdam, where he would board, with no ceremony, a KLM flight to New York. It restricted him to a period of one week in New York City with no excursions for sight-seeing or any activity outside the city's environs. His business was to sing the role of Mario Cavaradossi in Puccini's *Tosca*—the third act only—at the Metropolitan Opera House on the Night of the Tenors. It would be his debut outside the USSR. The cultural minister thought it a singular honor for Sergei and had given it his special attention and authorization. The invitation came directly from the Cultural Affairs Division of the U.S. Department of State in Washington, D.C.

In Russia the name Petrov was revered. He was Russia's greatest tenor, although his repertory was mostly Italian. He had copied the old tenors—Caruso, Gigli, Lauri-Volpi, Martinelli—from old 78 rpm records. His favorite role was Cavaradossi, so he was delighted with the prospect of giving the Americans a taste of his art.

The minister need have no fear of Sergei Petrov defecting to the West. Petrov was a Leninite. A true follower. A believer. From childhood he had promised himself and his family he would follow in the doctrine set forth by that fine, astute man. He would make Russia proud of the name Petrov. Now, with his trumpetlike tenor, he would herald the nobility of communism with his singing. Russia had given him everything. He would pay his debts with his voice.

O, thou billowy harvest field of grain,
Never mayest thou be mown at a single swath,
Never mayest thou be bound in a single sheaf!

The Russian words set to music by the expatriate Sergei Rachmaninoff were a ribbon of gold, emanating from the throat of the tenor on the platform at the far end of the vast armory. His voice filled the hall—forte to piano and back to forte, ending with a cadenza to a high B, causing a crashing wave of applause and cheers from the audience. The crowd—30,000 strong—was already standing for this, the End of Harvest rally of the Ukrainian People's party. This was *their* festival. The Ukraine. The wheat supplier of the motherland. Outside, thousands more milled about the meeting area of the communal farm, hearing Petrov's singing over loudspeakers. The social structure of Leninism was never more apparent. Never stronger. Never more self-evident. It was here. The power of the party. Equality. Strength. Unity.

They were applauding their tenor, their music, their Russia. Sergei Petrov had returned to his home city of Kiev on

20

the Dnieper River as its proud standard bearer to the cosmopolitan center of art and culture in the USSR—the Bolshoi Theater. He was home to assist in the party festivities. He was their native son. Tenor Petrov. Number one.

Sergei was pounded on the back and kissed full on the mouth by scores of men before he made it to the black Chaika limousine where his traveling companion, Anton Vlasov, and Sergei's father, Sandor, were waiting.

"Must you go back so soon?" his father asked. "Three days isn't long enough. We have so much to talk about."

"I know, father, but I must prepare for my trip to the United States next week. I want to work on my voice with Madame Danielitch."

"And don't forget you have an appointment at the ministry for tomorrow evening. Very important," interrupted Vlasov, who reminded one surprisingly of Khrushchev, even to his mink hat.

"Ah, well, I'm proud of you, Sergei. Your mother would be too were she here. Her spirit must be joyous. Come to us soon again, my son. Your home is in Kiev."

Sergei kissed his father, and the Chaika pulled away, heading north from the city to the airport—final destination Moscow.

"You're aware the meeting with the minister concerns your trip to the U.S.," Vlasov began. "The bureau has done much for you, Comrade Petrov. I'd suggest you cooperate in every way."

"I know they wouldn't call me in for a chat. I'm a party man, comrade. I owe my career—in part, at least—to the committee. I'm grateful." He had spoken enough. He closed his eyes, as a signal that the talking had ended.

Sergei was not a coward, but he knew the strength of the party. He knew his place. He had learned to be silent—to listen was to be safe. In his present position he was staying on the top rung of the rickety ladder of opera. His sense of

21

self-preservation was perhaps more acute than that of his colleagues. At least that is how he justified some of his actions. Petrov's loyalty to the party served both sides: the bureau and Sergei's ambition.

Last year his refusal to sing with the American soprano Roslyn Shadur had enabled the Bolshoi administration to cancel her contract without remuneration. Sergei explained to *Pravda* that she was absolutely incapable of singing Aida to his Radames at the Bolshoi. Her voice was just too small. And he refused to cast his lot—his reputation—with an unknown and a beginner. Harsh. Unfeeling. This after but one rehearsal where everyone was marking. The fact that she was Jewish was never publicly considered.

MONDAY, OCTOBER 19, MOSCOW, USSR

The day after his return to Moscow, in a plain restaurant called the Pirojak, Sergei waited impatiently. He had drunk two straight vodkas already and the clock on the university tower across the boulevard read 1:30. Tamara Lambrovna was a half hour late. Not like her. Perhaps her rehearsals at the theater had lasted longer than expected. Sergei fidgeted. He hated to be kept waiting, feeling vulnerable, observed.

For several months he had been meeting Tamara in secluded out-of-the-way places: in the park, at a crowded coffeehouse, in the subway, where they stood, just holding each other, while the trains thundered past. The problem was the disintegrating marriage of Tamara, not yet dissolved. All parties were nervous. Sergei was instantly recognizable in public.

In a flurry, Tamara arrived, and every head in the restaurant turned in their direction. Sergei could have crawled under the table.

"It's over, I'm a divorced woman and able to kiss you anytime or anywhere I want."

22

The relief was so great Sergei couldn't speak. He just stood there and smiled. With Tamara Lambrovna he had everything he could have ever wished for: talent, recognition, position, and love.

"If it hadn't been for your backers at the ministry, I couldn't have obtained the papers." The words tumbled from her lips. She spoke with joy. "You're so important to Russia— to the party, Sergei. You're a wonderful artist. You are *Vlasti*— the Chosen One. And I love you."

"Don't put me ahead of you," he said, his tone reprimanding. "We're together. Forever."

"I know, but I am not a tenor." She laughed. "I'm not one in a million. I'm an everyday soprano. They told me that at the ministry."

They held hands as they went onto the boulevard. Tamara, petite and full of life, wore her red fox-fur *shapka* perched at a jaunty angle on her head. And Sergei Petrov looked not like the blond cossack of Russian legend, but divertingly Latin, with a prominent nose and black horn-rimmed glasses. His height and weight would be classed as medium—nondescript, had it not been for his fame as a Bolshoi tenor.

The assistant to the minister of cultural affairs ushered Sergei into the interview room of the Cultural Affairs Building on Dzerzinsky Square at precisely eight o'clock.

"Comrade Petrov, may I present Secretary Ivan Tchelenkov, who has important business to discuss with you." He wasted no time with trivia, this man, Sergei thought. Punctual. Precise. Exact. He liked that.

"Comrade Secretary," he intoned, nodding without offering his hand, since none was proffered to him. They sat on cue.

"First, I must say how pleased I am to meet you," Tchelenkov said. "My wife and I have been followers of your career for years. We liked you especially in *Pique Dame*. The end of the first act was thrilling."

23

The minister took over. "Please, Comrade Ivan, we have no time. Come to the point."

The smile, which was so pleasant in praise of Sergei, vanished from the little man's face. "Comrade, you have served us on numerous occasions without question. Your care in planting the illegal drugs in Eugenia Mischetsky's dressing room simplified our deportation procedures. She was far too popular at the Bolshoi for one whose politics were suspect. Also, we felt a Jewess should be allowed to reside in the 'Land of Milk and Honey.' "

Sergei did not challenge Tchelenkov, but he knew the soprano was not Jewish, and that she had never been allowed to leave Russia.

"We know your feelings toward the Semites and we honor that feeling and protect you from unsavory associations—such a great talent, yours. We, in my department, arranged for the deportation of the tenor Mischa Mischenko, who was making an audience for himself with his performances at the Bolshoi. When you made it known to the director that you wanted the part of Dmitri in the new production of *Boris Godunov*, we managed it by permitting Mischenko to take his family and leave Russia. I believe he spent four years trying to obtain a contract at the Vienna Opera before giving up and emigrating to New York City." The pause in the flow of his speech was calculated for effect. "We have far-reaching influence, as you can see—even in Vienna."

"I couldn't understand why the director of the esteemed Bolshoi Theater engaged Mischenko in the first place, knowing he was a Jew." Sergei was irate at the memory.

"Because he had a good tenor voice and he was born in Moscow. Also, his uncle is the most famous impresario in America . . . an association we cannot afford to lose."

"I see," Sergei sighed, sitting back in the leather wing-backed chair.

"Comrade, you will help us on your trip to New York?"

"Without asking what it is, I will help you."

24

"A mission, uncomplicated, simple," the secretary continued. "No risk at all. You are given the first of many opportunities to be heard by the American audiences at the Metropolitan Opera in New York. They have heard no one like you, comrade. You are untouchable. And because you are untouchable, you will be able to move without obstacle, without interference. You will function without being observed—officially—by the Americans." He paused to open a desk drawer and produce a waterproof, pigskin capsule smaller than Sergei's little finger.

"A roll of microfilm is ready for transport. That is all the information you need, for your own safety; and ours. It is a vital mission to us. That is why we chose you—the least expected courier. You were my personal suggestion. You must not fail."

Petrov felt his heart beat faster. He felt tall, strong. "Have no fear. I can do it. I will be proud to do it."

"You will arrive in New York on Tuesday of next week. You will stay at the Salisbury Hotel on West Fifty-seventh Street. On Wednesday morning at ten o'clock a car will come for you to take you to the Metropolitan Opera House at Lincoln Center for your rehearsal, which is onstage with orchestra, in costume and makeup. A full complement.

"After the rehearsal you will have a midday meal with the opera management and then be taken back to your hotel. At eight o'clock you will go to the Russian Tea Room for supper. It is a restaurant just across Fifty-seventh Street from your hotel. At nine-fifteen precisely you will leave the restaurant, turn left to Seventh Avenue and left again, walking south towards Times Square. Walk on the west side of the street. At about Fifty-fourth Street, a prostitute will fall in step with you." His hand shot up to stem any questions. "One moment, comrade. The prostitute is one of our best agents. She is blond. Very beautiful. She is a very good prostitute. High-priced. Loyal. Unknown to the CIA.

"She will guide you to a side street in Times Square—a

doorway, perhaps—as if to discuss terms for her services. She will hand you microfilm, and you will deliver your microfilm to her. She will disappear into the night. You will proceed to discover the decay of the capitalistic system by looking about Times Square. You will find it depraved. You will then return to your hotel. Your job is done."

Sergei liked the idea of being a courier. Adventure. He felt a tingling along his spine. Just like in *Tosca*. Political conspiracy. Thrilling!

"You will be returning to America many times, Comrade Petrov. You will be of great service to us." The balding man rose, bringing the interview to a close.

"Sing well," the cultural minister said.

Scene 5

THE GENERAL MANAGER

WEDNESDAY, OCTOBER 28, NEW YORK, NEW YORK

The route of Peter Camden's habitual matutinal trek to the Metropolitan Opera House began at his home at the corner of Madison Avenue and Seventy-second Street, entered Central Park at the Seventy-second Street transverse, turned south, cutting over to the treeless, flat, amateur playing field called the Sheep Meadow, and passed the Tavern on the Green restaurant to exit the park at Sixty-seventh Street and Central Park West. The hike, in all seasons except the dead of winter—when he preferred to take a cab—took twenty-five minutes, which brought the general manager to his office suite punctually at nine o'clock, ready to do the best he could at this virtually impossible, frustrating, always alluring job.

Peter's pace that Wednesday morning was considerably faster. The air was clearer and cooler than usual—one of New York's invigorating fall days. Peter was only half aware of the bright morning. His eyes were fixed on a distant point ahead of him, and he methodically attempted to clarify his feelings about the scene he had just had with Jill, searching for justification for his affair with Eva, and weighing the ramifications of an out-and-out confession to Jill of his deception, his dishonesty.

As usual, he was dressed in the manner reflecting his position as administrator and guardian of the world's most esteemed opera house and the fragile, professional lives of its artists. He could not have been anything but elegant, from the dark blue, vested suit to the silver-gray tie to the shiny black half boots to the polished mahogany cane with its pointed metal tip—his only affectation, and that for a margin of protection on his peregrinations. He was born to the taste. He was the boss.

A smile crossed his face as he passed the Tavern on the Green and glanced across Central Park West to see the canopy of the Café des Artistes restaurant. He had been determined to forget the ugliness of the morning and the canopy accomplished just that, for his thoughts went to his luncheon with Eva Stein scheduled for tomorrow.

He entered the stage door of the opera house, blew kisses to the ladies at the telephone switchboard, who knew more about the business of opera than most of the administration. Crossing the stage, he greeted the head carpenter and the master electrician of the stage crew, who were preparing to set up Act 3 of Puccini's *Tosca* for the first rehearsal of the Gala at eleven o'clock.

"I hear we're sold out for the Gala. Great idea, boss," Seth, the ingenious lighting technician, said in his friendly way.

"Wait until you hear this Petrov today, Seth. Hell of a

27

tenor!" Peter tossed the words over his shoulder as he made for the elevator to the floor marked EXECUTIVE AND ARTISTIC.

The pride Peter felt as the helmsman of the Met had begun many years before when he was in prep school at Bosford in Connecticut. He had studied piano from an early age at the insistence of his mother, who had at one time aspired to a career as a concert violinist and had given it up to assume the role of the full-time wife of Erik Camden, sole owner of Camden, Inc., which published music of all kinds.

Peter became a student of voice, an ardent tenor, who traveled into New York every Saturday from his home in Darien, Connecticut, for a two-hour lesson in voice pedagogy and art song literature, with Madame Sylvane Rosenthal-Kopek. After prep school he was admitted to the Yale School of Music and found his love—opera. The dean of the school discouraged him as a voice major, but accepted him for his background in piano. Still, he read about and listened to and played and continued to try to sing opera. Anything pertaining to his favorite art form fascinated him.

His father came to his rescue with a job at Camden Publications, as executive vice-president, which at the age of twenty-five required him to do little more than occupy an office and receive a modest salary each week.

The event that most affected his professional life was the offer of a position as president of Candlewick Productions, which was the tax umbrella for all the music publishing, recording, composing, and allied activities of the prolific opera conductor Wieslaw Kopek, who had no time in his hectic schedule to handle his lucrative ancillary enterprises. It was a challenging offer and brought Peter into all aspects of the music business—especially opera—and close to the genius himself, ever hoping that some of that knowledge and talent would rub off on him. He remained as head of Candlewick Productions until his appointment as general manager of the Metropolitan Opera. He never mentioned to Kopek that he had once been a voice student of his estranged wife, Sylvane.

During his Candlewick years, he married Jill van Arsdale, fresh out of the New England Conservatory of Music, who had every intention of continuing her musical life. She was from the town of Proctorsville, Vermont. To pay for her piano studies, she applied for a job at Candlewick Productions, at the suggestion of her teacher, and was hired by Peter Camden for life. The interview—neither could speak without stammering—and a magnetic attraction to each other, coupled with the world they had in common, was all that was needed. Brief courtship. Marriage. Two girls: Janet and Jackie.

"I'm to call Portia Williams back when you come in, Mr. Camden. Do you want her now?" The question came from his secretary, Hilda, as he exited the elevator and entered the executive suite. She followed him down the long hallway to his office.

"Any problems?" Peter asked.

"I was on long-distance to Munich. Horst Ludwig missed his plane and won't be here until tomorrow."

"He has a rehearsal scheduled for tomorrow, damn it! We'll have to change it." The corners of his mouth seemed to droop, along with his shoulders. "Damn Ludwig. Always something! Charron rehearses the *Roméo* tomorrow evening— seven P.M. Ludwig will have to be content with a piano rehearsal on C-level on Saturday afternoon. Friday is out because Maestro Martinson is busy with chorus and orchestra rehearsals. We have Corsini and Prince with piano on Saturday morning. That's really cutting it close. All right, call Madame Williams on line one and wish me luck."

As he sagged into his maroon leather chair, he put into focus the familiar face of the music critic of the *New York Telegraph*, whom he had known for many years in a polite, professional way. Portia Williams was the foremost critic in New York. Powerful in the arts—venomous when she disliked an effort, constructive when she knew it was needed. Soft-spoken in public. Knowledgeable in music, as well as the allied arts; her critiques were vital to the success of the Met.

29

Peter thought her attractive, with her blond hair—just a touch of gray—always in a tight bun at the back or the side of her head, though he had never ventured anything but courtesy.

"Do you want this *thing* reviewed, Peter . . . love?" The voice came on the line as if they had been conversing all morning. Peter heard the first sensual slur. He pictured the half-empty martini glass he was certain she held in her hand. It was 9:15 in the morning.

"This *thing* you speak of is sold out. And, yes, I would like it reviewed. And, yes, I would like to take you to lunch someday soon after it's over. And good morning, sweetheart." All the conscious charm he could muster.

"God, your wife must eat you up!"

"Things aren't so good on that end, but I won't bore you with that."

"Oh, beautiful! Get a divorce. And never marry again. I never will. Remind me to tell you how my first one blew up. I was married to a tenor. Basket case! Is your wife seeing a tenor?"

The pause that followed was obviously long enough for her to drain her glass. For Peter, it was just long enough to muster composure.

"On paper it looks like a morbid evening in the theater. Whose idea to do five death scenes?" Portia asked.

"I hadn't realized we had programmed death scenes. I guess it just never occurred to me. A tenor Gala was my idea, but the repertory is the committee's. Each tenor will be featured in a scene from an opera for which he is renowned. It's what they do best."

"What? Die?" Portia laughed.

"No, sweetheart. We just happen to have five great singing actors who are known the world over for these particular roles. The fans are going to tear the place apart. And I, personally, can't wait for the competition."

"O.K., you win. You'll get your review, but I'll have to bend some. I've liked Prince, since I got to know him personally . . . in the flesh." Again the sensual slur. "Under the bravura lurks a real artist with almost as much charm as you have. I *never* hear the Texan twang in his singing. Don't know the Russian. François Charron always sings with that beautiful, arching line, but I can't abide the barking of Ludwig, nor the inartistic commerciality of Corsini—every note to the gallery with no visible artistic integrity."

"Thanks, Portia. I promise lunch next week."

"By the way, my prince charming, I understand Eva Stein is working with you on the Gala. I'd suggest you stay away from her. She had a big, big affair with Walter Prince. And besides, she's too damned sexy!"

Peter blushed. His hand trembled. "I didn't know you were doing a gossip column, too," he said, as the line went dead in his hand. He stared at the phone. What made her mention Eva? he asked himself. What could she know about us? Walter Prince! Ah, well, if there had been an affair between Eva and Walter, it was none of his business.

On his desk was the draft of the program for the Gala. He removed the heavy jade paperweight that fastened it to the polished surface. Five death scenes. He checked them off with pencil and made notes in the margin after each scene.

Sunday, November 1, 1987

GALA

Randolph Martinson, conductor
Jonathan J. Jeffreys, stage director—*James Lee*, assistant

I

Tosca—Act III (omit shepherd)   Giacomo Puccini

Mario Cavaradossi . . . . *Sergei Petrov*
Floria Tosca . . . . *Angelina Lombardini*

II
Roméo et Juliette—Boudoir Scene
and segue to Tomb Scene   Charles Gounod

Roméo .... *François Charron*
Juliette .... *Angelina Lombardini*

III
Götterdämmerung—Death of Siegfried   Richard Wagner

Siegfried .... *Horst Ludwig*
Hagen .... *Frederick Horne*

Intermission

IV
Cavalleria Rusticana—Final Scene   Pietro Mascagni

Turiddu .... *Walter Prince*
Alfio .... *Richard Clark*
Lola .... *Ariel Bybee*

V
Otello—Act IV   Giuseppe Verdi

Otello .... *Renato Corsini*
Desdemona .... *Francesca Zandonai*
Iago .... *Sherrill Milnes*
Cassio .... *William Lewis*
Emilia .... *Shirley Love*
Lodovico .... *Paul Plishka*
Montano .... *John Darrencamp*

The evening could easily turn into a wake—a tribute to operatic death. Only a critic with such an analytical mind would hit on that not so obvious continuity in the program. Peter settled into his chair, sucking on the blunt end of the gold ball-point pen his administrative staff had presented to him at the end of his fourth season as general manager.

"A terrible thing, jealousy," he mumbled.

He rose and walked to the window that looked out on the seldom frequented, deserted park at Lincoln Center with the equally desolate bandshell blocking the view of the tenements on Tenth Avenue. He had speculated on various occasions that the building had been erected precisely to blot out the last vestiges of the ghetto that was once known as Hell's Kitchen.

At this moment you let yourself in for a psychological jolt from a music critic's comment, he thought. Whether it was intentional or not, you'll never know. Now, you're Prince's boss at the Met. You like him; he's never let you down. He's not the cause of your jealousy. You are! Are you going to let the past stand in your way? Make a decision. Is Eva Stein going to take the place of Jill in your life?

"I don't know," Peter said aloud.

There was a great deal of paperwork to do. The basket on the desk was full, but Peter went to his wall cabinet, where he kept a dossier on every artist who had sung a major role onstage at the Met in the past twenty-five years. He found the ones he wanted and returned to his desk.

François Charron
Debut—1969—*Roméo*

AGE GIVEN AT DEBUT: 39 (born 1930)

ROLES PERFORMED AT THE MET: Des Grieux, Hoffmann, Don José, Roméo, Faust

REMARKS: The best lyric tenor we have in the French repertoire. *Cancels* often because of ill health. Oversensitive to colleagues, especially women.

Horst Ludwig
Debut—1973—Walther von Stolzing in
Die Meistersinger

AGE GIVEN AT DEBUT: 33 (born 1940)

ROLES PERFORMED AT THE MET: Siegmund, Siegfried in
Götterdämmerung, Lohengrin, Parsifal, Walther von
Stolzing

REMARKS: Outstanding heldentenor. Belligerent to colleagues, especially conductors and stage directors.
Intolerant of American politics. *Homosexual.*

Renato Corsini
Debut—1964—Otello

AGE GIVEN AT DEBUT: 34 (born 1930)

ROLES PERFORMED AT THE MET: Manrico, Pollione, Radames, Otello, Enzo, Calaf, Ernani

REMARKS: The successor to Caruso. Intensely passionate
in performance. Will not rehearse. Reclusive personality. Antisocial. Deeply religious. Inherited
Corsini Automotive Industry. Owns fifty-one percent of the stock. Active in politics.

Walter Prince
Debut—1973—Turiddu in *Cavalleria Rusticana*

AGE GIVEN AT DEBUT: 35 (born 1938)

ROLES PERFORMED AT THE MET: Rodolfo, Cavaradossi,
Pinkerton, Stewa, Ghermann, Dimitri, Macduff,
Turiddu, Arrigo, Gabriele Adorno

REMARKS: Has been called on to save an average of ten
performances per year, usually at the eleventh hour.
Most reliable. Short fuse. Violent temper. Brought
up on charges before AGMA for brawling in and
out of theater. Brief, successful Broadway career.

Peter put the dossiers away in the cabinet. His mind was clouding, like those nimbuses moving over the river on the wind from New Jersey. He turned from the window not wanting to see the sun obliterated.

Scene 6

THE ISRAELI

WEDNESDAY, OCTOBER 28, NEW YORK, NEW YORK

David bar Ephraim squinted into the morning sunlight streaming through his windows overlooking Washington Square. The smaller-scaled replica of the Arc de Triomphe lay to his right and the gray buildings of New York University to his left. He had just returned from his morning jog to his third-floor apartment in one of the town houses bordering the park on the north. When the phone rang, he snatched up the receiver.

"Yes," he mumbled, mopping his glistening forehead with a handkerchief.

"The target has arrived. He has a rehearsal at the Met at eleven o'clock this morning. He is staying at the Salisbury Hotel on West Fifty-seventh Street. The money for your assistance will be left with the doorman at the Park Avenue address I gave you. Ask for the envelope for Eagle Wing Deliveries." The crisp, female voice hummed through the receiver.

David bar Ephraim, still standing, still gazing through the window framing the students, loiterers, lecturers, and panhandlers spotted helter-skelter throughout Washington Square, adjusted his square gold-framed glasses on his nose and used the handkerchief to dry some of the perspiration from his salt-and-pepper beard.

"I have it," he said, and continued: "I have good help and we, the friends and relatives of Roslyn Shadur, Mischa Mischenko, and Eugenia Mischetsky, have waited a long time for this. Read the papers, good friend."

He hung up the receiver and began to strip off his green-and-white sweatsuit. "Sergei Petrov indeed!" he said to the empty apartment, a smile emerging through the heavy beard.

Scene 7

THE GENERAL MANAGER

WEDNESDAY, OCTOBER 28, NEW YORK, NEW YORK

Hilda's knock interrupted Peter's reverie. "Mr. Camden, may I introduce Sergei Petrov." Peter rushed forward to take Petrov's outstretched hand, genuinely welcoming the tenor. "My heartiest greetings, Mr. Petrov. We're extremely grateful for your participation in the Gala. You honor the Metropolitan Opera by your presence, for which we again express our indebtedness."

Petrov had not understood one word. Peter's smile faded quickly with sudden comprehension. He looked sheepishly to Hilda for help and was rescued.

"Mrs. Conrad is waiting in Mr. Petrov's dressing room to translate for us and to serve in any way she can."

Peter took Petrov's arm and guided him to the elevator, across the set of the third act of *Tosca*, and to the tenor's dressing room—S-8—where the makeup director, Paolo Palmieri, the costume coordinator, Franco del Villagio, and the tall, striking Katarina Tomassy-Conrad were waiting to prepare Petrov for the first rehearsal of Sunday's tenor Gala. Peter thanked the trio for their assistance and made his way into the auditorium to join Eva, Mimi, and Felix, who were waiting for him.

The great golden curtain of the Metropolitan went up as the orchestra began the prelude to the third act of *Tosca*. Mario Cavaradossi is discovered on the set gazing out over the battlement of the Castel Sant'Angelo in Rome. Stars twinkle on the grand cyclorama deep stage and Mario pauses in the composition of a difficult letter to his beloved Floria Tosca to contemplate the beauty of the night around him.

Since the performance was not until Sunday night, with ample time to rest, Sergei decided to give the orchestra, stagehands, and Peter Camden a full-throated preview. His voice surged and flowed through the aria. Resonant. Impassioned. He ended with a heartrending sob—*"Mai tanto la vita"*—and the entire orchestra rose to cheer. Even the conductor, Randolph Martinson, allowed himself a smile, however brief.

In the darkened auditorium, Eva Stein held fast to Peter's arm as he applauded and shouted his praise. Eva squeezed him tighter. Mimi Charron piped, *"Bravo,"* then Peter, in an even louder voice, *"Bravissimo."* Felix Conrad turned to him and laughed. "Not very dignified for a general manager." Eva was gazing with unconcealed admiration at the man whose arm she clung to.

"I don't care, my friends. That's one hell of a voice. What a night we're in for!"

Peter asked Felix and Katarina to co-host the private luncheon for Petrov in the Opera Club, excusing himself to see to a full agenda of appointments that afternoon.

As he kissed Eva's cheek, he whispered, "Don't forget tomorrow."

"How could I?" she answered.

THE RUSSIAN

WEDNESDAY, OCTOBER 28, NEW YORK, NEW YORK

After lunch the car was waiting to take Sergei back to the Salisbury Hotel. He had a long wait until the evening's activities began. He was feeling a bit weary from the time change, which was something like nine hours, yet he had sung "E lucevan le stelle" far better than anything they had ever heard. He deserved a respite.

He spent the rest of the afternoon reviewing the service he could do for his country. He would probably be awarded a medal and an opportunity to take a vodka with the premier himself. And he would sing whatever he wanted at the Bolshoi, where the rehearsals were much more serious and formal than the one at the Metropolitan Opera that morning.

At the Russian Tea Room, he dined on very good hot borscht, *côtelette Kiev*, and three Moscow mules. He liked the busy atmosphere and marveled at the number of people who could afford to dine away from home at such astronomical prices.

At 9:15 he paid his check, walked to Seventh Avenue, and turned south. He crossed to the Sheraton hotel on the west side, paused to look around him, and proceeded toward

Times Square. He walked slowly, intrigued by the strange-looking people: derelicts, whores, pimps, well-dressed businessmen with furtive eyes, hippies with much stubble or Tsar Nicholas beards, teen-age girls with enormous breasts hanging loose under athletic sweatshirts. This is New York? Sergei was not favorably impressed. He stumbled against some foul-smelling garbage bags stacked waist-high at the curbside.

At Fifty-third Street, from out of nowhere, stepped the most beautiful blond woman he had ever seen. She was his height, wearing exaggeratedly high-heeled red shoes, which branded her for what she was.

"Fun, darling?" she asked in English. She took his arm and smiled, continuing without breaking pace toward Times Square. And then in Russian, "I know you don't understand. Come," she said quietly, still smiling.

She guided him across the avenue and into a passageway next to a theater which was showing a pornographic movie. He couldn't read the title, but he was startled by the blowup of a naked girl on all fours, her melon-sized breasts hanging almost to the floor. His blond companion indicated that he should ignore the loitering men, who appeared worse than tramps, circling the theater. She embraced Sergei, kissing his ear, and dropped the pigskin capsule containing the microfilm into his outside breast pocket. He thumbed the identical capsule he was holding in his right hand into the deep cleft between her ample breasts.

"Push me away," she whispered in Russian.

Sergei gave her a shove, which she converted into a spin, staggering against one of the bums and falling to one knee.

"Lousy, fucking pervert," she snarled. "Go back to Chicago or wherever you come from." She spat at him but missed. Then she disappeared into the exit door of the porno theater. Not one of the rheumy-eyed men paid any serious attention to the exchange, though they had heard it all.

He patted the capsule in his pocket and strolled around Times Square, which wasn't a square at all. He couldn't believe the filth of the streets, the people, and the subhuman entertainment promised by the neon-lighted marquees.

The street sign said Forty-third and the crossbar read Eighth Avenue. He had walked a good distance. He waved his hand for a taxi, but it was caught in midgesture by a black man, who looked to Sergei like a mountain. The arm was pinned behind him. He was pulled across Eighth Avenue so fast his feet hardly touched the ground. On the west side of the street another black man of equal build flanked his other side, and they marched him smoothly west on Forty-third Street, across Ninth Avenue, and for half a block further, into a dilapidated brownstone and down a flight of crumbling stairs to the basement. Fear had silenced the voice of the great tenor Sergei Petrov. He wasn't certain what he was afraid of, but the size of his captors was reason enough.

He faced a small man with a heavy salt-and-pepper beard and gold-rimmed glasses, seated on a low stool in the middle of the room. A single, bare bulb hanging from the ceiling afforded a weird light. The hovel had a toilet bowl recessed in one corner and a pallet on the floor. The only furnishings. Sergei thought it might be a cell.

"O.K., King, let him go." The beard opened and closed as the little man spoke.

The man released his arm. Sergei had not realized until then why he couldn't focus on anything. The pain in his arm was beginning to blot out his consciousness.

"You speak any English?" No reaction. "O.K., I just want him to know why he dies. Show him the gun, King."

The black strongman produced a double-barreled, sawed-off shotgun. He held the weapon against Sergei's temple. Fear swelled, rolled, and swamped him like a great, cresting wave. His eyes glazed. His legs were numb. He could produce the capsule or he could get rid of it. Protect the party. He had not been trained for this. He was a spy, trapped.

"One barrel is for Roslyn Shadur, whose career you ruined, whose life you destroyed." The beard moved, but Sergei understood nothing. "The other is for Eugenia Mischetsky, for the same reasons, and all because of your fucking anti-Semitism, you Jew-hating Commie!"

David bar Ephraim was about to signal the execution when Sergei lunged for the toilet bowl, extracting the capsule from his pocket. He threw the microfilm into the bowl and flushed it in the same motion. The capsule would not go down. It floated. In that split second the other black thrust his hand into the water and retrieved it.

"Give me that." David bar Ephraim pried the top off of the capsule and held the film in front of the bare bulb. "The lady didn't say anything about this." He flipped the capsule and the film back into the toilet bowl and made sure it was flushed down. "If that's high-level U.S. information meant for Moscow, it can't hurt anybody in the sewer."

Sergei bolted for the door, but the black man called King seized his suit collar, hurled him into the corner, and pointed the shotgun at his head.

"Waste him," the beard growled from behind the gold-framed glasses.

The discharge of both barrels rocked the room. Petrov's face disappeared. In its place was a sieve, ejecting a spray of blood. Bone and brain splattered the wall from floor to ceiling. The beard strode out of the cell and onto the avenue. King and the other man had been instructed to dispose of the body in the Hudson River, two blocks to the west, but there was not enough left of Sergei Petrov to bother with.

Beard and glasses spoke quietly and briefly with the black patrolman on the beat, who waited fifteen minutes to investigate the sound of a shot from the brownstone down the block and report his findings. Identification of the body was next to impossible. The officer couldn't read the name on the blood-soaked Russian passport. The remains were carted all the way to the warehouse that serves as a morgue for unidentified corpses in Lower Manhattan.

Scene 9

THE GENERAL MANAGER

THURSDAY, OCTOBER 29, NEW YORK, NEW YORK

Hilda broke Peter's concentration, announcing the baritone Frederick Horne.

"Let him wait a minute, Hilda. I'd like you to write a letter to Paul Gregory asking him to take his retirement at the end of this season. He's been with the Met for thirty-five years. Make it gentle. And then drop a brief note to Felicia Maxwell, thanking her for her suggestions on the opera she'd like us to stage for her return to the Met. Please say we're considering *Das Wunder der Heliane* or *Joseph's Legend.*"

"But we would never do those operas at the Met."

"I know, but the possibility will give her something to talk about with her friends, and keep her out of my hair. She served us well for many years, but her days are over. Now, please send in Freddie."

Peter sat back in his chair, assuming the businesslike manner of the general manager, who balanced on his fingertips the careers, the lives of scores of singers, conductors, stage directors, and technical people. An awesome, powerful position. Some of his tasks were onerous, distasteful. He awaited his most difficult duty as an administrator.

42

Frederick Horne was six feet two inches tall, muscular, and thoroughly midwestern in speech and dress. He had a shock of unkempt, sandy hair, and the large rawboned hands of a lumberjack or a farmer which protruded from his beige windbreaker were an indication of his strength. His voice matched the rest of him. It was big and rough. He was typecast as the fierce, malevolent Hagen in *Götterdämmerung*, which the Gala audience would hear him sing on Sunday night. The anomaly in his psychological makeup was not always apparent. At times, whether deliberately or inadvertently, his homosexuality would surface. Lately Peter had watched Freddie's public façade peel away far too often in performance.

"Thank you, Hilda. I'll talk to Freddie alone. Please close the door." He reached into the side cabinet and brought out a black file, which he placed before him.

"Sit down, Freddie." He tried to smile, but it didn't work. "You're a fine artist. Eight years here in the house. Good record, in most cases, and I'm not being judge and jury. I'm just quoting what I see here."

"I think I get the gist," Freddie said harshly. "Lennie said you had nothing listed for me next year. And I know how far in advance you cast. What's the problem?"

Peter tapped the folder, stood, walked around the desk.

He changed the subject. "What are you studying?" he asked, indicating the thick briefcase at Freddie's side.

"O.K. You caught me." Flipping the latch, Freddie revealed the tiny Sony tape recorder. He was smiling.

"I shouldn't even give you the courtesy of a meeting," Peter said. "You underestimate us here. Turn it off." Anger had crept into his voice even though he tried not to show it. "I know all about the discrimination laws: age, sex, religion, what have you. But I could pass them all by with just one reason: vocal deterioration. I do it all the time. But your situation is more complicated. We've had complaints about you. I have here letters from members of the board. I have staff here—musical and technical—who are willing to stand up against you, if necessary. Discretion seems to be your weakest hand."

"What a crock of shit!" Freddie was livid, upright in his chair. Battle-ready.

"Good vocabulary."

"You've got real fags hanging from the flies. Closet queens, as close as Lennie Kempenski's office. Talentless ballet boys patting ass in the showers. And dykes by the busload, trying to pass off their roommates as platonic relationships. This is crocked-up shit, Mr. Camden."

"You propositioned Jason Kraft, one of our most important board members, who may look a little fey but just doesn't swing your way. Did you think you could improve your lot in the house by screwing backers? He's a close friend of mine. And whatever you're doing is showing up onstage—in your acting. You swish, Freddie. Are you trying to impress your friends in the audience?"

"Well, there are plenty of them, brother."

Peter's face was beet-red. "I am hardly a relative of yours." He had to pause for a deep breath. "The last straw is that one of the stagehands, you made a pass at, wants to go to the union about you. You're lucky someone hasn't clobbered you. End of interview."

"What about the Gala?"

"I have Marius Brendel standing by in case you don't want to go on or can't. You've still got the best voice in your category, but I'm afraid we can't use you after the Gala. You'll get work. I'll write to Hans Schober in Munich. He's Horst Ludwig's agent. But mind your manners there."

"Oh, I can work in Munich, all right. All I have to do is suck up to that asshole Ludwig. I know him up close and personal. He'd let me sing with him anytime." To Peter, his sarcasm was abhorrent. "What I'd like to do is throttle the son of a bitch," Freddie raved. "You're on your knees to him,

Camden, just because he's a tenor. Why, he's as queer as pink ink. And your conductor for the Gala? Who forced you to take him? Martinson's Ludwig's lover."

"You're finished here," Peter said.

"You said it. End of lecture. Fucking, crock of Met shit!"

Exit a Wagnerian god. Hagen at the Gala. His exit omitted the swish. It clearly exhibited the hate.

Scene 10

THE GERMAN AND THE MAESTRO

FEBRUARY 1967, KILLINGTON, VERMONT

The February sun glaring off the hard-packed snow tortured the eyes as the three skiers, forming a tight triangle, swooped down the trail properly named the Outrage. The two blond men led the Titian-haired girl by four ski lengths, handling the moguls and gullies like professionals. The slope was the steepest and the longest at Killington Mountain, specifically reserved for the best of alpine skiers, although this was Vermont, not Kitzbühl.

The trio disappeared behind a stand of pines and whipped into the last long downhill run to the bottom, where the ski lodge and gondola station stood. With one final lunge off their poles, arms extended above their heads, the conquerors of the Outrage breezed to a graceful stop. With smiles and accolades, they pounded each other on the back.

"That's the best hill in the world," said the German in

an almost accentless English. "Better than Bad Gastein or Gstaad. Thank you both for bringing me here."

"Horst, the pleasure is ours," said the other, who was exactly the same height as the German. "Jill was so anxious for us to come here. This is her territory—Vermont. I did my skiing out in Colorado, which is pretty good, too."

Randolph Martinson, the blond from Boulder, was a skier from childhood, having been born and reared under the Flat Irons near the campus of the University of Colorado, where he graduated with a bachelor's degree in music. He was not in the least frightened by the always inherent danger of a skiing accident. He couldn't remember not having skied. Randolph was good. And this trip to Vermont from Boston was the ideal way to entertain his friend and colleague Horst Ludwig after a winter concert tour together, which had taken them to major cities across the United States.

Randolph was aware of the attention Horst was giving Jill. Horst had purposely skied in her wake most of the day. Randolph was not displeased.

"Let's have a beer, my friends. I'm thirsty," Horst said as they deposited skis and poles on the rack outside the glass-and-cedar ski lodge at Mount Killington's base. "That sign says they have my home town's special beer—Münchenbräu. Let's go."

"Sorry, Horst, it's good beer, but it's made in Milwaukee." Jill van Arsdale laughed and artlessly swung her hips as she preceded them into the bar. Randolph held her hand. Jill's fingers squeezed his firmly in return. She adored her lover and teacher.

Dropping parkas, goggles, and caps on empty seats in the lounge, they elbowed their way toward the mass of chattering skiers to order a pitcher of beer and three glasses. Horst paid and they gingerly made their way back to a table.

"Jill's skied here all her life," Randolph said. "She was born over in Proctorsville and only recently left to come to school at the New England Conservatory."

"You're a pianist?" Horst intervened. "Where did you study?"

"In a little town called Ludlow near my home," Jill said. "My father drove me over three times a week, since I was five—about the time I started skiing. When I wasn't on the slopes, I was at the keyboard."

Jill pulled her mass of thick, red hair over her shoulders and took a long drink of Münchenbräu. "I hope this beer seems as good to you as our skiing, Horst. We want you to like us."

Horst Ludwig, perhaps the most promising heldentenor in the operatic world, basked in the adulation lavished on him by his two young musician friends. He liked the skiing. He liked the company. But above all he would be returning to Germany with many U.S. dollars.

"This fresh air has repaired my voice," Horst said, using the words as a vocalise. "I was getting hoarse in Cleveland because of the air pollution. Thank God for your good Vermont air."

Jill and the twenty-five-year-old Randolph beamed their pleasure at being able to please and entertain the young tenor from Munich. They realized they were sitting in the glow of fame, and cherished the moment.

Randolph Martinson was still nervous in the presence of this Wagnerian. He knew he was only a year or two younger, but the heldentenor had already sung in most of the operatic capitals.

Randolph had made something of a name for himself as an accompanist in the Boston area, but had never dreamt he would be called upon to play for anyone so famous—at least not this early in his career. The invitation, the engagement to accompany Horst Ludwig on a concert tour, came from an artist's agency in New York.

Playing the piano was as easy as skiing to Randolph, but his predominant desire in life was to conduct. Specifically, to conduct opera. And more than that, to conduct Wagner. He had studied *Der Ring des Nibelungen* with the foremost authority on Wagner in America, Andreas Schoenberg, spent hours at the piano playing through scores, and conducted for even longer periods, emulating the recordings of Fürtwängler, von Karajan, and Toscanini.

The key to his future success and the fulfillment of his ambitions was sitting across the table swilling beer and talking wanderingly about his accomplishments. A blond god with the key to Wagner's Hall of the Gods—his heldentenor voice.

Randolph dearly wanted the favor of this rightful heir to Valhalla, who could open the door for him with a snap of his fingers. A career conducting Wagner, perhaps at Wagner's own theater in Bayreuth. Randolph would please him. And Randolph would sacrifice his honor for him.

It happened that night at the Black River Lodge in Vermont.

Jill van Arsdale was forced to witness the coupling of her exalted idols. Randolph had locked the door to his room and hidden the key. She viewed the unimaginable and she could not close her eyes. They had forgotten she existed. Her beloved teacher and lover—perfidious, ardent, and commanding—and the besotted God-hero of Wagnerian myth.

Randolph drove Horst to Boston, where Horst boarded a plane for Munich via London. And, after a brief visit with her family in Proctorsville, Jill took the bus to New York City. She had said no good-byes, and she had shed no tears.

Scene 11

THE GENERAL MANAGER

THURSDAY, OCTOBER 29, NEW YORK, NEW YORK

The memo on Peter's pad read: "Thur., Oct. 29—C II." The last item appeared to be a Roman numeral, but in fact was part of a code quite clear to him. Even in the opera world, some coding was necessary to ensure privacy and avoid gossip. Everyone was aware that cast lists, future acquisitions of name singers, salaries, and illicit affairs around the Metropolitan were somehow discovered by ushers and opera buffs long before the press and members of the company, and parroted all over town for free and often not for free. To Peter the "C" meant a café or restaurant. In this case the first "I" indicated the Café des Artistes, at 1 West Sixty-seventh Street, and the last "I" easily translated to "one o'clock."

There seemed to be more political spying at the Met than in Washington, Moscow, and Bonn all together, Peter laughingly told himself as he tore the memo in half, depositing it in the wastebasket. *I truly enjoy the company of Eva Stein. She's stimulating, knowledgeable in the complex ways of getting a Broadway show produced, while opera espionage—sabotaging or building careers—is my territory. Keep everybody guessing, especially singers and secretaries.*

Peter slipped out the side door marked EMERGENCY EXIT— ALARM BELL WILL SOUND, used only by certain members of the administration, who knew no alarm bell was attached. He exited the underground garage onto Sixty-fifth Street and walked east to Central Park West. It was another one of those perfect New York days, the buildings casting shadows across the canyons filled with sharp patches of sun.

The Café des Artistes, not well known to out-of-towners, but cherished by artists and art lovers for half a century, was just off the park. Peter admired the two nude models—one blond, one brunette—who adorned the walls, immortalized by the brushstrokes of Howard Chandler Christy. The paintings were so sensual they gave one an immediate sense of intimacy without guilt or shyness.

Peter arrived first. It was only 12:30, but he wanted to have a quiet drink and be alone with his thoughts before giving his full attention to Eva. Sequestered comfortably in the corner, sipping a Rob Roy, he felt insulated against the world.

Besides Horne, the morning had held its problems. He had set up a board meeting to discuss union problems, fund raising, and a possible second tour of Japan—the first was in June 1975. And he had dictated a terse letter to a leading tenor who had not bothered to ask for a release from his contract in order to sing the high holy Yom Kippur services back in September. The Met was seeking remuneration for the performances he had canceled. Religion was one thing, but contracts were another, as far as Peter was concerned.

The agent Tony Garbatini had called to say that his client Melinda Martinez, who was to sing Aida the following evening, had been assailed by painful menstrual cramps and would not be able to perform. Peter told Tony to check on her periods next time before coming in for contract discussions, hung up, and dialed the private number of a superstar.

He heard her sleep-filled voice on the other end of the line. "Yes?"

"Dee, sweetheart, sing Aida for me tomorrow night. Miss Melinda just got sick and cut out." Peter had been more than persuasive, knowing his subject. "I'm sorry to wake you, especially after the super performance—I heard it reported— you gave in Philadelphia last night."

"I've got a little sore throat," she said, and after a pause: "O.K., Peter, only for you. What's Melinda getting?"

"Four thousand."

"I'll take eight, considering the time element."

"You'll take five, won't you? For me?"

"Right, five. See you tomorrow."

"Thanks. Sorry again to wake you."

"It's all right. I'm still in bed, but I've been awake for hours."

A second call announced the indisposition of Giulio d'Ancona, the Radames in the same production, by his blubbering wife—the loss of the fee was devastating to her. It necessitated a call to Chicago, where Peter located Sandor Miyhalski, who said he would fly to New York that afternoon to "save their skins." Another thousand over the fee. That's five thousand plus an air fare, Peter thought. Budget? There shouldn't be a budget.

Peter was just finishing his drink when Eva Stein leaned across the table to kiss him. Then she squeezed close to him on the banquette. She ordered a Cutty on the rocks and rested her hand without pressure on his thigh. "You're doing a marvelous job on the Gala," she began. "All on the committee are delirious! What you probably don't realize is that we've struck a positive blow for womankind. We're assembling the five most wanted men in opera onstage and all at once."

"True," Peter said. "They certainly explode the image of the fat pasta-gorging wine guzzler. We can't find enough tickets." He sat back, drained his second Rob Roy.

"Has it occurred to you that each of our stalwarts is a bachelor? I know François Charron was married to Mimi. And Ludwig was married once. But now they are all free. I'm sure there will be three times as many women as men in that audience on Sunday night."

"I don't think Ludwig is a candidate. As Freddie Horne says, Ludwig is as 'queer as pink ink.' Those were his very words, at the height of his rage."

51

"What happened?"

"Just a mild confrontation. Nothing that should occupy our luncheon conversation. But between Freddie and Ludwig, there's no love lost."

"Will their war hurt the Gala? It's going so well."

"Nothing to worry about. And I'm happy the committee is pleased."

Eva fondled her glass, running her index finger around the rim as she said, "It's a good deal of opera in one evening, so no one can say they didn't get their money's worth. None of us will ever forget that this Gala is your idea, and we're all grateful to be included. We love you," she said and kissed his cheek.

They ordered the house specialty—*sole bonne femme*—a green salad, and another round of drinks.

"I have to talk to you about something . . . about Jill . . . about us." Peter hesitated and began speaking much slower than was his normal propensity. "You know how I've made it a point not to compromise my marriage, fought down malefic desires. We've known each other for a long time. You've seen what an old-fashioned marriage I have. It's what I always had in mind. And I really was succeeding." He paused, as if he might not want to go on, fighting the trembling in his voice.

Eva held his hand in both of hers.

"Then we began work on this Gala last year. I saw more of you, Eva. I felt things I've never felt before for Jill or anyone. There's so much depth and understanding, so much humanity in you. I look in your eyes and I see joy; but there's pain there, too. And great inner strength. I hope you don't think I have to have three drinks to get up the nerve to say these things."

She smiled, her eyes shining. "You may say anything you want to me, Peter. I'll listen."

"That's one of the things that scares me about you. I feel you already know what I have to say and draw it from me.

When we make love, I feel you leading me, guiding me where you know I've never been. It's not easy for me. I know I have to end my marriage, but I'm afraid it would kill Jill and probably destroy the girls. I'll do it if you want me to. I love you desperately, Eva. And I want you for all time." Peter was visibly shaking.

"Don't you realize you have me? As much as I can give or have given anyone, I've given to you. I don't want to break up your marriage. I only want to give you what you want. I've been married twice. I've had lovers. I've never had much luck with longevity. And I'm too old to go through your divorce, the recriminations, the anguish. We have each other now. That's enough for me."

Their waiter was hovering over the table. "A Mr. Leonard Kempinski is at the door," he said. "He wishes to tell you something important." Peter nodded, not really comprehending.

Leonard Kempinski, one of Peter's assistants, ambled across the restaurant. He seemed painfully ill at ease, his thin face sporting a badly trimmed moustache, which could not conceal the fact that he was not yet thirty—twenty-eight was the considered opinion of the not too complimentary singers, whose lives were in many ways guided by this young man.

"I'm dreadfully sorry to intrude," he said, twisting the end of a garish tie.

"What's the problem?" Peter asked, not trying to hide his irritation and thinking that there are no secrets at the Metropolitan; that the codes are too damned simple; that this nincompoop had intervened at a most inauspicious—even traumatic—moment.

"Martinez and d'Ancona have both canceled for tomorrow night. Ron Robertson is nowhere to be found. His wife says he's here at the Met and the rehearsal department says he's not. And I just received a hysterical call from Nadine Powers. She knows she's the first cover for the Aida, found out Melinda is sick with a fever, and informed her agent that she wants this performance. Her career depends on her singing *Aida* at the Met. She may never get another chance and, if she doesn't get the chance—if she gets screwed—she'll sue the shit out of us. Unquote."

Peter forced a smile. "Calm down, Lennie. I'm aware of the situation. If you'll look in the 'in' basket on your desk, you'll find an interoffice memo apprising the department of the sickness and its cure. The Aida tomorrow night will be Dorothy Curtis, God's gift to music. Let Nadine Powers try to sue us. She'll find herself in court without the judge. As for Robertson, he is scared out of his shoes to sing the role. He's probably riding the subway back and forth from Coney Island to the Bronx, hoping we can't find him. When he learns we've alerted Sandor Miyhalski in Chicago, he'll show up."

"If we're not going to use the covers, why do we pay them?" Lennie asked.

"We use them in the roles they can manage. They're our insurance against a cancellation. We're not in the business of doing favors for people." Peter's tone was condescending, a teacher to a slow student. "They rehearse well. They accept the financial security. They learn. They punch the clock like factory workers. Some grow and become stars. And I don't mind pushing them on, if someone becomes hoarse halfway through the opera. The audience is judge and jury. We owe them the best, and when we have time we give it to them despite the egos. The audiences pay the salaries—mine and yours. Now go back and mind the shop while we finish our lunch."

"You are very good at what you do," Eva said.

"Yes, I'm good at running the Met, but not very damn good at running my personal life."

"I don't buy that at all. But the mood's broken. Can we continue our discussion at my apartment this evening, say seven o'clock? I might be able to ease some of the guilt and confusion to save your life."

"Or complicate it." Peter smiled.

"Or complicate it," Eva said.

Scene 12

THE AUSTRIAN WOMAN

AUGUST 1939, SALZBURG, AUSTRIA

The war had cast its shadow over Salzburg. Mozart's birthplace had lost its gaiety, its color. Officers of the German *Wehrmacht* and their mistresses replaced the handsomely dressed nobility at the concerts in the Mozarteum or at performances of *Die Zauberflöte* in the Festspielhaus. Although there was still freedom of movement for residents, vehicular traffic was restricted to the German military.

With her strong legs pumping mightily and with blue dirndl skirt tucked up tightly between her thighs, fourteen-year-old Eva Stein propelled her bicycle through the army traffic of Neutorstrasse, through the Neutor tunnel, past the Festival Theaters on the right, and through the winding streets and across the bridge over the swollen Salzach River, bringing her to the Hotel Stein, where she worked at the desk as an apprentice day clerk. Fourteen was a young age for such responsibilities, but Eva had proven herself capable to her employer, Uncle Wolfgang, during the summer season. She was quick, practical, and spoke fluent English and French, which she had learned at the *Gymnasium.*

Uncle Wolfgang did not have to ask her to wear the traditional Austrian dress for the sake of the customers. On the first day of her school vacation, Eva arrived in the dirndl with apron, skirt below the knees, and tight-fitting bodice with matching long hose, looking as if she had stepped out of the pages of an Austrian tourist magazine. Everyone was impressed by her dark beauty. Especially in awe of her was Wolfgang's son Manfred, who was the same age as the more mature Eva. If Manfred had been her blood cousin, it would have been highly improper for him to pursue her so ardently, but the Steins were her adopted family since 1935, so it was all right. Manfred was fun, thought Eva.

Young Manfred was at the front desk when Eva ascended the back stairs, having deposited her bicycle in the cellar. "You're right on time," he said. "*Vati* would like to see you in his rooms. He has a black face on today. Better hurry."

Eva mounted the stairs of the Hotel Stein two at a time. The hotel was only six stories tall. It had a rickety elevator, but Eva knew a black face meant she hadn't a minute to lose. She liked her work far too much to dally.

The door to the hotelier's apartment was almost invisible, set in a corner of the top story of the hotel. Eva found it in the dimly lit corridor and rapped sharply. The door swung in, revealing a stockily built, balding, green-jacketed man with indeed a sad face. Eva feared that look.

He didn't motion her inside. Rather, he turned and walked to the window, which framed a magnificent view of Old Salzburg across the river. She followed and stood quietly behind him.

The rain had stopped an hour ago. Clouds hung low over the city, but through a tiny aperture rays of the sun reflected off church towers inlaid with brass or gold or silver. The promenaders and amateur fishermen along the river put away their umbrellas. Children, on and off bicycles, were able to enjoy the respite in the inclement weather.

"What do you see?" His bass voice rolled over the room. His brows thickly obscured his black eyes. He did not expect an answer, so Eva just looked out the window.

"This city of culture, city of artists, was one of the last unbiased, unprejudiced places a Jew could live. Salzburg. Democratic. Unpolitical, except when it comes to music. Affluent. Everything a man could want. Thirty-odd years I've owned this hotel. My father brought us here from Moscow, just like your grandfather brought your real father fifty years ago." He turned and eased himself into a dilapidated overstuffed chair, indicated another chair for Eva.

"Out that window is the Salzburg of yesterday. Today every artist and conductor and stage director belongs to the Nazi party. The painters are relegated to doing portraits of *wehrmacht* commandants. It's the end of the world. In my business I hear everything. I have many friends, thank God. Hitler is going to make it unbearable for all of us Jews. I know it looks peaceful and harmless over there on the Getreidegasse and on the Mozartplatz, but believe me I know. Soon, the little man from Linz—right down the road—will make his ultimate move. He wants supreme power; and we free thinkers—especially Jews—will suffer the most."

"What do you want me to do, Uncle Wolfgang? I know nothing of politics except what I hear in school."

"You must leave. Your father and I have known it for some time. You're much too much in evidence. An extremely beautiful girl, highest grades in the *Gymnasium*; and it won't matter that you were not born a Jew since my brother legally adopted you both. If you stay here, by this time next year you'll have disappeared like many of our friends and relatives. Our cousin, Aron, isn't visiting old classmates in Vienna, as you were told." Wolfgang Stein pulled Eva to her knees in front of him and clasped her hands in his. "*Schatze* Eva, he's dead. Murdered by the Nazis for his politics and for being a Jew."

Eva was so stricken she could hardly speak. Her tears spilled from her eyes through her entwined fingers. "What will happen to my sister? And Manfred? And you?"

"Eugenia is only seven years old. She can't go with you. She'll be kept by the brothers at the Catholic orphanage at the abbey in Melk on the Danube. She'll be safe there. She is a Mischetsky, as you are. You mustn't keep the name Stein. No more. Do you hear, Eva?"

Eva nodded.

"I will send Manfred into the Dachstein. If he's to survive, he will do it there. The Nazis will never find him. But you! Run, Eva. Run."

She did as she was told. She ran.

The train south to Villach near the Italian border was jammed with men, women, babies, soldiers, so Eva found herself totally inconspicuous on the first leg of her journey to safety. At Villach, after an entire day's travel over a distance that in normal times would have taken no more than three or four hours, that August night she slept on the ground in the park of a hotel, not more than half a mile from the train station.

" *'Raus. Schnell machen.*" A voice cut through the night and then a flashlight blinded her, as she was roughly pulled to her feet. She was barely awake. A lone German soldier was conducting an inspection of the park. She could see other German soldiers lounging along the low stone wall that separated the park from the hotel.

"Warum schlafen Sie hier? Was machen Sie hier?" He searched her suitcase for God knows what. "Identification." Eva had none. She shook her head. "Where are you going? Where do you live?" Fourteen-year-old Eva Stein was stunned, speech-

less. Her interrogator dug his fingernails into her arm, leading her in the direction of the waiting truck outside the gate.

"My name is Eva Mischetsky. Mischetsky," she sputtered, doing as Uncle Wolfgang had instructed her.

"Are you a Jew?" the soldier asked.

"No. Catholic," Eva answered.

She was lifted off her feet and hurled into the back of the truck, landing on top of two sleeping women. At dawn the truck crossed the Italian border south of Villach; it's destination: the German military medical complex at Udine, Italy.

Until now, Eva had never known it was bad to be a Jew. Did bearing the name Eva Stein endanger her life? She was afraid for her father and Uncle Wolfgang and Manfred. And she was deeply afraid for herself.

Scene 13

THE GENERAL MANAGER

THURSDAY, OCTOBER 29, NEW YORK, NEW YORK

Peter should have felt on top of the world. The lunch with Eva was, as always, beguiling. *She knows how to make a man feel important, needed*, he thought. *Why, then, should I have this gnawing pang of fear? I'm on the verge of asking Jill for a divorce, asking Eva to marry me, and Eva says she doesn't want marriage. "We have each other now," she said. Why does it have to be so damned hard? I guess I really am old-*

fashioned. I can't love two women at the same time, so I've got to upset the whole world. I was certain being with Eva today would ease my fears, my nagging guilt; but it was just the opposite. Christ! I'm losing my mind.

There was a rap on the door, and Hilda was at his side ready to work.

"What's it look like?" Peter began, his head splitting from the Rob Roys he drank at lunch.

"François Charron arrives on the SST from Paris at four o'clock."

"Is someone meeting him?"

"His agency is taking care of everything. They booked his favorite hotel, the St. Moritz."

"Did they arrange the party for him at Mamma Guardino's for tonight or did Mimi?"

"World Artists again. Of course, rumor has it that neither can stand the sight of the other, but they'll have to be together at the party. She's on the committee, after all."

"See if you can get Mimi on the phone. I won't see her at the party. I'm meeting Corsini's plane at ten-thirty at Kennedy."

The phone console buzzed. Peter picked up. "Mimi, it's Peter Camden." He smiled broadly as he heard the chirpy coloratura soprano of Mimi Charron. "I need your help, Mimi. François is arriving this afternoon, will rehearse at seven o'-clock, and then go on to his party at nine. I can't be there because Corsini's plane comes in at ten-thirty. So I must ask all the committee members to attend the party. Felix and Katarina will be there. And Eva will be late, but she's promised to make it." Peter remembered the seductive look in Eva's eyes when she had suggested: "Seven o'clock. My apartment. I'll save your life. Or complicate it."

While Peter's thoughts strayed momentarily to Eva, Mimi was talking in a flurry. At last she stopped.

"Mimi, I had no idea you felt so strongly. You always

speak well of him. . . . I'm really sorry to have put you in this situation . . . but please, try to be there. Nothing will happen. Bring an escort. But please . . . I beg you . . . go to the party. You know how important this Gala is to me . . . to all of us." Peter paused again to listen.

"Don't cry, Mimi. Be brave, dear. And accept my gratitude for your help, and for your support. Good-bye, Mimi. Thanks."

What a mistake! Peter thought, staring at the receiver in its holder on the desk console. I should have vetoed François Charron just to keep from causing Mimi pain. We could have easily omitted him from the Gala. His is a beautiful instrument, but there are others we could have included. But it's done. Mimi has courage. This is one situation I didn't read well. I thought when she agreed to serve on the committee, it was a free indication of interest and commitment. Now I find I'm causing her anguish. Maybe each dossier should include information on wives and lovers.

Peter stood and walked to the wall cabinet. He thumbed through the dossiers to the one marked *François Charron*.

François Charron
Debut—1969—*Roméo*

AGE GIVEN AT DEBUT: 39 (born 1930)

ROLES PERFORMED AT THE MET: Des Grieux, Hoffmann, Don José, Roméo, Faust

REMARKS: The best lyric tenor we have in the French repertoire. *Cancels* often because of ill health. Oversensitive to colleagues, especially women.

What do we really know about you, François? Peter thought. You're a mystery.

Scene 14

THE FRENCH WOMAN

AUGUST 1965, PARIS, FRANCE

The sounds and smells of the river Seine wafted languorously through the oversized window on the Quai d'Orléans over-looking the Quai Béthune and L'Eglise de la Notre Dame. The window was thrown open to the romantic panorama of Paris on a star-filled summer's night. In the clear air, Notre Dame's floodlit gargoyles and flying buttresses were that much more inspiring. And, yes, that much more mysterious as seen through that window on the Quai d'Orléans by Mimi Doger-eau—quite naturally named by her entrepreneur father for the heroine of the Puccini opera *La Bohème*.

For Mimi, Bohemia was perhaps in Montmartre, perhaps on Rue Saint-Denis or around the Gare du Nord, but certainly there was no evidence or hint of anything less than affluence in her father's villa on the Ile Saint-Louis. To obtain a house in their particular neighborhood one would have had to inherit it or have influence in very high government.

Mimi's phonograph was heralding the marriage of Roméo and Juliette from a recording starring the young tenor François Charron of L'Opéra de Paris. Her father, as newly named assistant director of the opera, had heard Charron in Aix-en-Provence and nurtured and guided him to his debut as the star-crossed Roméo at the Theatre National. She couldn't remember the name of the Juliette. Gounod's music filled the room and soared out over the Quai Béthune and the placid Seine three floors below.

Mimi could hardly wait for the record to change, trans-porting her from the nuptial meeting in the rooms of Friar

Laurent to the boudoir of the newlywed teen-agers. She could feel herself being caressed by the hands and the voice of her Roméo. She would be, if he wanted, his real-life Juliette. How she longed to meet him!

The next morning, a noisy Monday, Mimi was up early. She took breakfast in her room, gazing through that magical window to her outside world. Her maid, Yvette, told her that her father had left for the opera house and would expect her to join him at one o'clock for lunch.

"Mademoiselle, your father said you will have a surprise today. Something very special. You will not miss your appointment with him at Restaurant Joseph. Dominique will take you, so you'll be on time."

Mimi was not overly mystified. She knew her birthday was less than a week away, and her father had lavished gifts on her on all of her eighteen birthdays. She enjoyed his pampering. But this time he could not give her what she wanted.

I'm surely old enough and ready enough for Monsieur François Charron now. He couldn't be more than twenty-five. Perfect! And he's not much taller than I am. We could be brother and sister. She laughed to herself. No, that would never do.

She leaned from the window, her elbows on the sill, staring at the monumental cathedral across the Seine and felt herself tremble. "We *are* Roméo and Juliette," she murmured.

At a quarter to one, Mimi stepped into the limousine chauffeured by Dominique, who had driven for them as long as she could remember. He drove her father to the Opéra Comique, to the Theatre National, to his mistress in Neuilly-sur-Seine on Tuesdays and Fridays. He drove her and her father and sometimes the mistress to Aix-en-Provence in the summer for the music festival, which lasted two months. Today the trip was fifteen minutes from the house on the Ile Saint-Louis to the luncheon appointment with her father. When he let her out, her heart stopped.

He was there! Next to her father. Just rising to meet her. He was smiling. Oh, God, that boyish smile! Her father was saying his wonderful name—François Charron, François the First—the name of the street on which stood this hallowed restaurant where Roméo and Juliette were meeting for the first time. His lips moved. His glorious, warm, smooth tenor voice. *"Bonjour, mademoiselle. Enchanté."* She thought she would surely faint. Her father had given her the present she most wanted after all.

Mimi, trying her best to control the butterflies in her stomach, managed to reach her chair and maintain conversation throughout the meal: an Amer Picon, a shared bottle of Pouilly-Fuissé with the *saumon,* a shared bottle of Musigny 1937 with the *côte de veau,* and a double Rémy Martin with her *café américain.* Somewhere during the course of the conversation with the pride of the French nation, she mentioned how she admired his art and especially his interpretation of the role of Roméo. He in turn, after thanking her for her enthusiasm, complimented her for her inspired conversation and her taste in clothes. And then her Roméo said, "You are exquisitely beautiful."

Gabriel Dogereau, one of Paris's most elegant and sought-after widowers, single after twelve years of marriage, motioned for the bill, signed it, and rose. "You two seem to be getting on well," he said. "So I'll excuse myself and get back to work. François will see you home, Mimi, and I'll see you Wednesday. If you need me, you know the name in Neuilly. *Au revoir, François.*" He kissed his daughter's hand and disappeared into the bright sunlight.

Before her birthday, Mimi discovered her Roméo to be as charming between meals as he had been at Joseph. She discovered he was really a young-looking thirty-five years old. She found out how much they had in common and how conversant he was about all things cultural. She discovered how much she knew about making love without any previous experience. She discovered he was just as eager to wed her as she was to bed him. And, to her disappointment, she realized François Charron, although an ardent lover, was not going to be enough Roméo for her.

They were married in Notre Dame Cathedral in the small chapel of Saint-Clement. They were divorced before Christmas three years later.

Mimi gave up the boy, but she would always love his voice.

Scene 15

THE FRENCHMAN

SATURDAY, OCTOBER 24, PARIS, FRANCE

François Charron chose the Boccaccio that evening purely on recommendation and intuition. He had heard it was quiet and thorough, with a better than usual staff of talented, experienced girls who took their work seriously. Feminine soft fingers and companionship was what François sought that night. Almost every night, especially after a performance.

The taxi with the garrulous driver braked in front of a building. There was no indication from the street that a business of any kind was housed there. The driver assured him the address was correct. Thirty-three Avenue Victor-Hugo. Discreet. Residential Paris.

Two rings brought a crack in the door, the release of a chain lock, and the permitted entry. François' eyes took in the emerald green decor in one glance. The woman before him smiled with appreciation at his approval of the accommodations. She spoke quietly and escorted him to a room with a massage table in the center and mirrors on walls and ceiling. He was happy he had taken the recommendation seriously.

Stepping out of his clothes—black tie, tux, and patent-leather shoes—he wrapped a four-foot-long towel around him—armpits to ankles—and followed the woman down a long hallway to the bath. She was in a floor-length, tight-fitting gown, which accentuated a perfectly rounded derrière. He stared at the undercurve, longing to touch her as she swung her hips with practiced skill, aware of his gaze.

She opened the curtains on a sunken bath—ten feet square and four feet deep. In the bath, smiling toward him, was the face of a young Oriental girl, perhaps twenty-one. She was nude, with high firm breasts. He felt an immediate awakening in his groin.

"*Bon soir, mademoiselle,*" he said to the young woman in the pool. The older woman relieved him of his towel, drawing her fingernail in one sensual motion from the hair on his chest, to the hair on his stomach, to his pubic hair.

"*Que veux-tu?*" the girl began.

"*A vôtre discrétion, cherie,*" he answered. The true gallant.

Many women in Paris would have gladly taken him to their beds, and many had; but it was frustrating for both, as it often ended in anger and tears. The tears would be those of François Charron. He was unable to perform unless he was total master. And to be master he found he had to pay. He preferred the professional woman, not only because of the experience extant but for the lack of emotional involvement required. With a prostitute he never felt he had to perform and was never threatened with rebuff. "Thank God for my voice," he said.

The hotel was called the Vieux Port. It was directly on the quai. It was not big, but it was busy. And it was surrounded that midnight, as usual, with prostitutes.

Madeleine Sauvet looked like the others. She was not the youngest, nor the prettiest, nor the busiest, nor the cleanest. She was not the best nor the worst of anything, and she didn't care. Like many of the others, the dark roots of her hair were surfacing at temples and crown from lack of attention. She was giving up trying to be someone else. She was a nonperson of the war. She just wanted to survive, as did all the *putains* around her.

Her room was on the fourth and top floor of this elevatorless building, perhaps the oldest hotel on Marseille's "Old Port." The lodgings were dismal, but the food in the neighborhood was surprisingly good and remained cheap to accommodate the German occupation troops. The port was too shallow for large ships or the German navy, but the fishing fleet was large and enterprising.

The Hôtel Vieux Port was used as a safe-house for some of the Resistance fighters, and Madeleine found herself privy to not a little clandestine information and activity: the drowning of a drunken, whoring *Oberstleutnant*; a fire on one of the German navy frigates moored at another pier; the bombing of a German communications center; and the passing of hundreds of refugees and political activists from peril to safety.

Madeleine loathed the fish-breathed German who now had mounted her, cursing and drooling. She detested herself, at that moment, for not finding a means to castrate him. His breathing was coming in irregular gasps, as he held her buttocks with both hands, calloused and hard, and watched his penis disappear and reappear.

"Why don't you say something? Why don't you come?"

he screamed. He flailed her ass with his thick leather belt. He crushed her breasts in those scaly hands. "Beg me to fuck you, you whore. Beg me."

Mercifully, he climaxed, roaring like a bull, and was quiet.

The German soldier, whose name she never asked, was one of the many who came regularly to Madeleine. No love ever voiced. Love never appearing. She had lost her virginity in that room above the quai. To whom? She couldn't remember. They were all just faces now: clean-shaven, stubbled, bearded, pockmarked, acne-cratered, dead eyes, bleary eyes, crazy eyes. She hated them all: German, French, Turks, and Italians. It made no difference. A dam of bitterness had broken inside her, engulfing her, drowning her.

Almost four years after moving into the Hôtel Vieux Port on the quai—July 1945—Madeleine found she was infected, punished for her sacrifices, for her very existence. She inquired and was told of a doctor in Aix-en-Provence, Dante Charron, who would be willing to help her. The information was freely given by her friend André Charron, the concierge at the elegant Hôtel Splendide and a first cousin of Dr. Dante Charron.

SEPTEMBER 1945, AIX-EN-PROVENCE, FRANCE

Fortunately, François Charron had been a child during the hostilities in Europe, and even more fortunate was the remoteness of the minuscule hamlet of Plaçon tucked away in the hills near Aix-en-Provence. Luckily, too, was his father's profession, as the most trusted practitioner in Aix. Villagers hailed the doctor as he rushed along, coattails flying, on his bicycle, calling at the homes of patients in Aix and surrounding secluded farms and crossroads. Because of his father's intervention, François was relatively oblivious to the rumors—fact and fiction—of the war.

Theirs was a family of five children. All were female except for François, so the addition of a twenty-year-old girl to do the odd chores and take care of the younger girls, four, six, eight, and ten, was not a major event in their life.

Their father introduced the girl one morning as Madeleine. That's all. Just Madeleine. She began her tasks in earnest. François tried to make conversation with her, but she only nodded. He thought her beautiful, like the raven-haired Madonna above the altar in the cathedral. She was a shade taller than he was, too, but he was certain he would grow some more; he was only fifteen. There was something in her eyes. They were different. They were a strange color of green; but it wasn't that. Was it pain he saw in them? Sadness? He couldn't fathom it, but François was determined to make her his friend.

He studied piano in the town of Aix, and after some coaxing, Mademoiselle Madeleine would permit him to bike her to the lesson, sitting on the handlebars. His musicianship was a source of great pride to the delicate-featured lad. His piano teacher, Madame Boky, welcomed the comely visitor, who sat in silent, rapt concentration as the two played four-hand sonatas. Then François would pedal Madeleine home on his bicycle.

Often in the evening, after the meal, the family would gather around the piano to sing. François' voice would soar above the others. Madeleine, although not singing, seated herself beside him on the piano bench. And François watched the sadness in her extraordinary eyes slowly vanish.

During the dark, silent, predawn hours of a cold February morning, just six months after her arrival, the inevitable happened. Mademoiselle Madeleine slipped up the stairs of the Charron country house and into the bed of the sleeping François. It was the finish of his naïveté and the dawn of his desire.

It was the termination of Madeleine's loneliness and the awakening of their love.

Mademoiselle Madeleine, with the gentle magic of her lips, her tongue, fingers, lifted the vulnerable François to ecstasy. She never seemed to waver in her propensity to satisfy him, but she would not allow him to please her, to penetrate her body. He had not the experience or the knowledge to question her proclivity. His love held no question. She was an angel sent from heaven, to be his forever.

Two years passed. François' father, the much revered physician of Aix-en-Provence, died. The healer of hundreds, perhaps thousands of people over the years, could not cure the cancer that destroyed his lungs. They buried him on the side of a hill overlooking the hamlet of Plaçon.

"François, your father wrote this letter to you on his terrible bed of pain before he died." His mother handed her son the sealed envelope, her hand trembling. Her eyes were red-rimmed from weeping. She pressed her kerchief to her nose and mouth as she left her son's room.

My dearest François,

My only son, my life, I must leave you. You are already a man. Seventeen years constitutes manhood. And, as man to man, I write to you.

I saw the love you hold for Madeleine begin, flourish, persevere. It was not my want, until now, to interfere. Madeleine assured me that her feelings for you were genuine, that she loved you deeply; but, because of your age and her condition, she has chosen to wait to consummate your love. Believe me, my son, I know it is wrong to intervene in something so serious, so personal. Forgive me. If I did not tell you, you would never forgive me.

Madeleine is an unknown, a displaced person—a victim of the war. She is not of our faith. She is a Jew. In surviving the early years of the war, she succeeded by engaging in

prostitution in Marseille. That is all I know about her. My
information comes from my cousin André. He sent her to me
to cure a venereal disease she contracted. It is curable, but it
is a slow process and can reoccur. You are young. Your future
will be in music. Think well on your relationship.

    I leave you and all I cherish—with great love.

Your father,
Dante Charron

The following afternoon, Madeleine's belongings were placed in the road in front of the house. François had locked himself in his room. When Madeleine went out to inspect the disarray, his mother slammed and bolted the door. Madeleine Sauvet gathered her meager goods and walked back to Marseille.

Scene 16

THE GENERAL MANAGER

THURSDAY, OCTOBER 29, NEW YORK, NEW YORK

Peter settled back into the heavily cushioned seat on the drive across town from the Met to Eva's Fifth Avenue duplex in the limousine made available to him so that he might meet Renato Corsini's ten-thirty plane.

    On the short ride through the park, Peter's mind raced as fast as his pulse. You need Eva, he thought; but are you certain she needs you? She's an independent, self-sufficient woman. And every moment you spend with her is a step away from Jill, your marriage—and maybe the girls. It, assuredly, hasn't been a casual affair. But how one-sided is it? Can she love you, if she doesn't even want to discuss marriage? Damn it! You're not going to be able to handle the guilt. You're not going to be able to look at yourself in the mirror. Is this old-fashioned idea of "no sex without marriage" going to stop you from having a wonderful relationship? Grow up!

The driver deposited Peter at the Eighty-second Street entrance to Eva's apartment building. "I'll be ready at exactly nine-thirty," Peter told the chauffeur. "The plane I'm meeting arrives at ten-thirty; but my traveler has to pass through customs and wait for baggage, so it may be after eleven before we can come back in." Peter dismissed the driver, who returned to the garage.

Peter was afraid his lack of composure was showing. Maybe a strong Scotch is what I need, he told himself. Am I talking myself out of a good thing? My God, I'm like a teen-ager on his first date. A fifty-five-year-old teen-ager! Be more cavalier. Relax! What Jill doesn't know won't hurt her; and, surely, at your advanced age, you can control your guilt. If not, learn!

Eva answered her door buzzer with a tumbler of Scotch on ice, which she handed to Peter. She closed the door and held Peter in a brief embrace, her head against his chest.

"You read my mind," he said. "I need this drink. Sorry I'm late."

"I do read your mind, Peter, because I feel so close to you." She led him to the living room, sat beside him on the oversized couch.

"I hope you don't mind missing the Charron party," Peter said, lighting up a good panatella. The smoke roiled up, partially obscuring the Monet floral that hung above the couch. It left in haze, too, the framed original letters and manuscript excerpts of such composers as Verdi, Puccini, Massenet, Berg, and Stravinsky decorating the paneled walls, a collection painstakingly acquired by Eva's late husband, Manfred Stein.

Eva laughed. "All through lunch today, I was planning how I would entertain you, once I had lured you here. I'll tell you right off, as if you didn't already know, I have nefarious designs on you. Charron's party has a low priority compared to you."

Peter looked into Eva's unusual green eyes. "It bothers me you don't want to hear about marriage. I want you so badly I would end mine tomorrow. Am I old-fashioned? Or just way out of line?"

"Neither, Peter. Holding on to my men has been my problem. Manfred died after five years of marriage. We were cousins, you know. No, not by blood. We grew up together. The war separated us. He hid from the Nazis in the Dachstein. My foster father and Uncle Wolfgang never survived the camps. I ran for my life—even though I'm not a Jew. My birth name is Mischetsky. My parents were Russian. When I was seven years old, they attended some sort of rally in Munich, and never returned to Salzburg. My sister and I were adopted by the Stein family. Uncle Wolfgang told me much later that my parents had been trapped by the Brownshirts in an anti-Fascist mob, and were beaten to death."

"My God, what a story!" Peter said, wondering why she had not told him this before. He had heard bits of it, but never so directly.

"Then, many years later, Manfred found me here in New York. I was producing my seventh Broadway show. I asked him to stay here with me, although he owned a small hotel not far from here. And we were eventually married; so I had the name Stein forever. It was not a marriage made in heaven, but he was a good, considerate husband. He's been dead for two years."

"At lunch you said you were married twice."

"That I don't want to talk about. It was a morbid time in my life. I'd rather forget it."

"What about us?"

"We have more right now than I've ever had, Peter. I said it before. I'll say it as many times as is necessary. We don't need a piece of paper that says we're in love."

Peter didn't press. He changed the subject. "I know I won't be missed at the Met this evening. *La Traviata* almost performs itself—at least technically. I hope I don't load you down with too much personal garbage when we're together— too much self-pity and guilt."

Patiently, Eva took Peter's hand and led him up the stairs to her penthouse bedroom. At the foot of the king-size bed, she kissed him, holding his face in her hands. And gazing hard into his eyes, she whispered, "Undress me."

Scene 17

THE FRENCHMAN

THURSDAY, OCTOBER 29, PARIS/NEW YORK

The Air France stewardess in the first-class cabin was doing her training-school best to entertain her distinguished passenger. Had he not been the VIP François Charron, he would still have merited her full effort. He was the sole person in her realm.

François couldn't stand her smell. What is it with my countrywomen? he thought. When they perspire they stink, and they never seem to realize it. Not only Frenchwomen. What about that Romanian soprano in *Manon* at the Metropolitan? No one could get within arm's length of her, but in the performance I was forced to. And the pretty Canadian in the Montreal *Tales of Hoffmann*, who fucked somebody every lunch break and would return disheveled and clammy to rehearse the love scenes with me. He put the glass of Cognac under his nose, eyes firmly closed, inhaled. And the soprano who had made a debut as Thaïs with him as her Nicias at the Opéra Comique in Paris, married a wealthy wine distributor, and retired to the Trocadero—what an odor that was . . . nerves. Perhaps the wine distributor had a sinus condition. François swilled the Cognac and signaled the girl for more.

La petite Mimi, he thought. I wonder what bargehand or sailor she's fucking today. No doubt I'll have to see her in New York.

From his short marriage to Mimi, François felt he understood her very well. His Juliette, as she urged him to call her, would fuck the balls off anyone who called her that. She had named her boutique on New York's Madison Avenue Juliette, speaking of tastelessness. François imagined that Mimi had caused a decline in high-class East Side prostitution. By all accounts, she was giving it away.

The SST flight, originating in Paris, was due to arrive at JFK International at four o'clock. François was counting on punctuality. He had wired ahead his arrival time; and Tony Garbatini, his personal agent at World Artists, would take care of everything. He would have him booked into the St. Moritz. He would have spoken to the head of customs at their office on Fifth Avenue. He would have a car waiting at the airport. He would have placed a packet of American dollars at the hotel desk for François' use, along with the rehearsal schedule at the Met and at least one pair of good tickets for the Gala. He himself would have called Mamma Guardino to arrange for the back room of her restaurant for the party. And Tony would have the right people there.

"I despise Italian cuisine," he mumbled to himself, "but

75

everyone I know in New York swears by Mamma's pasta, so I'll just hold my nose."

The final task expected and performed by his agent would be a discreet phone call to Jacquelyn de la Ville to inform her of François' pending arrival. No more than: "How are you? François arrives at four P.M. this afternoon." For all this effort the World Artists Management would garner 10 percent of his earnings while he was in the States and Tony another 10 percent, which François always gave him in cash, tendered normally over lunch or an after-theater drink.

"Clockwork-smooth." François spoke out inadvertently to the desk clerk, who was checking him into the St. Moritz.

"I beg your pardon, Mr. Charron?" came the polite reply.

"Nothing. Everything is in order."

In his room, François had shaved and was just toweling off after his shower when the knock came. He found the new terrycloth robe—courtesy of the hotel to François Charron and very few others—folded neatly in a drawer beneath the washstand. He hurried the robe onto his shoulders and was knotting the cord as he opened the door.

Jacquelyn entered. The exquisite creature, who greeted François in the French style with a peck on each cheek, would shame a goddess. She swept into the room, giving her long blond hair a flip with her hand as she turned to face him. François could never get used to the sight of her. It was obvious that she was a ballerina by the way she moved, the way she glowed. She was a star, the rocketing star of the American Lyric Ballet. Not tall—five feet four. The same as François. And a face that had been sculpted by a master.

She removed her light coat as she glided into the bedroom, dropping it on the floor, oblivious to form or fashion. A princess. The blouse and fringed Russian skirt were next, and she was free. She shone there, clad only in her black high-heeled boots, proud and alive. With a charming smile

76

she wafted like a floating feather onto the oversized bed with the rich, emerald green coverlet. She was still on extended point as she stretched her ballerina's legs toward François. In a move he was on his knees to remove her boots.

Jacquelyn was every inch a blonde, from her almost white-blond hair to the peach-blond fur that covered her pubic region.

She lifted her hips to simplify the first insertion of his tongue.

Jacquelyn dressed carefully, collecting her clothing item by item, kissed François on both cheeks, and pirouetted to the door. François pointed to the money on the bureau. Jacquelyn curtsied.

"You are coming tonight?" François asked from his sitting position at the foot of the bed.

"I'll be there, whenever and wherever you want," she said, as she closed the door behind her. The clock showed almost seven. He would be a little late.

A smiling François Charron, arriving at the Metropolitan, kissed every cheek offered, shook hands extended by familiar and unfamiliar acquaintances, and took the elevator to C-level stage, where his piano rehearsal would take place. The orchestra run-through on the main stage was scheduled for the next morning.

C-level stage is part of the third basement in the labyrinth that is the underground Met. It lies below the orchestra-pit level, which belongs solely to orchestra players, with dressing rooms, warm-up rooms, and card rooms, and the principal conductor's suite—a cubbyhole with bathroom in a sequestered corner.

B-level houses the music library, and the archives, which has less space because C-level below is actually over two stories deep in order to provide a warehouse for the storing of the scenery, the orchestra rehearsal hall, the ballet rehearsal studios, several offices, and the mammoth hall known as C-level stage. Here stagehands can mount the entire free-standing scenery of any opera, minus the backdrops and lighting.

Peter Camden, waiting on C-level stage, welcomed François and left the theater. The stage director, Jonathan Jeffries, the conductor, Martinson, and the pianist, Foster Stevens, all greeted François. Angelina Lombardini, standing near the piano, did not. She stood aloof, waiting. A pert beret was carefully perched on her head, concealing only part of her new French-style haircut. Her chic, black-knit suit was folded out stylishly at the waist to help hide the thick waistline, but not the more than ample breasts.

Angelina Lombardini was actually French, not Italian, in spite of her aristocratic name—née Lombard, she was a true Monaguesque. Either language was easy for her, however.

François had sung with her before. He recognized this "diva syndrome" immediately and, since his mood was high, he summoned all the Gallic charm he so abundantly possessed and swept across the room to confront her.

"Diva," he whispered, which broke down the wall of protocol instantly. He kissed her hand, both cheeks—lingering slightly—and then tenderly, professionally on the lips. Angelina had no words. The rehearsal began.

Except for Martinson's caution to Angelina "to not sit on every high note," the boudoir scene went well. François was marking all the while because he felt less than brilliant vocally after the tryst with Jacquelyn less than an hour before. His nostrils were still full of the sweet perfume of her body. Even when we're married I'll pay her, he thought. I'll pay her whatever she wants.

In the tomb scene, Angelina was singing full out, pouring forth that limpid sound that was rapidly making her the darling of the New York public. Jonathan Jeffries was enjoying it, too. He made only a few small suggestions about the staging, since he had created this spectacular Met production five years before and both artists were familiar with it.

Roméo drinks the fatal potion. And Juliette, discovering him, despairing, stabs herself. They end the scene in each other's arms, stretched out on the steps of the funeral bier, pleading their eternal love even in death. Maestro Martinson thanked them with a curt handshake, closed the conductor's score, and left.

Then Angelina began. "Jonathan, I'm too small to jump off this bier by myself. It is not graceful. Please go back to the original staging. When I awake, Roméo must help me out and then lift me down the steps and onto the floor. It is so romantic. So right."

Silence. Jonathan looked to François for support. A sharp pain in François' lower back began again. Emotional recall maybe. Too recent history maybe. Self-preservation? Decidedly.

The sympathetic vibration caused a quick flashback to the night of Angelina's debut in the part. He had attempted to lift her according to plan, but had not correctly calculated the overall avoirdupois, which was considerably more than at present, thanks to a Swiss doctor and two months on his starvation diet in a converted *pensione* near the famous bear pits in Berne. The accomplishment cost him several weeks of intense pain caused by the dislocation of two vertebrae and secured him the weight-lifting championship of the opera world. He was known for his voice, not his Olympic ability. What Roméo was?

"I think Jonathan had a sort of sleepwalking, somnambulistic feeling in mind for when you awake, Angelina. It's much better. It's more like a dream," he said.

"I look like a frog, leaping down from that height."

"No, Angelina, you're wrong. It's a lovely moment. And I don't feel Roméo should interfere. He's too stunned to react immediately. I shouldn't touch you."

"Bullshit!" she spat at him, her true spirit surfacing. "You're a pantywaist, weak-tit! Afraid to use your balls. Well, you're not going to make me look bad again. Why do I have to sing

79

with this midget? Get Walter Prince to sing this part. He would lift me down. He's bigger! Why can't I sing with him on this Gala?"

Her eyes were glowing. François hoped it was irritation of her contact lenses. He tried to take her hand, but she snatched it from him and stood by the bier.

"Look at this. It's almost my height from the top to the first level. I'm not a high jumper. Get me a ladder. Get me a step. Two steps."

"A step? What kind of step?" Jonathan broke in. "They don't put steps on funeral biers because corpses don't climb up and down." He paused. He could have eaten his words. "We have to keep some authenticity, some sense of style even in this opera house. Even with divas." He headed out the door and slammed the door to the men's room across the hall.

"Bullshit!" she screamed after him.

"We'll work it out," François said. "I'll get you down, don't worry. I'd better see to Jonathan. I don't think he's too well." He went to aid the stage director.

"Fags or tenors. I don't know who's worse," Angelina shrieked.

She patted her beret into place, found her score and purse, and took the elevator to the floor marked EXECUTIVE AND ARTISTIC.

Jonathan popped two Valium tablets into his mouth and splashed water after them and then onto his face. He was standing with his head against the cool tiles of the men's room wall when François found him.

"Do you know what I'm going through in this house, François? Did you see that rehearsal of *Tosca* with Petrov yesterday? He didn't do one goddamn thing I asked. I'm supposed to stage each scene for the Gala. Talk about 'instant opera.' Pour it in a bowl and stir. I'm so tense I could shit! And now Madame-the-Diva-Superba-Lombardini! I saw it coming. She wants to rule this place. She's probably up in

Peter Camden's office crucifying the lot of us. They sanction her every whim."

"It's all right, Jonathan. Take it easy. Let's just get through the Gala in peace. I'll do her staging some way. Maybe I'll get a truss like Lauritz Melchior wore to support his diaphragm. It'll support my back."

"You're a prince!" Jonathan put his arms around the Frenchman.

"I hope you know you're invited to Mamma Guardino's tonight—anytime after nine o'clock. Bring your friend Tony Sidney and come," François said. "Do you good."

Jonathan shook his head affirmatively.

The idea of Angelina Lombardini and Peter Camden closeted together discussing him made François guffaw. He wondered if they ever exchanged anecdotes. She was his Diva Superba. Surely Angelina would never confide, much less admit, that he had turned her down on numerous occasions—offers of torrid romance between acts at the Met and, also, during the long spring tours. He knew she had a paramour she was keeping out of sight at the Ansonia Hotel for her illicit use, but as the Diva-Superba of the Met she was conscious of her public image. The paramour stayed at home nursing his feelings. She has a husband, too, somewhere. She would never know the real reason for her failure to seduce him. It was not her weight, nor her looks. It was the god-awful mixture of cheap perfumes she wore.

François left the Metropolitan by a side door and hailed a taxi to the St. Moritz to prepare for the evening. And in his mind he was preparing, planning, concentrating on a new Utopian life for himself. A life with Jacquelyn de la Ville, the only woman on earth who didn't offend his sensibilities.

It might as well have been the Feast of St. Gennaro at Mamma Guardino's Restaurant. Tony Garbatini was hosting the evening, having introduced the Gala committee members to the assemblage. The agent made certain each guest had a drink in hand when François, attired in tux and black tie, arrived at 9:30. Mimi Charron had come with a hulk of a man in tow. His dinner jacket bulged at shoulders and biceps, unsuccessfully camouflaging his Mr. America potential. She was all smiles and pleasant repartee. He was all frowns and confusion in this society.

In Peter Camden's absence, the Met was represented by his assistant, Lennie Kempenski. Jason Kraft and Felix Conrad represented the board of directors of the Metropolitan, and Jason was accompanied by the statuesque Francesca Zandonai, whom François knew only by name, never having had the opportunity to sing with her. Even one of the Met physicians, Dr. Alberto Danieli, was there. A devoted opera lover, this elfin, Toulouse-Lautrec figure was purported to be the protector of hundreds of great throats, including the tenors Corsini and Prince. Mr. and Mrs. Felix Conrad had found place cards across from Jacquelyn and her Roméo. Eva Stein was not in attendance.

François had sent the car for Jacquelyn, who made her late, well-timed entrance to an accompanying chorus of "oohs" and "aahs" and not a little appreciative applause from all the gentlemen present.

The guests were served a good Italian Soave and would dine on specialties for the evening named after an opera heroine or hero: Fettuccine Alfredo, Insalata Giulio Cesare, Pollo la Tosca, finishing off the meal with Manon and Carmen cakes with the Espresso Lola.

François had located and sent ahead by messenger three bottles of his favorite French wine. Like the Italian cuisine, he could not abide the too sweet Italian wine. Tonight, for his exquisite Jacquelyn and himself, he had procured a rare Musigny. The three bottles had cost one thousand dollars.

François was having a most wonderful time, delighting in the conviviality, inhaling the remarkable bouquet of the

Musigny, and pausing to kiss the fragile lips of his Juliette at his side. He poured a bit of the precious wine in his glass and tasted it.

"My Juliette, are you happy?" he asked tenderly.

"Happy forever for you, my Roméo."

The last words François Charron heard on this mortal sphere were "my Roméo." His mouth agape, his eyes registering disbelief, he lurched forward into eternity. His head struck the edge of the table with a stomach-churning slap. He fell from his chair and lay in a fetal heap at the foot of his Juliette.

Act 2

"*Un baiser et Je part.*" (A kiss and I go.)

—*Roméo and Juliette*
Charles Gounod and Jules Barbier
and Michel Carré

Scene 1

THE GENERAL MANAGER

FRIDAY, OCTOBER 30, NEW YORK, NEW YORK

The phone in his study was ringing. Peter scrambled to find his door key and the lock. There was no need to hurry. The caller was patient. The ringing continued. He managed the apartment door and went quickly into his study, fumbling for the switch on the desk lamp and lifting the receiver at the same time.

"Peter Camden here."

"Mr. Cámden, hold on for Lieutenant Pasing." The speaker went off the line. There was a click and not much time for Peter to speculate.

"Camden, this is Lieutenant Pasing, New York police. Homicide—Special Unit. We've been trying to find you for about an hour. Nobody home at your house."

He didn't understand. Why hadn't Jill heard the phone? "Can you hold one minute? I've got to check something. I'll be right back." Not waiting for an answer, he put down the phone and went into the bedroom. The lamp beside the bed was on, but the bed had not been slept in. The electric bedside clock showed 12:50 A.M., Friday, October 30. Peter went back to the study, his mind racing.

"What's the matter, lieutenant? Is it my wife? She's not here."

"No, no, Mr. Camden, I just want to talk to you, have you identify someone." The pause he took seemed, to Peter, interminable. "I want you to come to the medical examiner's office. Near Bellevue Hospital. First Avenue at Thirtieth Street."

"Now?"

"Yes, sir, now. We've got an employee of yours. A François Charron. One of your singers. A probable homicide, Mr. Camden."

Peter's gasp cut the man off. His heart leaped from his chest to his throat, pulsing madly. "Jesus God!" he said. "What happened?"

"I'm not sure yet. He died at Mamma Guardino's restaurant. I closed the place until morning. You'd better come on down here, Mr. Camden. First Avenue and Thirtieth. First floor. Pasing. One s, said like a z. You have it? You know the place?"

"No, I don't know the place."

"Take a taxi. I'll be waiting." The phone went dead in his hand.

The driver grunted his acknowledgment of the address, so Peter sat back in the rear seat of the Yellow Cab and tried to think calmly. It was virtually impossible. Jill's absence, coupled with François' death, was enough to send any sane man screaming into the streets. It was all so vague. So out of nowhere. However, one thing was definite. François had been alive at his rehearsal last evening and now his golden voice was silenced. Irretrievable.

Four hours ago, he had wanted to shout to the whole

world that he was in love, that he didn't need to lean on his wife for psychological support. He had discovered peace and place in the arms of Eva Stein that night. Now he didn't know where he was.

He had taken the rented limousine from Eva's apartment to the airport to meet Renato Corsini. He had helped the tenor through customs and to the Mayflower Hotel. And then he had gone home. To this!

The taxi drew to the curb in front of an ominous building on First Avenue at Thirtieth Street. Peter was more than ready to get out. He handed the driver a five-dollar bill and, not waiting for change, hurried up the steps. He mentioned the name Pasing, signed his name in a ledger, produced his driver's license for the guard, and was courteously guided to the back elevator and told to push the button for the subbasement.

He was just noticing the television eye focused on him from the ceiling of the elevator when the door slid open to reveal another uniformed official, who led him down a dark corridor and opened a door marked HOMICIDE.

"Welcome, Mr. Camden. I'm Lieutenant Theodore Pasing." He indicated a chair.

Peter sat down, finding the chair with his leg, like a well-trained actor, unable to detach his gaze from the man standing behind a desk, lighting a meerschaum pipe. The lieutenant was shorter than Peter's six feet. He was wearing the vest to his three-piece suit and was fishing a lighter from his jacket, which was hanging over the back of his chair. Peter was impressed with his calm demeanor. His hair was clipped close, receding and chalk white. He could have been around sixty. He finished lighting his pipe.

"Please feel free to smoke, Mr. Camden. I smoke a pipe, but there are cigars in the box there on the desk; also cigarettes, if you wish."

The air in the room was permeated with smoke. Peter was grateful for the respite. He took a cigar with a thankful nod. His eyes fell on the shoulder-holstered weapon that lay on the desk. The lieutenant caught his expression and laughed.

"Second war, snub-nosed .45," he said in explanation. "Usually wear it to bed, but I've been waiting around here for over two hours. It's very heavy—especially for a man of my age . . . more deadly than a magnum, if you know how to handle it. It's old-fashioned, but it gives me a lot of comfort."

This man is certainly not the stereotypical, cigar-chomping, hard-nosed detective we see on television or in the movies, Peter thought. He reminds me of my composition professor at Yale. But Peter was aware of his well-muscled arms and shoulders, which revealed a man of action beneath the tranquil façade.

Lieutenant Pasing began to strap on the piece. "I can fill you in as we go. I just want you to get hold of yourself, because I can see this is all new to you. Believe me, you spend one day with me around this town and nothing would bother you. Come this way." He flipped his jacket off the chair and started for the door. Peter followed.

They walked further along the dimly lit corridor, one of the guards following discreetly behind. Peter didn't know whether the cold he was feeling was caused by anxiety or the subterranean, windowless chill. He soon found out. The lieutenant pushed open a swinging door, and the cold hit him in the face like a wind, carrying with it a starchy, disinfectant odor, which he knew, instinctively, was the smell of death. He felt suddenly weak, but caught himself. Fear of the unknown. That's all it is.

They were in an autopsy room standing between two empty metal tables, scrubbed shiny clean. Each table had a drain four inches wide and three inches deep around the perimeter. Metal sinks were along one wall. There were no windows. An instrument case was open on the far wall. Peter closed his eyes to the impersonal room.

Pasing guided him to a third table, where a body was covered by a sheet. He rolled down the sheet and then tossed it back in place. A glance was enough. The gray mask the lieutenant had uncovered was certainly that of François.

"That's Charron," Peter managed to say.

"A personal formality, Mr. Camden. Everyone knows it's Charron. His ex-wife was there. I sent her home. She was hysterical."

Lieutenant Pasing motioned to the guard, who went through a door marked PRIVATE and returned with two men in galoshes and rubber aprons. They wheeled François out through the swinging doors.

"Give me a rundown, Sam, as soon as possible. I'll be back here about four A.M. I'm going to take you home, Mr. Camden."

Pasing led the way up a flight of steps to another underground level and down a stark cement-block corridor to the parking garage. He located a dark blue Plymouth, which had no police markings, slapped the top with his hand, indicating possession, and got in. Peter made his way to the other side. They were out of the garage and on the way uptown before Pasing stopped the incessant pulling on his meerschaum.

"I'm pretty sure it's poison, Mr. Camden. I'll know later, but I've seen it many times. So far, I don't have any idea who might have wanted him dead. Do you?"

"I can't imagine! Charron is one of the world's greatest singers. His death is a calamity."

"Was one," the lieutenant corrected. "I'm well aware of the loss. One of the reasons the commissioner asked me personally to take this case is my longtime interest in the arts. I'm an opera buff, Mr. Camden, as my father was before me. And my wife, Lissette, is a bona fide balletomane. Although we don't attend the opera and the ballet as much as we used to because of the god-awful high-priced tickets."

Although surprised at the anomaly of a New York cop with such a varied background, Peter wasn't able to comment. "I'm sorry" is all he wanted to say.

"The girl Charron was with tonight is a dancer," Pasing continued. "Pretty thing. She's in shock. Knows nothing. Most of the people at the party speak Italian or French. Do you speak French or Italian, Camden?"

"A little."

"Mamma Guardino and her son were about to come apart at the binding. Either there is a real pro involved or your opera people are all damn good actors. Everybody—about fifty people—all going crazy, shouting and waving their arms, as if they were performing. Regular circus! Any one of them could have dropped something in Charron's drink. He bought some special wine for himself and the girl."

"Could this be some kind of vendetta against the Met, against the Gala?" Peter asked, wishing he felt as calm as the dauntless force sitting beside him. "It's crazy to imagine anything so drastic . . . but it is possible in light of Charron's death . . . isn't it?"

"Very possible. I was on the same wavelength." The lieutenant emptied the cooled ashes from his pipe out the window and began to pack it again, using his right hand only. "I'd like to count on your help on this. I don't think this comes from outside the opera world. It's far too pointed, direct. I just want permission to tap your brain. I need to know all about those people connected with the Gala. Yes, I know about the big event. I told you I'm a fan, and I read the newspapers. And there are hundreds, perhaps thousands, of employees at the Met—singers, stagehands, musicians. Any one of them might want to sabotage your project. I'm going to need you, Mr. Camden."

Pasing swung onto Madison Avenue, driving slowly. The traffic was light at that hour. Peter stared at the dashboard.

"Yes, Mr. Camden," said Pasing, puffing his freshly lit

pipe, "there seems to be a lot of ammunition aimed in your direction."

Peter felt perplexity and fear mounting inside him. "What do you mean?"

"We had a killing Wednesday night over on the West Side. It was an execution, probably political. Probably JDL. You know: Jewish Defense League. They select targets very carefully in their war against anti-Semitism. This was a well-planned assassination. And we had a hell of a time identifying the man. Nothing left of his face. He had a passport. Unreadable because of the blood. We finally got a make on it. Checked with the Russian embassy. They verified. Checked with the hotel."

"Good God." Peter couldn't believe his ears. His comprehension was quick and horrifying. "Petrov?"

"You got it, Camden. Home run. Another one of your singers. We've got him downtown."

"You say it was an execution?" Peter's mind was spinning. "A vendetta!"

"Just that. Lined up against the wall. Firing squad."

Peter had his face in his hands. He felt his temples throbbing.

The car eased to a halt in front of Peter's apartment building.

"We have a few homicides every night."

Peter didn't get out of the car. "Do you want me to identify him?"

Pasing took a long look at the pale, strained countenance of the Met's general manager. "No. You wouldn't be able to recognize him anyway. What I really wanted to do was talk to you." He paused, scratching the bowl of his pipe against the stubble on his cheek. "Have the other tenors on the Gala arrived yet? Are they in town?"

"Oh, God!" Peter could not repress a sob. He thought: There are only three of them left. He said: "Only Renato

93

Corsini, lieutenant. I met him at the airport earlier tonight. I hope I can keep him here when he hears about Charron and Petrov. He's already nervous about being in New York."

"What do you mean?"

"All the way into the city he was mumbling to himself, asking himself why he was here. He kept crossing himself and kissing a picture he held in his hand. I thought it was an icon or the medallion of a saint, but it was the photo of a girl. He asked her for strength to face the *ombra*."

"What's an *ombra*?" Pasing asked.

"It's a singer's superstition. It's the hostile audience—the black void a singer faces when he's on the stage. The darkness makes him feel alone, vulnerable. It's stage fright. With some singers it's an obsession. Some singers have had to be literally forced onto the stage at the Met for a performance. That's why you hear one singer say to another: '*In bocca al lupo*' before going on. To which the reply is: '*Crepi al lupo.*' "

"Which means?"

" 'Into the mouth of the wolf,' which is the same as the *ombra*. And the answer is: 'To hell with the wolf.' "

"I have many of Corsini's records. My father collected Caruso records, and I collect Corsini. To me he's the successor to Caruso; but he hasn't sung here in ten years. What's the problem? Don't tell me stage fright."

"I'm not quite sure. He's a very rich man, so he doesn't have to sing. He's been mixed up in politics in Italy. He's chosen to be reclusive, not to face the public. Maybe it's fear. Maybe something else. I just don't know."

"There is something I'm aware of that probably hasn't concerned you," Pasing said. "When Corsini was singing here in the sixties and seventies, he associated himself with some pretty shady characters. Perhaps it was because he was first and foremost an Italian, but he was often seen with powerful underworld figures such as Sonny Altabelli and Mario 'the arm' Lupetin. But he was a star. He attracted the money and

94

the power to him. And he was not unknown in Washington circles."

"Well, we can consider ourselves blessed. We're lucky to have him for whatever reason. And we will be able to herald his 'farewell performance.'"

"Did you learn that tonight?"

"Yes, on the way in to the hotel. He's not the same Corsini who sang at the Met in the glory days. He's closed off. Inside himself he's suffering terribly, whether it's from fear or guilt or whatever, and he's ready to quit. I just hope he can sing. I'm taking a big chance, lieutenant."

"I'm going to keep a close watch on Mr. Corsini and all his associates," Pasing said. "*Vendetta* is an Italian word."

Scene 2

THE ITALIAN

JUNE 1954, SPOLETO, ITALY

Gian Carlo Corsini stood on the majestic promontory overlooking the verdant Umbrian valley. Below him was the old viaduct, built by the Romans some twenty centuries before—a marvel of architecture and human ingenuity. To the northwest was Spoleto, with its winding streets, stone battlements, the stately *duomo*, inspired and built by the Franciscans. His elbows rested on a portion of the western wall of a palace built by the Borgias, now serving as a prison and sometime tourist attraction. Every evening at sundown that spot on the promontory was implicitly reserved for the personal meditation and aesthetic contemplation of the sixty-year-old Gian Carlo Corsini, the most powerful man in the district.

Today he watched the fair-haired young woman approach him. She was in the center of the walkway three hundred feet above the rocky crevasse when she paused to look about her and take in the grandeur. Gian Carlo noticed the delightful jutting of her breasts and the fullness of her hips—her summer frock clinging to her from the heat of the day—and her determined assault on the slope to the promontory. Gian Carlo smiled. He didn't feel old at all, although his white hair indicated time's passing. Life has held so much unfulfillment for me, he thought. Could it have been any different? If I hadn't lost Anna Lisa at such a young age, would it have been any different? If Renato were more serious, closer? Perhaps I can be more of a father to him. But how? Love? We all need to constantly seek and find love. Daydreams of an old man? Perhaps.

"*Buona sera.*" The girl had reached the promontory and spoke to Gian Carlo.

"*Buona sera,*" he said, looking squarely at the most voluptuous breasts in the world. "You are seeking Gian Carlo Corsini?"

"Yes, I came on the train from Rome. Signor Beltrami, the attorney in your office, said I was to join you here in Spoleto. He said you have much need of a secretary and assistant. I do hope I have not made the journey in vain." Her prepared, halting, slightly accented speech, delivered in a charming manner, produced a warm smile on Corsini's face.

"I can assure you your trip was not in vain. If you can write letters and make some sort of order in my home and office, you'll have steady employment. And I believe I shall erect a ten-foot wall around my house to discourage the young gentry of Spoleto. I need assistance, not trouble." His smile remained and his voice brimmed with sincerity and interest.

"My name is Margarita Secchi. My home is in Rome. My great ambition in life was to be an artist, a painter, but my father insisted I go to business school." She laughed a melodic arpeggio. Seeing Gian Carlo's smile, she continued. "My parents are dead."

"I know. I've been told. You are highly recommended. You are formerly from the Tyrol—consequently, your accent. You'll stay here with me at my villa just up the hill from the Piazza Duomo. It is quieter here than in Rome. Some of my work is secret, or at least private, and so Spoleto suits my purposes best." He continued to stare at her, amazed at her beauty. "I know who comes into the city and who leaves and how. This has been my family home for over one hundred years. My stronghold. I hope you will grow to love it as I do." He at last turned to look out over the valley toward Assisi and Perugia in the far distance. "This place is my love, Margarita. Umbria. My love. My entire life is cradled here."

They walked together side by side down the road to the viaduct and entered the city.

"During the war, Margarita, my factories were making tanks, not automobiles. My home from 1938 to 1946 was in Milan. When Mussolini was hanged, Generale Badoglio, who then governed Italy, insisted I retire to Spoleto, where I would be relatively safe. Who would not be safe in these peaceful streets?"

As they reached the villa, a disturbance in the distance brought Gian Carlo about-face to look in the direction of the piazza in front of the *duomo*. A green Corsini 700 had throttled from a narrow side street into the piazza, which was forbidden to vehicular traffic, and disappeared down another alley the width of a donkey-cart. Still in the distance, the engine holding its level of noise, it precipitated an outburst of obscenities from the old man. Then control. Then a philosophical mien.

"That's my son Renato in that car. I almost hope he smashes into a wall. Something to force some sense into his

97

head. I have no control. He won't listen to me. I think he hates me and I don't know why." Again he used the most sincere, thoughtful tone.

The Corsini 700 reappeared and jolted to a stop in front of the Villa Corsini. An Adonis stepped from the automobile. A god. To Margarita, he was the most astonishingly handsome man she had ever seen. His smile shamed the sun, lit up the twilight sky.

"My son," Gian Carlo said, looking at him. "You see why I can't be angry long. He's blessed by the gods. The image of my beloved wife, Anna Lisa. Perhaps a boy without a mother can develop into only half a man."

Renato noticed her. He saw how her eyes burned into him, undressing him. Scalding, green eyes. He knew it all. He had seen it all before. Women worshiped him until they spread their legs for him, and then possession and jealousy destroyed the relationship. He kicked each wide marble step on the way to his third-floor suite.

Anyone can see why she's here, he thought. Blond whore! She'll be after the old man in the flick of an eyelash. Well, he's worked hard, lived like a monk, and probably deserves a little now and again. Only about thirty years' difference in their ages. He laughed, rolling onto his huge double bed, thinking what a workbench the bed would be had he the courage to bring one of his conquests into the family villa.

The only thing one could consider polished about Renato was the automobile parked outside. The green Corsini 700, a gift from his father, or at least his father's automobile factory in Milan, was the most important thing in his life. He felt his heart surge proud and virile when he drove it.

"The old man didn't even realize I was gone," he said aloud to the four walls, as he tossed his jacket and silk scarf across the marble end of his unmade bed. "Just as well. He wouldn't approve of the way I spend his money, humping the beauties of Rome. He's Italian, but his conscience is ever Catholic."

Renato had spent the last three days and nights hanging about the Spanish Steps, trying to break his personal record by sleeping with thirteen prostitutes, one at a time, and he had done so with scant pleasure and obvious disdain. One of them had produced a searing ache in his prostate area and yellow-green secretion from his penis. He knew it was a temporary illness. He would visit the Spoleto Hospital tomorrow morning for the quick cure. Dr. Danieli would give him a needle full of multiple cc's of penicillin. Alberto Danieli, dwarflike and serious, had been the Corsini family physician for many years; he was the most discreet of men.

Two fateful events evolved during the first year of Margarita's employment at the Villa Corsini in Spoleto. The first happened as a not too minor miracle.

The day began simply enough. Renato, looking bored, hands thrust deep into his pockets, slouched down the steps of the villa, heading in the direction of the *duomo*. He hadn't been to church in some time—perhaps years. He had not made confession since his confirmation. He was drawn, however, by something like a magnetic force. He crossed the piazza—the bright Umbrian sun burning a hole in his back—passing the Caio Melissa to stand looking up at the *duomo*.

He knew nothing about art or architecture and little enough about religion, but at that moment, with the rays of the noonday sun heightening the myriad colors of the stained-glass windows, he felt humbled. He pushed open the heavy, carved mahogany door and went inside. Now the sun reflected the colors in a kaleidoscopic sequence on the walls, on the saints in their niches, on the worn pews, and finally on the ornate altar, glowing with inlaid gold and semiprecious stones. Renato dropped to his knees.

How long he had been kneeling there when he heard the voices from above and behind him was uncertain to him. A boys' choir? Yes, but augmented with older men's voices. He looked up to them. He could see the cherubic faces of some twenty young boys concentrating on the music they held before them. He was drawn to them, ascending the narrow wooden steps to the choir loft. The director of the choir was a tiny Franciscan brother, who motioned for him to sit with them. One of the boys, whose face was that of a miniature David, sculpted in alabaster, handed him a sheet of paper with strange-looking symbols and words written on it. He couldn't read the notes, but he read the words *Regina Coeli* from Mascagni's *Cavalleria Rusticana.*

The organ peeled forth at a sign from the Franciscan. He waved his hands in a pattern—down, across his stomach, out, and then up to a point above his head—and the men and boys broke into song. And Renato Corsini, inspired, sang with them. Every angelic face turned in his direction. The sun shone brighter, turning the interior of the *duomo* into a glorious rainbow.

Renato's life gained purpose. His attitude and his personality traversed the entire spectrum of change. Black to white. He had direction. Ambition. He sang every day, tirelessly, either with the choir or solo. The Franciscan father, Leo, who directed the music at the *duomo*, taught him how to best use his voice. Renato's father endowed the church with vast sums of money. And it was not long before everyone in Spoleto knew and had heard the God-given instrument of Renato Corsini fill the holy *duomo* with wondrous sound.

At this time, the old Spoleto opera house, which had long before fallen into disrepair, was to be refurbished and used as a school and training theater for the Rome Opera Company. Renato applied, auditioned, and was accepted. The following year, after much preparation, Renato made his debut in the *spinto* role of Pollione in the opera *Norma*, which to

100

most tenors was a true test of vocal prowess. Renato soared over the hurdle. His success was overwhelming. His future in opera was secured. He was twenty-five years old.

The order of incidence of the second fateful event was, to Renato, both unimportant and unknown. What was important was the inevitability of a union between Gian Carlo and Margarita. Renato saw it, observing the progress step by step. Acquaintance. Communication. Companionship. Intimacy. Love.

The old man and Margarita were together all the time, except for Gian Carlo's daily trip to the promontory above the city. The valued moment for contemplation of his life, which was happier now with Margarita than ever before, was reserved each evening for him, alone. He had so much more to think about now besides his beautiful Umbria, his home: Margarita, *con grande amore*. With monumental love.

She was a genius at organization. Spending each morning on the telephone to managers and accountants of his factories, she kept a close watch on every facet of the Corsini empire. She labored over a most accurate ledger, answered hundreds of letters each week, and began an extensive and intricate filing system, centralizing the entire operation in the Corsini villa from its separate offices in Rome, Milan, Bologna, Genoa, Venice, Naples, and Palermo. She needed no staff in the villa. She worked alone.

The nights were simple enough. Dinner was served in the elegant salon, with its ornate crystal chandelier. Easy conversation flowed. There was anisette in the garden in summer, and in the fall they sipped the best French Cognac in front of a glowing fire when frost covered the ground. Friendship and respect. Then inevitably, as even Renato could witness: true love. Margarita and the old man. As a Catholic, Gian Carlo felt he could not marry again. But their love was real.

Renato was occupied with his studies: voice, repertory, solfeggio, and acting. He spent his days at the tiny Spoleto opera house engrossed in his singing. He could not explain his feelings about his work even to himself, but he was deeply, joyously resolved. He loved to sing. To let his golden sound escape his throat. He sang at every opportunity. After the sessions at the opera house, he would join his young colleagues at the Trattoria Mercante—a small restaurant in the center of Spoleto, in the marketplace—for a flask of red wine and warm conviviality. And sing some more. He forgot about Rome and his whores.

The old *spinetto* piano, played by Dr. Alberto Danieli—one half-tone flat, with a sound like a banjo—was used for the accompaniment of Italian drinking songs. Renato would be called on to lead off with the Libiamo from Verdi's *La Traviata*, and after a long pull on the flask of *vino rosso*—one foot on his chair and the other on the table, his voice threatening the safety of the structure of the small establishment—he would throw back his head and let fly the glorious high tones of "Viva il vino spumeggiante" from *Cavalleria Rusticana*.

At some point, his baritone friend Memo would take over with the drinking song from the first act of *Otello*. The festivities would continue into the evening and then spill into the streets, as the opera stars of tomorrow made their way home. If a sore throat was the result of too much singing, Dr. Danieli would switch from keyboard to his black bag to administer to the troubadours.

Renato's contracts began to pile up in his room, sent on to him by his agent in Rome, who had signed him to a contract after his Spoleto debut. In 1958 and 1959 he repeated his favorite role—Pollione in *Norma*—in Palermo, Florence, and Venice. He sang his first Manrico in *Il Trovatore* in Naples in the winter of 1960, and again in Genoa and Rome. His fame spread.

One day he opened his mail to find the Metropolitan

Opera offer that would be emblazoned on his brain forever. The contract requested him to debut at the esteemed house on Thirty-ninth Street and Broadway in New York City as the black Moor of Venice in the fall of 1964, and continue throughout the season. It was two years away, but Renato would learn the role and try it out in any of a number of theaters, to be ready. It was like a dream to him. He signed that day and marched to the main post office at the bottom of the hill near the railroad station to make certain the letter was dispatched immediately to his agent.

Making his way slowly back up the steep hill, he passed the little record shop where he bought every record of such tenors as Caruso, Gigli, Lauri-Volpi, Tamagno, Bonci. He thought seriously of his heritage. A tenor. No, a world-class tenor. Renato Corsini. In Italy, in the world, he would be king.

Continuing his climb, he waved to a prostitute who stationed herself near the Albergo Umbria, Spoleto's only *primo* hotel. Renato had not frequented prostitutes, he realized, since God had touched his vocal cords. He had confessed and done hours of penance. He had his aura. He was purified.

He turned, approached the girl, and slipped two ten-thousand-lire notes into her hand, leaning over to kiss her forehead.

"Grazie mille, Signor Corsini," she said in her scratchy voice, pocketing the money.

"Niente, cara. Salve." He continued up the hill. He noticed the tears in her eyes as she turned away. They were forming in his, too.

At the foot of the steps to the Villa Corsini, Renato paused. Coming toward him from the house was his father's attorney from Rome, Signor Beltrami, whom he had not seen in almost a year. He did not know the man's first name—just Beltrami. A man in his fifties, dark suit, dark tie, somber. A fringe of hair over his ears, protruding at right angles to his head, gave him the look of a monk with a shiny, white skull-cap. His expression was stern.

Beltrami took Renato's arm in a strong grip, belying the attorney's fragile outward appearance. He walked Renato back in the direction the younger man had come, toward the *duomo*, and then into a narrow street leading toward the center of town.

"My car's in the marketplace, but I must speak with you before I return to Rome." Renato was impressed with the educated mien of the man. He couldn't recall ever speaking with him at length before.

"The Trattoria Mercante is quiet this time of day," Renato said.

"Excellent. Come."

The afternoon crowd had departed and the evening diners not yet arrived, leaving the small restaurant deserted except for the daughter of the proprietor, who took their order of a flask of chianti.

"Your father asked me here today to change his will," Beltrami said, patting his briefcase and sipping wine. "He's leaving the bulk of his estate to his secretary and—only assuming—his one love, Margarita Secchi." Renato's mouth fell open, releasing the pent-up air of disbelief. "There's a trust fund for you, of course, but it's merely a token compared with what you would acquire from the old will. I, too, will suffer because I will not be retained and will have no share in the estate. Even the villa goes to Margarita. He must love her very much."

Renato placed his hands over his face. Beltrami lit a cigar and sat back in his chair, his eyes on the young man.

"The entire Corsini Auto Industry goes to Margarita. You become a ward to the whims of Signora Secchi. Contemplate that. Chew on it. It's up to you," Beltrami continued. "You have an important career ahead of you, but who knows how long it will last. You'll make money in opera, but it is nothing—

a pittance—compared to Gian Carlo's fortune." He paused, letting his use of Gian Carlo's name, instead of a reference to him as father, sink in. "Gian Carlo is too old. Margarita will close the door on both of us. You must prevent it."

"How?"

"You'll think of something. It must be soon. I won't begin a new draft of the will until I hear from you—yea or nay. I'm going back to Rome."

Beltrami stood, placing his briefcase under his arm, and crossed the Piazza Mercante to his car.

Renato's mind was in turmoil. He wanted to cry out in despair. He wanted to run. If the woman, Margarita, had been near at that moment he would have strangled her. He stood thinking of his past, of its comfort, and of the future that held only his voice—and he knew how ephemeral singing could be. Then he thrust his hands into his pockets and shuffled his way toward the villa.

Aimlessly, Renato rounded the corner into the Piazza Duomo. His eye caught the figure of Gian Carlo as he cleared the last step of the villa and turned right up the hill toward the old Borgia Castello—off on his daily walk over the old viaduct to the promontory above the valley. The unexplained forces of good and evil that would guide the life of Renato Corsini were activated. He was drawn after the old man.

The pace the elder Corsini set was more brisk that evening, as if a weight had gone from his shoulders. His thoughts were of Margarita and the beauty of the countryside around him, which seemed to be more sharply in focus with a vision of her omnipresent in it.

Margarita, of course, was unaware of the generous gift, a present of a new and worry-free life. She would know only after his death. But he believed he would be around for a long time. He was only sixty-eight. He wanted to see the sunset on this beautiful day from the heights and then hurry home to her arms. Some evenings Margarita would read to him, a part of their nurtured, deepening companionship.

Gian Carlo crossed the viaduct and took his place on the aerie, marveling at the display of colors painted on the hillside: bottle green in the shadows, yellow green where the sun still spilled on the trees, and a sort of opaque, misty green when the two met, as if viewed through a crystal goblet. He could not see the tortured face and figure standing in the trees on the town side of the viaduct. For that shredded psyche the wait was far more than a solitary half hour. It was forever.

As Gian Carlo began his descent, the shadows were longer, so he had to look twice to discover the approaching man. Renato was no more than thirty feet away when Gian Carlo recognized him. Surprise was in his voice as he asked why Renato was there, on the viaduct, at this time of day. But Renato did not answer. He grasped his father's shoulders and spun him over the railing of the viaduct, into the fragrant evening air, plunging him three hundred feet onto the rocks. Gian Carlo's head was split open on a moss-covered boulder the size, the color, and the shape of Renato's automobile.

Legs churning, the breeze blowing his thick, dark hair, Renato made his way back to the Trattoria Mercante. He ordered wine and settled himself into a corner to salvage, to clutch at his life . . . his sanity.

The announcement of the death of Gian Carlo Corsini came only twenty minutes after Renato had begun to consume his second flask of chianti. The daughter of the proprietor and her lover, Luigi, had heard a noise outside the old, deserted sheep shed under the viaduct, where they met each afternoon. They were startled by the unexpected crash. It took moments to locate the cause. But there, half on the rock and half hidden in the rushes, was the crushed body of Signor Gian Carlo Corsini. The sight of the blood-drenched white mane of hair tripped the consciousness of the proprietor's daughter, and, as she fainted, her lover ejected his midday meal into the thick foliage. As soon as Luigi could revive the girl, they made their way back to the Piazza Mercante to spread the shocking news.

At the funeral, held at the *duomo*, Signor Beltrami took Margarita Secchi into a side chapel and presented her with a check for one year's wages and a railroad ticket to Rome.

Renato moved downstairs to the second floor of the Villa Corsini and promptly arranged for Signor Beltrami to take over the Corsini Automotive Industry. Two years later the thirty-four-year-old tenor galvanized the Metropolitan Opera audience with his portrayal of the murderous Moor of Venice.

Scene 3

THE GENERAL MANAGER

FRIDAY, OCTOBER 30, NEW YORK, NEW YORK

Jill, holding a large bell of Cognac, was sitting on the living-room sofa when Peter let himself in.

"Portia Williams called. Eva Stein called. Mimi Charron called. Doris at the switchboard called. The rehearsal department called. It seems you have your share of problems." Her voice was startling in its volume, cutting the silence.

"I'm glad you noticed. I'd say that, yes, two murders in about twenty-four hours, annihilating two of the finest tenors in the world could easily pass as 'my share of problems.' "

"*Two* murders! Oh, Peter. I had no idea . . . oh, my. . . ."

He poured himself a drink and plopped into his comfortable wing chair, looking, he was certain, for all the ponderous world, as drained as the corpse he had just seen. He decided not to elaborate.

"Where were you tonight?" Peter asked.

Jill countered, incredulous and confused at his abrupt change of subject, "Following you, my Don Juan."

"You were *what*? What for?"

"Because I'm a fighter. You think I'm going to sit back and watch you make a fool of yourself over a sixty-year-old widow. Not on your life! I'm not the naïve housewife you make me out to be. I followed you from the Met to Eva Stein's apartment house, waited half an hour, and gave it up. I hope your recreation was fulfilling."

"That was a business call. She is a committee member . . . on my Gala. What an underhanded thing to do!"

She shook her head angrily. "Come off it. You sent the limo away. This has been going on for the better part of a year, hasn't it?"

"How do you know that? Why haven't you said something before?"

"Because I didn't know for sure until tonight. When I left you there, seeking your pleasure, I called Randolph Martinson. Yes, we speak occasionally. I forgave him long ago for that night in Vermont. He took me to dinner at Il Vagabondo. And he verified my suspicions of Eva Stein."

"How would he know?"

"Everybody knows, it seems. Except me. *I* didn't know. I thought we were growing apart because of your job. I didn't know it was an affair in progress. For God's sake, Peter. Eva Stein is older than you. In a few years she'll really be old. Do you think I'm going to let you indulge in your middle-aged change-for-the-sake-of-change and destroy our marriage? You have two daughters, who love and admire you, and a wife, who loves you and understands you. Have your fling, but don't think I'm going to step aside without a fight."

He felt himself blushing; remorse and guilt joined in his

brain. "I didn't know you still spoke to Randolph Martinson. You said that was a sordid part of your life, that business with Martinson and Ludwig."

"It was a long time ago. I loved Randolph. You knew that. We've spoken on the phone over the years. He knows I'm your wife."

"Yet you've never mentioned him as a prospective Met conductor."

"Of course not. I don't know how good he is. And I've never meddled in your business."

"Well, I never would have chosen him for the Gala. I wanted Jimmy Levine, but my committee was unanimously in Martinson's favor. I don't know why."

"Maybe you should have asked me to join your committee. I know two of your artists personally."

"Would you have voted for Martinson?"

"Yes."

Jill handed Peter her empty glass. Peter took it, and refilled it at the sideboard, pouring another drink for himself.

"I've just identified the body of François Charron," Peter said. "After I met Corsini's plane at Kennedy, I received a call from the police. We have two murders, Jill. Two of our stars are dead. I have no idea why. I'm beside myself. I think I have to cancel the Gala."

Her face showed disbelief. "Oh my God—Petrov too? You may not cancel the Gala!" she said, taking his hand. Her voice was filled with compassion. "You've got to be strong. You've been preaching to me how important it is to you, your credibility, your job. There are still three great tenors to carry on on Sunday night. I agree it's horrendous. But you have a kinship with your singers that other general managers, the world over, can't cultivate. Stick by them. See to the others, Peter."

Peter felt the strength of her voice flow through him, knew she was right. "Lieutenant Pasing said essentially the same thing. I know you're both right. Thanks for standing by me. I'm afraid I've been awful to you. I'm sorry."

She smiled. "I wish you'd concentrate on just getting the Gala on, for the sake of us all, and stop searching for someone to bolster you. You don't need Eva Stein. You have me."

He finished the Cognac in one burning gulp, replaced the glass on the sideboard, stood, and, with a short cry of pain and love, pulled her to him and held her in his arms.

Scene 4

THE ITALIAN

DECEMBER 1969, MILAN, ITALY

When Renato Corsini was thirty-nine years old, long after the death of his father, Gian Carlo, sometime after his heralded debut at the Metropolitan Opera, and a short while after he was acclaimed to be the greatest tenor since Enrico Caruso, he met Francesca Zandonai.

It was in December 1969 that Renato parked his two-seat, underslung, sporty Corsini 1000 next to the curb in the narrow street beside the Teatro alla Scala in rainy, dreary Milan. His rehearsal was to begin at eleven o'clock, and he was punctual, one of his obsessions.

Immediately the car was surrounded by fans, waiting for a glimpse of him. Renato hurried through the mob, holding a scarf across his throat and mouth, mainly so he wouldn't have to greet the people. They took it as protection of a golden voice against the elements. He shook hands with Antonio, the elderly concierge, and strode on stage at exactly 11:00 to the applause of chorus, supers, and stagehands.

Lightning flashed, and the stage filled with a surging mass of people on a wharf on the island of Cyprus, watching the ship bearing the victorious returning army of the black Moor of Venice. The storm, described in glorious musical invention, finally subsided, and Otello's galleon reached its moorings. There, on the deck high above the tumultuous, adoring throng, appeared the conqueror—Renato, with his scarf still wrapped around his throat.

"*Esultate! L'orgoglio Musulmano sepolto è in mar!*" The human trumpet was Renato's voice. His sound rocketed like a silver projectile to the far reaches of the theater, thrilling every ear, touching every heart. Even in rehearsal, the magic was all there. Verdi. Shakespeare. Corsini.

Once the act was over, a three-hour lunch break was called. Almost as if the magic of the scene were still there in effulgence, a statuesque redhead, her figure perfectly proportioned to her height, was at his elbow.

"I want you to take me to lunch. If you don't have money, I'll take you." The sincerity, the lilt of her voice, and the obvious promise of physical reward stopped Renato in midstride. He looked into her da Vinci face. His smile would have blotted out the sun. Hers matched his.

"I have money and I'll take you. Biffi alla Scala next door is reasonable."

Over the meal, Francesca told Renato that she was one of the corps of singers at La Scala, and that she had wanted to introduce herself for months but hadn't had the nerve until that day. She had understudied Desdemona in *Otello*, and hoped one day to have the privilege of singing it with him. "I'm a long way from being ready to sing with Corsini," she said, showing that winning smile.

She had been in the company at La Scala for only two

years, but she had undertaken several years of apprenticeship in the San Carlo Opera of Naples, Maggio Musicale in Florence, and the Teatro Massimo in Palermo.

She was from Venice, where she began her singing in a small cabaret, forced to make a living by the death of both parents when she was seventeen. She did not mention how they died. She thought she was distantly related to the composer Riccardo Zandonai.

That evening at midnight, Francesca moved her things from the tiny Pensione Sparafucil, in the street that bears the same name, to the penthouse apartment of Renato in the Residence Elite. From that day, for seven years she never left his side. She relinquished her own career in deference to his, her own life to his. Her care over her tenor was almost servile. Every problem she swept aside to ensure his well-being mentally and physically. Renato had never needed anyone until then. But he had had no true idea of what he might have been missing in his solitary life. Francesca was to show him. Ten years younger than he, she was to make those seven years, years of wonder.

His singing became more expressive. He laughed at almost everything. He even permitted Francesca to have the villa in Spoleto cleaned and aired and the exterior painted a sparkling white.

They went everywhere together, not only to sing. A favorite place was the little town of San Benedetto on the Adriatic Sea, where they lived near the beach, turning the color of the natives, who looked far more Greek than Italian. They ate clams, shrimp, and octopus especially prepared for them in the Trattoria Bianca on the Via Regina. They swam in the Adriatic and they discovered and rediscovered each other.

On one of these trips, Renato told Francesca the complete story of his father's death. Haltingly, feeling the pain and guilt, which had never left him, he poured out his tale, knowing it would never go further than his beloved Francesca. He confessed that his dreams were infused with visions of his father cursing him and swearing God would silence his voice, as retribution for his deed.

At first, Francesca could not believe him. It was unthinkable that this gentle human being, hugging his knees, sitting in the sand on that deserted beach, was capable of killing his father. My God, she thought, how could he hide such a thing? She remembered reading somewhere that sentimentality, among Italians, was, in truth, suppressed brutality.

"Renato," she said, searching for some way to console him. "I can't play God. *He* is the one you must go to with your guilt to ask forgiveness. I can only love you and try to help you. And you must forgive me that I can't accept the responsibility of this secret. It's too much for me. But, this I know: I love you, and I will try." She knew he, too, cherished their love above all things. But she knew that her love would never erase for him the images of his father's disbelieving face.

Renato revealed the dark responsibilities he inherited as head of the Corsini Industries. With bitter words, he spoke of his father's complicity with Mussolini in the war, his father's seclusion to escape discovery or indictment. The unwritten agreements in the industry not to hire or do business with Jews. And, finally, the vast sums of money his company was paying to support the neo-Fascist rightists who had shielded his father—Il Movimento Bianco.

Renato hated politics. He didn't know one movement from the other. But he did promise Francesca that he would do everything he could to extract himself from his father's past political machinations. "I promise you, Francesca, no more aid to the Movimento. *Giuro!* I swear," he told her. But it was only another lie. Like his father before him, he was trapped in his own web. And Francesca, too, was trapped, for despite his sins, she loved him.

THE INSPECTOR

FRIDAY, OCTOBER 30, NEW YORK, NEW YORK

"Yes, Mr. Camden, I realize it's only eight o'clock in the morning, and you've had a mere four hours' sleep. I'm sorry I called you so early. Would it make you feel better to know that Napoleon fought all his major battles on but four hours' sleep, and that I have had none?"

Lieutenant Pasing sat at his desk in his austere office, pulling on his tobacco-packed pipe. His face had much more than stubble, and under his heavy brows his eyes were red from lack of sleep.

"Mr. Camden, I have a commissioner who never sleeps. He wants some answers, and he doesn't care, as we do, whether you have a Gala or not. I'm about ready to give him two names, but I wanted to tell you first. I called the Conrads this morning to set a time for me to ask them some questions. For some damned reason they can't see me until tomorrow. The commissioner's given me twenty-four hours. They were the last people to speak to Sergei Petrov, and Mrs. Conrad was the only one who could communicate with him, the only Russian-speaker around."

Pasing exhaled a cloud of smoke. "I know they're respectable people. And I'll be as gentle as I can, but I have to touch all the bases. Mrs. Conrad is my only connection to Petrov, so far. I have to follow it up. And I've contacted Mimi Charron. Same thing, Camden. She's my Charron connection, for obvious reasons."

A uniformed officer entered Pasing's office, depositing a

114

sheaf of computer readouts on his desk. "Just a minute, Mr. Camden. Stay on. I'm checking something here." Reading quickly, he grinned. "Camden, did you know that Katarina Tomassy-Conrad was educated in Moscow, at about the same time Petrov was a student? Moscow University, Mr. Camden." There was a flurry of words from the other end of the line. Pasing sat patiently.

"I'd like your permission to nose about the Met today. There are others I'd like to talk to. . . . You'll be glad to know I've put my men on a twenty-four-hour surveillance of Renato Corsini. And when Walter Prince steps off the plane at Kennedy this afternoon, we'll be right behind him. Also, let me know when the other tenor is due. We don't want any more accidents. And we want those tenors there on Sunday night." He waited, listening.

"Oh, we're protecting them, all right. We may even be protecting them from themselves."

Scene 6

THE ITALIAN

DECEMBER 1977, SPOLETO, ITALY

There was snow in the air. Dark clouds hovered over the city, and icy wind, funneled down Spoleto's narrow streets, cut to the bone. It gets very cold in the Umbrian hills, so the populace hurries to home and hearth early in the afternoon. Except for a dog, the Piazza Duomo was empty. The new hotel—built in the sixties to house the summer tourist trade for the Festival of Two Worlds, founded by Gian Carlo Menotti in 1958—was closed for the winter. The Piazza Mercante, a beehive in the summer months, looked forlorn.

The Mercedes limousine, with government license plates and miniature green-red-and-white flags adorning the two front fenders, was too long to make the turn into the narrow alleyway leading to the Piazza Duomo, so the chauffeur parked directly in front of the medieval egress, blocking it off. A short man in a black Homburg made his way up the street to the *duomo* and across the piazza to the villa of Renato Corsini. He was followed by a hatless man in a leather jacket, carrying—in full view—a pistol. Two *carabinieri* from the town's militia emerged from nowhere to take up positions at either end of the street. A group of young boys, braving the cold, congregated near the limousine, chattering in unison, in obvious awe of the automobile.

Renato and Francesca met the dignitary at the front door of the villa and Renato helped him out of his heavy, fur-lined coat; following introductions and the offer of a chair near the blazing fire in the main drawing room, Francesca brought *espressi* and Cognac for Renato and his visitor from Rome. She then retired to her sewing room, adjoining the main hall. The young guard stood vigil just inside the heavy oak front door.

Their guest had traveled to Spoleto from his offices in the Palazzo Quirinale in Rome to speak to Renato privately, now confiding his hesitancy to write his message in a letter and his aversion to telephones. "Every phone in the Quirinale is tapped," he said, with no humor in his voice.

Renato had had only formal telephone conversations in the past with the official emissary. He knew his name was Professore Dottore Beniamino Grassi. And that he sat on the cabinet of *il presidente* Leone.

The impeccably dressed balding man settled himself in the wing chair nearest the fire, sipped Cognac and *espresso caffè* alternately, and spoke. "Thank you for receiving me in your home, Signor Corsini. I fear we in politics can never be too careful. I bear greetings from the president. I hear news, and I bear a serious request." He spoke the precise, lilting Italian of Florence, with not a trace of Roman dialect. Renato had heard he was a well-known authority on Dante Alighieri. But that must have been before he joined the president's men.

"I am certain you didn't come so far in this weather unless you had serious business."

"We of the republic have long been grateful for the aid, the support you—and your father before you—have given us. Your father was a true patriot . . . *requiescat in pace.*" He crossed himself and continued. "Your father's industry has been the backbone of our economy since long before the second war. He supported us, and we supported and protected him. We do the same for you. We are proud of your success as an international opera star. But we must ask to be more thoroughly informed about your support of fringe groups."

"I've never had to explain myself before," Renato said calmly. "Nor did my father. The money we give is to help those who help Italy. They keep our society pure. They enable us to live in peace, in neutrality, without fear that someone will take my business from me, or worse, assassinate me. It has always been better that I alone know where the money goes."

"Have you ever heard the name H. Preston Hadley?" Professore Grassi asked.

"No."

"He's the uncle of the American boy who was kidnapped and held by members of the Movimento Bianco. We know of your affiliation."

"I didn't know you knew."

"We try our best to keep abreast, Signor Corsini. What

117

I don't understand is why this boy was taken. You could have personally given them the five million dollars they requested as ransom. Why did they take this chance? H. Preston Hadley is the richest man in the world. Consequently, he has power in very high places. We at the Quirinale must answer to the American State Department."

"I don't ask questions, *professore*. The association goes back to the days of Il Duce. My father established the connection. I merely carry out his responsibilities. I didn't kidnap the boy. Presumably, it was to show power, to defy the American capitalist government—their heavy-handed desire to dictate how we run our country. The Movimento protects us."

"The boy is dead, *signor*. My investigators say his body was found hanging from a wooden cross in the mountains above Fiesole. Both his ears were missing. They were mailed to his mother in Paris. His father is in seclusion. His uncle paid the ransom and wants his nephew released."

Renato's face was the gray of the marble fireplace, and as cold. He poured another Cognac for the professor and for himself.

"The uncle's lawyers have been making inquiries. He wants to know who's supporting this faction. You may be in grave danger. Hadley is one of the board members of the Metropolitan Opera. And he is a Jew. I'm afraid this incident has stirred up a hornet's nest, Signor Corsini."

"Who, besides you, knows for certain that I help their cause?"

"To my knowledge, no one."

"You've given me the news. What's the request?"

"That you confine your singing to Italy. It is for your own safety. We don't want to give fuel for a fire between America and Italy. We must let this incident be forgotten. You'll serve your country far better at home. Let it be known through your agent that you suffer from stage nerves in your approaching middle age. It's a common phobia among tenors, so I'm told. Or better still, that you have developed a fear of flying."

Professore Grassi rose, shook hands with Renato, and walked toward the front door.

"This is a beautiful home, Signor Corsini. I have long wanted to be invited here. I am sorry it was not for a happier occasion."

Renato helped him into his coat and watched him disappear into the street leading to the center of the city, where his limousine was waiting. The young bodyguard bounced along after him on springy athlete's legs. The snow fell thickly.

Renato didn't see Francesca standing at the door to her sewing room until she spoke, her voice full of indignation and anger.

"Son of the father! Infamous coward! How could you do such a thing?"

"I've done nothing. How dare you eavesdrop on my private interview!"

"Oh, no, you can't turn your back this time. I couldn't help hearing you. Thank God I did, or I might have continued to love you. I might have learned to condone the murder of your father. You were so pathetic, so remorseful. You did penance every day of your life for that deed. I loved you, so I forgave you. But now? I'm afraid for my own life, Renato. You're a murderer. You say you did nothing. You might as well have driven the nails into that poor boy's hands. Damn you forever!"

"What do I care what the Movimento does. They make it safe for me here. Who's more important—the Jewish kid and his uncle or Renato Corsini?"

"I care. And I'm not going to stand here to listen to this bigotry."

Not knowing where she might go, Francesca moved toward the front closet, seeking her winter fur. Renato intercepted her, spinning her to him, raging. "You go nowhere! Who do you think you are? You can't walk out on me. I own you."

Near hysteria, Francesca slapped him across the face. The smack reverberated around the marble-and-stone foyer. Renato held her wrists. "You think I'm the only one who does this sort of thing? Don't be so naïve. The Mafia, the Movimento Bianco, the Brigate Rosse are all part of the government. This is Italy. I'm not a Fascist or a Communist. I'm Italian. We do it our way. How do you think I made such a big career?"

"With your voice," she managed through quivering lips.

"Merda!" he screamed. "I owe people. They owe me. You owe me."

"I owe you nothing. You're a murderer! Your heart is black. You will burn in hell, in spite of the penance you do."

With both hands, Renato seized her by the throat, forcing her to her knees. Francesca clawed at his hands as she struggled to breathe. Then, feeling her consciousness ebb, she used what air she had left in her lungs to scream his name.

"Renato, no!"

Suddenly she was free of his grip. She pulled herself to her feet and rushed out the door into the stormy night. Renato, dumbfounded, stood staring at his trembling hands.

Moments passed. Renato was drawn to the open front door, following Francesca's retreat. Oblivious to the swirling snow, which buffeted his face, he crossed the piazza and shuffled up the steps to the *duomo.* Inside, he dipped his fingers in the water at the holy font, genuflected, crossed himself. He lowered his eyes, not wanting to face the ornate altar with the Christ looking down from his cross.

Kneeling at the prie-dieu in the pew nearest the back of the church, he pummeled his clenched fist against his breast in the rhythm of his words: *"Mea culpa, mea culpa, mea maxima culpa."*

Scene 7

THE GENERAL MANAGER

FRIDAY, OCTOBER 30, NEW YORK, NEW YORK

From a source deep within himself, real fear was eroding Peter's foundation. The pangs were surfacing; Peter, with all the stoicism he could summon, was battling back. Consequently, his hike across Central Park that Friday morning was more than habit. It was crucial. He desperately needed time away from everyone to meld sanity and reason.

I am in love with Eva Stein, he told himself, setting an energetic pace. Of that one thing, on this brisk morning, I am confident. Jill can fight all she wants. At least now I don't have to hide. I'm free to pursue that which I know to be vital to my well-being. Yet, oh God, I love Jill too!

Seated on one of the bottle-green velvet couches in his office was the stunning Katarina Conrad. She extended her hand to Peter, but did not stand. "I'm grief-stricken, Peter. Over Petrov. Over Charron. I know you must be, too."

Peter nodded and sat beside her.

"Now it's not only the Cultural Affairs Department in Washington, calling me at eight o'clock this morning with inquiries, but the New York police. A Lieutenant Pasing was on the phone to Felix, asking all kinds of personal questions: Whom did we know in Washington? in Russia? Where were we born? Did I have family living in Hungary? Our connection with the Met. Practically everything except, 'How much money do you have?' "

Katarina's placid, blond beauty was wavering under the furrows of worry and confusion.

121

"I know," Peter said. "He called me, too, to explain his investigation. He showed me Charron's corpse last night. Horrible!"

It was as though she hadn't heard him. "Felix and I were there at Mamma Guardino's. I can't tell you everything that happened. It was all so unexpected, so fast. We saw the lieutenant then, but I don't remember saying anything to him. Felix took me home, as soon as the inspector would release us."

"The last few hours have been agony for all of us," Peter said. "We must help each other." He held her hands.

Scene 8

THE HUNGARIAN WOMAN

APRIL 1968, MOSCOW, USSR

The sign on the door was in Russian. It read: CREATIVE WRITING—ADVANCED STUDIES—PROFESSOR A. TCHECHELENSKY. The creative-writing class of 237 students that convened Monday, Wednesday, and Friday for two hours under the supervision of Professor André Tchechelensky almost filled one of the two amphitheaters situated in building A-21 on the Lensky Prospekt at Moscow University.

Professor Tchechelensky—all six feet six of him—shifting his sparse weight from one foot to the other, leaned at a precarious angle toward the students.

"Comrade Katarina Tomassy, where are you?" He saw a hand raised far back, on perhaps the twentieth tier.

"Please stand, comrade."

Katarina Tomassy, notebook in hand, white-blond hair cascading to her waist in back and covering one blue eye in front, came to her feet and stood like a model, in perfect composure, confident, serene in front of 236 of her colleagues.

"Comrade Tomassy, who are you?" The question was totally matter-of-fact. A question that would have provoked a titter in an American classroom evoked utter silence here.

"Comrade Professor Tchechelensky, my name is Katarina Tomassy. I am twenty-four years old. I am in my third year at the university. I was born in Budapest—in Pest. We lived two streets from the Duna on Becsi Utca, near the Margaret Bridge. My father is the writer Istvan Tomassy. One of his books, *An Honest Evaluation of Communism in Our Time*, won the Lenin Medal, presented to him by Khrushchev in person at the Kremlin. That was in 1959. He died in 1960. I was graduated from the Arts and Sciences Gymnasium in Vienna in 1965. I speak Russian, French, Italian, German, Czech, English, Romanian, and my own Hungarian."

The professor smiled. "You have inherited much of your esteemed father's talent. I have here two theses written by you, which I consider to be of outstanding merit. The paper entitled *Vietnam: Quicksand* is to my thinking a subject which could be augmented and published in book form. The second, which, students, is in large essay form, seems to come from deep intellectual insight. Its title is *Détente.* I am convinced I have not read such an enlightened analysis of the controversial subject heretofore. Congratulations Comrade Tomassy."

Applause echoed round the amphitheater.

Katarina heard the ring of the telephone as she turned the key in the lock of her one-room flat at 13 Nikolai Road. By the second ring she had flung her heavy parka on a chair and snatched up the receiver.

"Comrade Tomassy," she answered, breathless still from her climb up five flights of stairs.

"Here is Professor Tchechelensky," the familiar high voice hummed. "I have important business to discuss with you. I am only five minutes from your apartment block. I will come for you in my car. Please come down now, and do not speak to anyone. I will explain." The line went dead.

Katarina had been elated since the class in creative writing, but now her elation was replaced with a strange presentiment.

The car approached. The professor leaned across and pushed the door open for her. It had begun to rain. She barely got the door closed before he accelerated from the curb, made a sharp U-turn—there wasn't another vehicle in sight—and headed toward Dzerzinsky Prospekt.

"Just like a novel," she mused.

"Did you speak to anyone?"

"No."

"You must not be afraid. You are one of a chosen few who can serve Soviet Russia in a most vital way. You are of brilliant mind and philosophy. You are talented in many fields, especially in languages. We have been watching you for over a year. We need you."

"Does 'we' mean the university?"

"Oh, no. Much more important to the country. 'We' is the KGB."

Her gasp was audible. Katarina, at once shocked and complimented, thought of her premonition and gained her composure.

"I repeat, no fear," the high-pitched voice of her favorite professor continued, explanatory and consoling. "It is a great honor to be chosen by the ministry. You'll be able to pursue your career abroad. Your mother and your two brothers will be well taken care of in Budapest. The benefits are many."

Katarina was not naïve. She knew well how Soviet security and the KGB worked throughout the satellite countries. She would secure the safety of her family by cooperating in every way. Was there a choice?

"But how can I serve?" she asked, already knowing the answer.

"You'll find out at the school. We're on our way there now."

"But my belongings? My studies?"

"Everything will be taken care of. Your studies at the university are ended. Your degree is assured—*summa cum laude*. Your fellow students will hear that you've accepted a position abroad and have been allowed to emigrate. As a writer. You are on your way to a stimulating adventure, comrade."

Katarina was tingling. The initial jolt had been confusing, but by the time Professor Tchechelensky passed through the gate into the courtyard of the bizarre gray-green building near the Lefortovo Prison, she was self-possessed and eager to begin.

NOVEMBER 1983, NEW YORK CITY

Manhattan. Park Avenue. Menorca Publications. Le Voisin. The New York City Ballet. Broadway. The Metropolitan Museum and the Metropolitan Opera. What an exhilarating, heady place to live, to work! What a molding of artists, financiers, survivors, and creators! What a fortunate woman I am!

Katarina's high heels clicked on the pavement in a rhythmic, punctuated staccato as she hurried along West Fifty-seventh Street, having decided to walk from her apartment on Park Avenue at Sixty-ninth Street to the office of her publisher. It was a long hike, but Katarina liked the exercise and relished the hum of activity one heard and felt on Manhattan's busy streets.

Her friend and publisher at Menorca Music House, Boris Cherkassy, had rung at 8:30 A.M. to tell her he had new contracts for her to sign, so she left the apartment with her husband, Felix, politely refusing his offer of a lift, and set off at a hearty pace.

Katarina glanced at her blond hair, reflected in the glass door at 111 West Fifty-seventh, and found it presentable as usual. She took the elevator to the eleventh floor and, heels clicking along the marble corridor, reached the door marked MENORCA MUSIC HOUSE PUBLICATIONS.

Boris Cherkassy, formerly of Riga, kissed her on both cheeks and guided her to a chair beside his desk in his minuscule one-room office with the icon on one wall and assorted inscribed photos of artists, composers, and musicians on another. Some of the inscriptions were in Russian, some in Czech, some in Hungarian, German, or English. Katarina could read them all.

"Do you realize what a success you are, Katya?" Boris, who looked just as a Boris should look, with a full brownish-red beard flecked with gray, a skullcap of gray-brown hair, and an antique lorgnette worn on a shoestring around his neck, smiled at his most prolific translator of foreign operas into English. "Nine years you have been in this country, and no one in the field can compete with you. I have here a contract for a new English translation of Kodaly's *Hary Janos*. There's a new production at Santa Fe next summer. The San Francisco Opera wants to use your *Katarina Ismailova*. The Boston Opera has sent a contract for your *Katya Kabanova*. All for next season. And so it goes. Mind-boggling!"

"I'm happy, Boris. Everything's right for me in America. My husband is an angel. He knows exactly what to say to people in a social gathering, while I'm still too opinionated, especially about American politics, and find myself on the defensive. Felix inevitably saves me. My work is a joy! How lucky I am to be paid to do something I truly love. And Felix is a great support to me there, too. It's a happy life I have here, Boris. I hope it will never change."

Boris opened an envelope and passed a photo across the desk to Katarina. "Your mother and your two brothers are enjoying a prosperous, secure life in Budapest, dear Katya. Much of this comfort is due to your cooperation, as well as the extra money you send them. We're deeply grateful. The picture, if you are wondering, was taken one month ago."

"You know my loyalty, my convictions. For example, Felix is beginning the takeover of Sepek Oil. I thought you'd like to know. It's the American-owned company ostensibly headed by Sheikh Ali Ben Belar of Oman."

"Your sponsors will be pleased. And you may expect other commissions from Dallas, Detroit, and Miami. *Noblesse oblige, n'est-ce pas?*"

Katarina pushed back her chair. "Come to dinner next Saturday evening. I'm having Randolph Martinson and Walter Prince, boor that he is, and his present girl friend, Mimi Charron. Prince will be singing in a new production of *Jenufa* in San Francisco next season. They'll perform it in Czech, so I've already given him about thirty hours of coaching in the language. He has a good ear for languages and music but offstage he's opinionated and overbearing. God's gift to women, they say. Please come. I'll need help. Randolph Martinson is another supreme ego."

"I'd be delighted to attend, Katya. For you, anything."

"One more thing," she said. "The *Khovanchina* score you gave me to give to Maestro Martinson was delivered by him personally to Grigorov at the Royal Opera stage door on the seventh of October."

"Good. Any trouble?" Boris asked.

"None. Grigorov took the score without so much as a

nod. Martinson was furious at the snub. Poor man. He shouted at Grigorov, 'I'm not your fan.' Grigorov just turned and walked away. Martinson hates singers more than ever now."

"Thank you again. You realize how valuable the material was?"

"I know. And how clever to conceal it in a score."

Scene 9

THE GENERAL MANAGER

FRIDAY, OCTOBER 30, NEW YORK, NEW YORK

Peter helped Katarina to her feet. "Let's try to be calm and carry on in the face of this catastrophe. Please refer all inquiries to me here. I'll try to fend off the doom seekers and we'll get this Gala on, no matter what happens." He was trying his damnedest to be convincing. "My best to Felix, and my thanks to you both."

She was gone, gliding down the hallway. He turned to see Hilda, notebook in hand, awaiting his full attention.

Hilda followed Peter into his office, placed the *New York Times*, the *Daily News*, and the *Telegraph* on his desk—face up, headlines blaring: TENORS MURDERED . . . VENDETTA IN-VESTIGATION . . . GALA STARS DEAD. Peter didn't want to look. He sat on one of the couches and stared blindly in the direction of the Enrico Caruso portrait on the west wall.

"Do you want to hold a press conference about the Gala?" Hilda spoke softly, not wishing to intrude on his meditation.

"Reporters are insisting you make a statement. The television people are the most adamant. They want blood."

"Four o'clock this afternoon. We won't be able to avoid them." Peter was striving for control.

"Is there something I can get you? You look as if you could stand a solid Scotch on the rocks."

"No thanks, not so early. I'll be all right. I just have to realize this isn't a dream I'm living. These things have happened!" he said, color returning to his face.

"I don't want to add to your worries, but Horst Ludwig informed us he'll arrive on Saturday at noon—something to do with a slipped disc. He assured me he'll make the rehearsal Saturday afternoon and will be in stentorian voice for the Gala."

"I didn't realize he wasn't here. My God, with what's happened, it's a wonder *I'm* here."

"Oh, and Renato Corsini will come to his piano rehearsal this morning at eleven o'clock."

Peter looked into Hilda's eyes, his own red-veined. "Thank God for him," he said.

Scene 10

THE ITALIAN

FRIDAY, OCTOBER 30, NEW YORK, NEW YORK

Renato received the call on Friday that his was to be the only orchestra rehearsal of the morning. The voice was the familiar one of the rehearsal secretary, Arge Helder, who softened each early morning cast call with: "Good morning. This is the rehearsal department of the glorious Metropolitan Opera." Renato had to smile. It was a warm gentle welcome. He remembered it well. "Welcome back, Signor Corsini," Arge added.

Renato had confirmed to his agent in Rome that he would return to New York, after an absence of ten years, to sing the Gala. He knew he had thousands of American fans who begged for him. They had never ceased to flood his agent's mailbox with letters, pleading for news of his next appearance, next record release, newest photo.

But above all, Renato wanted to see the aging Dr. Alberto Danieli, who had helped Renato care for his voice in those early years and who had emigrated to New York, shortly after Renato's acclaimed debut at the Met.

The phone rang. It was the desk clerk. "Mr. Corsini, we have a large basket of fruit and several boxes of flowers for you. Shall I send them up?" Renato replied affirmatively.

A few minutes later the bellman arrived, and Renato sent him away with a generous tip. He examined each of the cards attached to the gifts. There was a card from the press department of the Met: "Welcome Back." A card from Peter Camden: "A Salute to the World's Greatest Tenor!" A card from a fan: "We Love You!" And a card with no name: "Your Father Would Have Been Proud of You." The words were printed in bold letters in Italian.

Renato's legs would not support him. He dropped into the nearest chair, staring at the card. "God in Heaven," he prayed aloud. "Forgive me. Purify me. Help me forget. Hail, Mary, Mother of God. Pray for me now."

He walked the few blocks to the Metropolitan and into the rehearsal of the last act of Otello in a self-inflicted fog. Through that fog he saw her. Francesca Zandonai. It was she, as if no time had elapsed. He shook his head, trying to separate dream and reality. Oh, God, make it a dream, he prayed. She was smiling. She was nodding, speaking. He heard nothing.

In his brain he heard: You're a heinous murderer, Renato. You killed that boy, as surely as if you drove the nails into his hands. You murdered your father. No amount of penance will ever save your black soul. It was Francesca's voice searing his brain, as she fled into the snowy night, escaping him, deserting him.

Maestro Martinson said, "Welcome, this is your Desdemona, Signor Corsini."

How can I go through this madness? he asked himself. How can I pretend she's Desdemona, knowing I could destroy her with the same conviction that drove Otello to end Desdemona's life, seeking to alleviate his own pain and betrayal? How simple it would be to crush the pillow over her smiling face, shutting out her life, as she shut out mine. If I touch her now, I'll kill her. God, have you forsaken me?

He heard himself say: "Forgive me, maestro. I don't feel well enough to go through with the rehearsal. It must be jet lag. I feel as if I might faint. I can't breathe. Air—yes, I must have air."

He avoided Francesca's eyes, seeing her in a haze. His eyes were tearing. I see her hate, he told himself. I didn't know she had come to New York. I've had no idea of her life since she left me. But now she, like my father, can haunt me, punish me. And she alone knows my guilt. She alone would want to see me in hell. Of course she sent the card: "*Your Father Would Have Been Proud of You.*" Vile, unfeeling witch! *Strega!* Isn't being alone to face the omniscient ghost of my father enough hell? Why now? Why?

Renato exited through the Met stage door alone, still in a haze, having refused assistance. His mind reverted to scenes of Francesca, to the viaduct in Spoleto, his father, Gian Carlo, and Margarita Secchi looking over their green Umbria at sunset. The faces of the two women blurred together. Francesca and Margarita—the betrayers! He had loved Francesca with a fierce passion. He pictured her kneeling with him at mass in the *duomo*. Or was it Gian Carlo and Margarita kneeling there?

In his room, he found the picture of Francesca he always kept near him. Fury forced his heart against his chest. His jaw was set in determination. His last act. Her life. Her silence.

"I looked to you for love, Francesca," he said aloud. "You've betrayed me." He stared at the card in his left hand, her picture in his right. "Please, God, tell me what to do."

There was no reply.

Scene 11

THE GENERAL MANAGER

FRIDAY, OCTOBER 30, NEW YORK, NEW YORK

The greenroom, situated down a long hallway leading from the stage-door entrance of the Met to the principal artists' dressing-room area, was far too small to accommodate the horde of reporters from the newspapers and television stations. The room itself—windowless, airless—housed a grand piano, a well-worn green couch, and several straight chairs. When Peter Camden and his entourage requested entry, four cameramen had to shift to the hallway to make room. There was much grumbling about the facility, but for the most part, there was eagerness to learn more about the murder of two world stars.

"Ladies and gentlemen," Peter began, "I am Peter Camden, the general manager of the Metropolitan Opera. May I introduce Mrs. Eva Stein, who is representing the Gala committee. And Mr. and Mrs. Felix Conrad, representing the board of directors of the Met and the Gala committee. They are here to give me physical and moral support, for as you can readily see or well imagine, I am ready for an institution." There was no laughter, nor was there meant to be.

"We don't know why François Charron and Sergei Petrov were murdered. But I do know, personally, there was no better way to wound—to decapitate—the opera world. That person—that monster—out there, who seeks revenge or thrill or whatever motivation, has succeeded. Oh my God, how he has succeeded! The opera world—mankind—has lost two of its heroes. We have lost the glory of sound that emanated from their golden throats. I can think of nothing more devastating.

"François Charron was to have returned to us in January of 'eighty-eight to sing *Werther* in a new production of that great lyric masterpiece by Massenet. After his acclaimed performance of *Roméo* here at the Met last year, we were looking forward with great anticipation to his return.

"We knew Sergei Petrov from his recordings only. But I must tell you, I had the privilege of hearing him sing the third act of *Tosca* Wednesday morning. It was a tribute to the vocal art. I would have given him carte blanche in future years to choose his roles at the Met.

"The loss is too overwhelming to comprehend. The ramifications too frightening to ponder. Two great singers are gone. Silenced forever. God keep the ones who loved them. In their honor the Gala will go on."

Tears coursed down Peter's cheeks. He elbowed his way past the reporters blocking the door and the cameramen in the hallway. Eva and the Conrads followed closely behind. There were shouted questions from the reporters, but Peter shook his head, negating any reply.

Eva held Peter in her arms for a warm, comforting moment, and Felix Conrad thumped him several times on the back.

Peter broke the silence. "Thank you for your support. Felix, do you think you and Katarina could do something to make certain Horst Ludwig is on that Lufthansa flight from Munich tomorrow morning? Slap a lawsuit on him. Anything." Peter's tears had ceased; replacing them was a determined, laser glare. "Do you realize we've totally ignored one of our stars? Eva, what's happening with Walter Prince?"

"He should be arriving about now at Kennedy. I'm to meet him for a drink at the Plaza at seven."

Peter couldn't quite catch Eva's eye as she spoke. She seemed to be avoiding his. "The Plaza?" he asked.

"I'll make sure he makes his rehearsal tomorrow," she said. "Don't worry. He's in good hands. Mine."

Peter watched her as she retreated down the hallway. *Walter Prince? Eva? I've got to get a handle on this.*

Is this getting to be a compulsory habit? Do I need to always keep abreast of every detail in this house? Or am I a worrying workaholic? I should see a psychiatrist. But what is it about this job that makes me suspect everyone of everything, and feel I have to know how everyone connected lives, breathes, and copulates? I guess I believe it's necessary, even to protect them from themselves. I didn't know enough about Charron to keep him alive. . . . I'm trying to play God.

Reaching his office, not having acknowledged anyone en route, he went straight to the wall cabinet and found the dossier on his American tenor star, Walter Prince.

Walter Prince
Debut—1973—Turiddu in *Cavalleria Rusticana*

AGE GIVEN AT DEBUT: 35 (born 1938)

ROLES PERFORMED AT THE MET: Rodolfo, Cavaradossi, Pinkerton, Stewa, Ghermann, Dimitri, Macduff, Turiddu, Arrigo, Gabriele Adorno.

REMARKS: Has been called on to save an average of ten performances per year, usually at the eleventh hour. Most reliable. Short fuse. Violent temper. Brought up on charges before AGMA for brawling in and out of theater. Brief, successful Broadway career.

Yes, Walter, you'll be in good hands with Eva tonight. You were there before; but how does one save you from yourself?

"You're damned right," he said out loud. "I'm jealous. And why shouldn't I be? She loved you once, you tenor bastard!"

Scene 12

IL MARITO

FRIDAY, OCTOBER 9, MILAN, ITALY

"We have a great deal to discuss, Signor di Giulio. Come, let's go into the bar. This late at night it is practically deserted."

The short, thickset man led the way across the lobby of the Hotel Duomo into the dimly lit bar. He chose a corner table. The tall man draped his raincoat over a chair and sat opposite his host. The tall man removed his horn-rimmed glasses, cleaning them with a handkerchief. He was nervous. The short man was not. Each ordered a beer.

"My phone call must have come as a surprise to you, Signor di Giulio, but I was instructed to find out some things about you before making contact. So I know you, but you don't know me. I'm afraid we must keep it that way. The name I gave you over the phone is not my name. Suffice it to say I am from Rome, and came here with one purpose: to offer you a job."

"That I can use," the tall man said. "I haven't had a job since I came here from Sicily eight years ago."

"I know. It must be hard, taking care of your two children while your wife is singing all over the world. Does she send you money?" The short man already knew the answer.

"Oh yes, plenty of money, but I've never liked the idea. I should be working, bringing home the money. She should be at home. You know she's a star, my Angelina?"

"How well I know! As does the whole world. Angelina Lombardini. La Diva Superba!" The stocky man paused to look about the small bar of the Hotel Duomo, which is situated next to the Galleria, not far from the Teatro alla Scala. Only one other table was occupied. He continued.

"Would you return to Palermo if you could?"

"Yes, to work. I work with metal. I'm very good. But there is nothing here."

"Would you take your children?"

"Of course. Why do you ask that?"

"Do you know your wife is unfaithful to you?"

The tall man gasped. "No. Impossible. She would never think to do a thing like that. Never! But I don't want to talk to you about her."

"Angelina is with her lover now in San Francisco."

"She's singing there."

"Yes. But her lover is singing with her. He is the American tenor Walter Prince. They've been together for two, perhaps three years."

"I don't believe you," the tall man insisted. "Not my Angelina. She's a good woman. She works very hard for her career. She's a diva!"

"Even angels fall from grace, *signor*. It pains me to tell you, but their indiscretion is well known. And you must put an end to it."

"If this is true, they should both be dead," Alfio di Giulio said. "If this were Sicily, not Milano, they *would* both be dead."

The short man took time to study the face of his guest. He saw confusion. He saw mounting fury. He knew his task was an easy one.

The smaller man spoke again. "Your Angelina is only one of many women who have been soiled and cast aside by this man, Walter Prince. Oh yes, she'll soon be part of his refuse, too. It's a pattern. He has no soul. Angelina is nothing more than an easy conquest."

"He spits on my doorstep. I will kill him."

"You will, but only him. Your Angelina must not suffer. It's not her fault. You'll defend your honor and serve my client in New York by removing the cancer that is Walter Prince."

"How do I do it?"

"Then you *will* do it?"

"*Giuro!*"

The stocky man removed a packet from his inside breast pocket, placing it on the table before Alfio di Giulio.

"In the envelope is twenty thousand dollars, American. There is an air ticket to San Francisco with a return to Rome and Palermo. Go to San Francisco. See for yourself the dishonorable affair. Follow Prince until you kill him. Make it look like an accident."

"What about my children?"

"Do you have relatives in Palermo?"

"Yes, my sister, cousins, many."

"Send the children to them now. You have the money. There will be more for you when you have completed your task. The children will be well cared for. My client is generous."

"Who is this person who wants the blood of Walter Prince?"

"That you need not know, for your own safety. Also, the passport in the envelope is false. You must not use your own name while in America, and you must escape detention. For a time you will be a criminal, Signor di Giulio. Think like one. Can you do it?"

The tall man nodded affirmation, collected the packet and his raincoat, and walked quickly out of the hotel, disappearing into the Galleria.

Scene 13

THE AMERICAN

SUNDAY, OCTOBER 25, SAN FRANCISCO, CALIFORNIA

The roar from the audience was deafening as the last chords of I Pagliacci echoed through the San Francisco Opera House. The great brocade curtain, a dusty gold color, swooshed closed.

Bedlam broke loose backstage as well, among singers, stage-hands, and management. Walter Prince, America's foremost tenor star, swept Angelina Lombardini, who had joined in the triumph as the flirtatious Nedda, off her feet. He whirled her around once, twice, and planted a passionate kiss on her lips.

"*Brava*, baby, you did it. We did it. What a success!"

He shook hands with everyone within reach. He was the only American tenor on the San Francisco Opera roster that season, so he could be indulged almost everything. He could even be forgiven his left hand, which was busy probing the left buttock of Angelina Lombardini.

"Mr. Prince, take your call, please." It was the stage manager, Ralph.

He slipped away from Angelina, past the bass-baritone Tito Valente from La Scala, who had sung the part of Tonio, and sauntered before the curtain. The sound crescendoed as Walter took his bows, lifting his clenched fist in a salute of utter confidence and victory.

"Walter, you were outstanding!" said the director, Rolf Feldman, holding Walter's arm and guiding him toward the dressing rooms. "We must discuss next season."

"Anything you want," Walter replied. "You know how I love to sing here."

Professor Dr. Rolf Feldman, from Vienna, who for almost thirty years as general manager had built the San Francisco Opera to world prominence, placing his stylish, professional mark on all aspects of the organization from artistic to technical, from fund raising to social decorum, led the way. A man of rare genius and personal appeal. Walter Prince swore by him.

The new productions of *Cavalleria* and *Pagliacci* had been coveted by every dramatic tenor in the world. It was a Jacques Delacroix concept, and no one knew opera better. Walter had gone after the parts with a vengeance. He auditioned for everyone connected with the project even though he had been for many years a well-known star at his home base, the Metropolitan. His agent hustled too. And talked. And cajoled. Until it was obvious Walter was the only one to tackle both parts: Turiddu and Canio. And he had succeeded. The audience was still applauding as he began to cream off his heavy makeup, removing the false lower-chin beard and leaving his own reddish moustache. The director had suggested a full beard, which made him look older, more vulnerable. As far as Walter knew, it was an original concept; but it had worked! They were still applauding.

Walter's thick hair was the color of his moustache. He was forty-nine, but the ladies said he looked closer to thirty.

"Where was Jacques at the curtain?" he asked his dresser.

"Across the street in the Court Room having his second Scotch, I imagine. He's always there when he knows he has a hit. No worries now."

"You know, Chad, I took a hell of a chance. I should have my goddamn head examined. I fucked the ass off Angie until four o'clock this morning. The wonder is I had any voice at all for tonight."

"I know. Most of us walk up to the girls and stick it in, but you Texans stick it in and then walk up. Isn't that the way it goes?" Chad was used to tenor braggadocio. They all did it. "You didn't sound tired. How was she?"

"Like always. A waterbed. Strong. Like too much of everything, tits and ass. Her goddamn voice is so loud I thought she could be heard from the Fairmont Hotel all the way to Chinatown. Jesus, what a night!"

Chad was smiling. Walter was sweating.

Walter Prince had rehearsed for three weeks before the premiere. Each time he visited the Bay City some esoteric, hidden part of him reveled in its beauty, its charm, and its atmosphere. The cooling, light fog and mist gave the nights an aqueous feeling of mystery much different from the hot, dusty atmosphere of his native Fort Worth. It was refreshing, too, after the heat and airlessness of the theater.

There were several fine restaurants on Nob Hill, but Walter frequented the North Beach area, where he discovered the Longhorn Grill. It boasted two-inch sirloins and Lone Star beer. It reminded him of home, and he liked his roots. Walter felt that the downhome attitude of the born-and-bred Texan was a hell of a lot better than the tight-ass ways of the opera world. His problem was he loved to sing.

Walter was known as a loner. He liked it that way. He had never been engaged, never been married. He was a good actor, with not a great deal of conscience when it came to women, so he could extract himself from any situation. He had had hundreds of one-nighters but preferred not to make love in his own digs, so he could be the one to leave. His system, thus far, had been infallible.

Fort Worth, the "Gate to the West," is a cow town where the front pages of both newspapers run pictures of prize heifers or black angus bulls rather than head shots of people. Walter Prince was born there in 1938 to divorcing parents. An only child, he was shuttled from one relative to another, attending seven schools before he graduated from high school. The most satisfying, mystifying part of his postpubescent years was his desire to sing, to open his mouth and let the tones pour forth. His talent was natural.

Between the Korean and Vietnam wars, he sought his doctorate in music in three universities on three different music scholarships, all because of his God-given, natural tenor instrument. When Vietnam was aflame he was too old for service, and his career blossomed.

Although he had not fought in a war for his country, he

talked as if he had. He called himself a patriot. A Texan. A Republican. A proud flag-waver when in a foreign country, whether singing or just visiting. Some called him a redneck, but never to his face. He stood six feet two with two hundred well-distributed pounds.

He sang without accent in French and Italian. From what source, besides his schooling, he had acquired his linguistic ability, he could not say. Nor could he account for his voice or musicianship, since his family had no musical history. Walter Prince was a very fortunate man.

"Phone call, Mr. Prince. Someone from the Met." Chad stuck his head in the shower-room door. "Take it in Dr. Feldman's office."

Walter threw on his terrycloth robe, slipped into clogs, and threw a towel over his wet head. He took the stairs at a lope, two floors up to the executive suite. Rhonda, the number one secretary to the boss, waved him into a cubicle where the receiver was off the hook. He blew her a kiss.

"Prince here."

"Hello, lover." A sultry voice came over, followed by a husky laugh. "It's Eva."

"Baby, baby, what a surprise! Where are you?"

"In New York. It's two A.M. I tried to get you all day, but they wouldn't put me through. Seems you were tied up." She paused for effect.

"Just sleepin', honey. You know I can't afford any hanky-panky on the day I sing. How long has it been? Five years? More? Jesus!"

"I know, darling. Too long. Needless to say, I've missed you like hell. But you got sidetracked. Let me down a little."

"Wasn't any cow shit clingin' to your boots either, sweetheart."

"That's my Walter. Time stands still. . . . Listen, I'm just checking up on you. You know I'm on the Gala committee?"

"Yeah? You're part of this jamboree?"

"Yes, I've got you cleared with Dr. Feldman for Friday through Sunday. It's really going to help the Met, and I'll get to see you again."

"Just like old times?"

"That's the idea."

"I'll be there Friday."

"Walter, try to keep healthy. There's a lot of money riding on this Gala. There's not a ticket to be had. With you, Charron, Corsini, Ludwig, and Petrov we have a guaranteed, colossal success. No cancellations, please."

"I wouldn't miss it on a bet. I've been laughin' about the five of us on the same stage. What a crazy fuckin' idea! Oh well, it's your funeral."

"On Friday, meet me at seven o'clock in the Oak Room of the Plaza, O.K.? I thought we might have dinner at Patsy's."

"You got it, babe."

"I need you," Eva purred. "Poor little me and all you great big egos."

Toweling his hair dry, he walked down the stairs to his dressing room. "What a ball-breaker," he mumbled half out loud. He shook his head, as if to clear away the clouds surrounding his image of Eva and himself together. What was their relationship? A moment ago it sounded as if she wanted to start up again. Convenience? Old time's sake? Money? What the hell was it? Walter didn't have the facts of her life. He hadn't cared much at the time. He thought maybe she was feeling old and wanted some security besides just sleeping with him. Her husband's name was Manny Stein. Hotel man. Big cheese from Vienna. He smiled. That's right. Read about it a couple of years back. The son of a bitch up and died on her. Choked on a large chunk of rare rump steak. Probably a Texas steer. Too tough for him. Served the bastard right.

"How old are you?" Eva whispered, as she traced a blue vein on Walt's half-hard penis with the long manicured, crimson nail of her left index finger. Her head was cushioned on his stomach and she pressed herself to him with the warmth of afterlove.

"Thirty-two in November. You?"

"Forty-five in August. The fifteenth. I love you, Walter. Not just your voice, although I do love that. I love to hear you on a good long B-flat. Confident. I love what you do to me. It's been a long time for me. I'm grateful for you."

She pulled him on top of her, draping her right leg over his left shoulder, and arched her back to meet his insertion. His hands gripped her shoulders. God, he was huge! The first feeling was of pain, which gradually wore away to a throbbing pleasure. She felt stretched to capacity and fully expected to burst into a fountain of pain and blood, but it never happened. Walt's eyes were turned inward as he drove with all his strength deeper into her. Eva's stomach muscles knotted into a huge ball as she screamed her release.

Walter was her star that year. One hundred and sixty-eight performances of Billy Bigelow in a revival of *Carousel*. Walter was not unlike the original Billy, John Raitt—tall, with wavy reddish hair and a similar voice, that of a tenor with baritonal timbre throughout the range. Eva Stein was the producer, and the revival was a smash. Eva had taken one look at the tenor at his audition and decided he would perform for her in bed as well as on the stage of the Prince Edward Theater.

Walter Prince proved his worth on Broadway. His soliloquy, "My Boy Bill," brought triumphant applause every night. And Eva never stopped applauding him either.

THE GENERAL MANAGER AND
THE INSPECTOR

FRIDAY, OCTOBER 30, NEW YORK, NEW YORK

Lieutenant Pasing was standing in Peter's usual spot, looking out on Damrosch Park. The ever-present meerschaum emitted a thin gray line of swirling smoke, and he a strong aura of concentration. Peter sat at his desk. It was 5:30 P.M.

"Thank you for not including me in your press conference, Mr. Camden. I'm not quite ready to make any kind of a statement. I have many theories, but few facts."

Peter sighed. "It was one of the most difficult things I've ever had to do. When I think of François and Petrov, I want to cry. It's not the manly image one would like to present." He paused. "What's to be done? Where do we go from here?"

"We question everybody who had the vaguest connection to Charron and Petrov."

"But that could take weeks!"

"Yes, it could. But we can shorten it by helping each other. You've got to let your thoughts and your imagination float free. If you think of something you believe to be pertinent, tell me. If you have a question, ask it. You have access to more information concerning these singers than anyone. And much of it is in your head. I want it, Mr. Camden. If we're to prevent another murder—and that is my worst fear—you're going to have to guide me."

"God, I don't know where to begin. You'd better ask the questions. You know I'm willing. First, I think I'll have a drink. Do you want one?"

"No thanks, no drink. I've got my pipe. But don't let me stop you."

Peter filled a glass half full of Scotch, added ice, and returned to his high-backed chair. Pasing remained at the window, pensive.

"Corsini had a visitor this afternoon. My man on the spot said his name is Dr. Alberto Danieli. You know him?"

"Yes, he treats singers and actors. Good throat specialist. He's from Italy. Been practicing here in New York for over twenty years. He's a dwarflike man—stature, I mean. We've had to call him to care for a singer on many occasions. He makes himself available, never complains of the inconvenience. He loves opera and he seems to love the singers."

"Then he'll probably be looking after Corsini's voice. He was sick at his rehearsal today. He went straight back to his hotel and called the doctor. Let's hope he doesn't cancel."

"Don't say it, lieutenant. Don't even think it. Dr. Danieli will take care of him. Walter Prince and Horst Ludwig could not carry the Gala. As it is, I've asked Eva Stein to beg Prince to sing the third act of *Tosca* in place of Petrov to begin the evening. Then we'll end with the *Cavalleria*, which he's already scheduled to sing. The *Götterdämmerung* and the last act of *Otello* will come in between."

"Prince should have arrived by now," Pasing said, "but you don't have to worry about him. I have a man at the airport who'll shadow him until he returns to San Francisco. And I need to know when Horst Ludwig is arriving. I'm worried about them all."

"Tomorrow, hopefully. He's somewhat unpredictable, lieutenant. He's late as it is, which isn't unusual. He has a traveling companion, in any case, which should be a measure of safety."

"I'll have someone on him. My head tells me there's a psychopath out there, not too far away, who wants to destroy

146

these tenors you've chosen for your Gala. And . . . consequently . . . the Gala itself."

Peter didn't answer. He stared into his glass.

"There's a plan," Pasing continued. "It's ingenious. It's diabolical."

"It's not a coincidence?" Peter said.

"I've never known one. Not completely. Not in the final analysis. I've been at this job in New York City for eighteen years and for the fifteen years before that with the San Francisco Police Department. In fact, I qualify for retirement; but the commissioner chooses to disregard that fact, says he still needs me. Well, Mr. Camden, in that long period of time, I haven't witnessed one bona fide coincidence."

"You've just caused the hair to stand up on my neck," Peter said. "We could all be in danger."

"Exactly. Anyone close to the tenors could be a mark."

"Then couldn't Katarina Conrad and Mimi Charron, or any of the committee, be victims?"

"That's complicating it too much. I'm going to meet all of your committee members tomorrow morning. You'll have to ask Martinson to see me, too. I'll ask a lot of questions, get some answers. I want you to come with me. You may have questions of your own. Together we'll come up with something. Of that, I'm certain."

There was a sharp rap on the door. After Peter's "Come in," Lennie Kempenski poked his head in.

"Our star of the evening has arrived in the theater. Says she's suffering stomach cramps, wants to talk to you immediately about making an announcement to the audience about her indisposition."

"I'll have a talk with Miss Costa," Peter told Pasing. "We have a soprano substituting tonight, singing Aida. She has a Callas temper, so I have to try to keep the lid on. I'll stay with her until the curtain goes up. Once she's on, she'll be all right. Most of them are."

"I'd like to stick around, ask some questions, get an idea of the effect these killings have had on their colleagues."

"You have carte blanche, lieutenant. Make yourself at home. And, if I can help, I'll be in my office most of the evening."

"One more thing. Have you had any inquiries, any word at all from the Russians?"

"You mean from the embassy?"

"Yes."

"Nothing official. No, it's strange. I hadn't thought much about it."

"It's my gut feeling—intuition again—the Russians want Petrov forgotten immediately," Pasing said. "They don't want speculation about an assassination. Your tenor might have been up to something besides singing on your Gala. Otherwise, why not an outcry, an international incident? He was their hero."

"Up to something? Oh no, lieutenant. That's utter nonsense! Absurd! He was a great artist!"

"He was a Russian."

Scene 15

THE AMERICAN

SUNDAY, OCTOBER 25, SAN FRANCISCO, CALIFORNIA

Walter Prince strolled through the lobby of the Fairmont, stopping at the desk only long enough to collect his messages.

148

After the success of *Cav & Pag* that evening, there would be love notes waiting for him.

The ever-ready opera groupies, he thought. Who could it be tonight? Assuming he could ditch Angelina. Maybe a trio? That would be a turn-on. Like that night in Dallas on the Met tour when Dan and Bill and I chose up sides and balled those groupies, two apiece, until the hotel cops broke up the party at five in the morning. I should write a book.

"Congratulations, Mr. Prince," said the hotel manager, coming up to him solicitously. "News travels fast. Connie von Bulow was all aglow on her way to the Revolving Bar. Told the maître d' you were a god. She's writing her review right now over in the corner. Why not drop by?"

"No thanks. Too much like suckin'. Never fucked a lady critic. She shouldn't be a writer. Not with tits like that. Should be a go-go dancer." He'd put the intrusive bastard in his place.

Pocketing the key, he found the elevator bank and punched the button for the sixth floor. Suite 600 was his. He was superstitious. Six and multiples of six kept him lucky. His apartment house bore the number 6 just across from Lincoln Center Plaza. His agent always called ahead to make the proper reservation in the hotel of his choice. When he gambled in Vegas or Reno, he rode number 6 for hours at the roulette table. And he won. Not always, but enough.

He changed quickly from his Neiman-Marcus jeans suit into his velvet tux with a blue shirt and big square bow tie he wouldn't be caught dead wearing in Fort Worth. His clothes fit as if they were stitched onto his lean, hard frame. It was not by accident. Walt knew about image and he had good taste, even when it bored him. He felt only pity and disdain for some of his male opera colleagues who looked as if they were off-work waiters or bank tellers.

The Italians were the worst. He could not think of one

tenor from Italy who was not supporting a rubber tire around his middle or who dressed with any degree of taste or whose public life had any more glamour than a banana peddler's. Not my problem, he told himself. I've got enough on my own plate.

The doorman signaled for a taxi that would take him to the opening-night party on Green Street, about half a mile from the Fairmont.

It was already well after midnight when Walt presented himself at the door of perhaps the most unusual house in San Francisco—an enormous converted fire station. The building dated back to 1880 and for many years had been the home of the wonderful three-horse hitches, the fire truck of the day drawn by two or three horses. The building had withstood the big quake and had been converted into a home—a marvel of Victorian charm and splendor.

There was applause as his hostess escorted Walter into the large party room. Everyone turned in his direction and he received the accolades with a full smile. He was the last of the cast to arrive—his timing was a source of pride onstage and off—to indicate to one and all his stature.

Walter kissed cheek after cheek, shook a hundred hands before he was taken aside by Jacques Delacroix.

"I'm glad it was a success for you," the director said. "You're good. Very good. And I thank you."

"It's your dream, Jacques. I'm just damned lucky you asked me."

He was congratulated by another well-known director from the Met and the National Theater in Munich, who had come especially for the premiere, and proceeded to the bar to order a beer. The crowd was already dense and oppressive. He shouldered his way through them.

"Hello, star!" It was Angelina Lombardini.

Walt set the beer glass on the bar and seized her, lifting

her off the floor. He kissed her on both cheeks and then full on the mouth.

"Walter, this is my husband, Alfio. Just flew in this morning from Milan for the premiere. Big surprise." She nodded toward the tall, broad-shouldered man with horn-rimmed glasses standing beside her.

Walter saw the punch coming, but it was too late. He took the blow on the forehead, ducking away, but it spun him half around. He gashed his cheek on a pedestal supporting an antique brass fire bell. He dropped to both knees and saw the foot in plenty of time. He clamped both hands around the ankle and twisted. His assailant went down, glasses shattering. The man held a knife in his hand, but it fell harmlessly on the floor. Walt was on his feet. He grabbed Angie's husband's hair and knee-lifted him off the floor, splitting the skin on his forehead, then let him fall hard.

Walter took Angelina's hand and guided her quickly out the front door before anyone quite knew what was happening. They reached the street and turned right up the hill to look for a taxi.

"What am I going to do?" she cried.

"Who gives a shit? Come on."

He told the driver to take them to Geary and Mason. There was a dark bar nearby where they could pull themselves together with a quiet drink. It was called the Blue Flame.

Once they were shown to a corner booth, Angelina went to the ladies' room, wet a paper towel with cold water, and brought it back to Walter, who immediately placed it over his wound. They ordered two beers. Walter downed his in one motion. They relaxed.

"I'm sorry," she whispered in the darkness. "I never expected him here. I don't know where he got the money to come. Somebody must have told him about us. Oh God, what are we going to do?" She was weeping.

"*We're* not gonna do anything. Not together anyway. You do what you have to do. Tell him anything. Cool him off, but keep me out of it. Asshole wanted to kill me!"

"He's Sicilian, Walter. He's going to want to kill me, too."

"Well, don't worry. We'll think of something," he said, as his hand searched under her dress.

She took his hand away, lowering her head into his lap. She found his already throbbing erection, fumbled open his fly and with urgency, brought him to climax. He moaned with pleasure.

"You deserved that! Star!"

Not one head turned in their direction. Not on Geary Street. Not in San Francisco.

Scene 16

FRIDAY, OCTOBER 30, NEW YORK, NEW YORK

The telephone in the East Side apartment was picked up on the sixth ring. The recipient of the call did not speak, but merely waited, listened.

"I'm aware of your failure, Signor di Giulio," the recipient said at last. "You're being paid to do a job. Walter Prince is no longer in San Francisco. He's in New York City. You'd better take the next plane here."

The recipient paused to listen.

"Your wife is not my concern. I don't know where she is. Why should I? Do what you're paid to do. And don't use this telephone number again. It will not be in service."

The recipient depressed the button, ending the connection, then dialed the number of Dr. Alberto Danieli.

Scene 17

THE AMERICAN

FRIDAY, OCTOBER 30, NEW YORK, NEW YORK

Walter was late for his date with Eva, but he had his excuse planned. He would tell her his plane from San Francisco had been delayed and the Friday traffic from Kennedy, along the Grand Central Parkway, had been predictably heavy. That story should suffice, since Walter had arrived at six o'clock Wednesday morning, escaping San Francisco on the red-eye flight after the second *Cav & Pag* performance, nursing his wound and his apprehensions suffered at the hands of Angie's irate husband. The skin-colored patch on his cheek could be easily explained to Eva.

He would be certain not to elaborate on his successful evasion of Angelina Lombardini and/or her phantom husband. Walter had dropped the affair, but he was not so confident about Angelina's predilection.

Eva was there. Ineffable. Ravishing, in a black cocktail

dress, cut low in front. Her hair was in a loose bun on the crown of her head—not the mode of the day, but individual and devastating. Her emerald eyes glistened. Could she possibly be sixty years old? She smiled and lifted a Rob Roy in salute. Here was a look with no reprimand, just genuine pleasure at seeing him after almost six years.

"The great lover returns," she purred. "I'll drink to that."

Walt leaned across the table, kissed her full on the mouth and, standing back, stretched out both arms in the corniest of operatic gestures and sang the first phrase of "Celeste Aida." Then he sat next to her amid laughter and scattered applause.

"That was a rare, if somewhat flamboyant tribute."

"Your kind of beauty, Eva, deserves far more recognition." The poet, having spoken, was all apologies for his tardy arrival, pointing to the bandage, and miming a fist fight.

"I was late, too," she told him. "You can imagine what we've been through."

"What's the matter? One of those famous tenors cancel the Gala?"

"Don't you know?"

"Know what?"

"Haven't you seen the papers?"

"No. I've been sitting in the goddamn VIP lounge on and off the flight, since seven this morning," he lied. "What's happening?"

"Get a drink first," she said, motioning for the waiter. Walter ordered a Löwenbräu. "The police found Petrov murdered in a cellar over near Ninth Avenue. And François Charron keeled over at a party at Mamma Guardino's."

"I'll be goddamned! It's a wonder you even showed up here. You didn't have to, Eva. I would have understood. I'll be double damned!" He tossed down what was left of the beer and ordered another round.

"I had to get away," Eva said. "The phones have been jammed. The police have been at me all day in my office, and I had to go to Mamma Guardino's, too. And Peter Camden asked me to represent the Gala committee at a press conference this afternoon. More like a wake! The whole thing is so sudden. So gruesome. They think it's a master plan. I think someone may be trying to sabotage our Gala."

"For Christ's sake, that's idiocy! I know it's rough on the Met, but it's a goddamn coincidence." He forced the mock-heroic tone, hoping it showed none of the nervous pangs his stomach engendered. Coincidence? Walter thought. I hope to hell it is coincidence, and not somebody out to get rid of tenors. Could Angie have had anything to do with Charron? An affair? Holy shit! Maybe Angie knows about Mimi Charron and me.

During dinner at Patsy's, he told Eva some of the events of his week in San Francisco. He did not, however, tell her who his predator was. "I hate to cut this short," Walter said. "But I'm exhausted and I got some unfinished business to do—calls and the like. Sorry!"

Outside on the corner of Fifty-sixth Street and Eighth Avenue, he held her close.

"It's all right," she told him. "It's too much to wish that we could forget everything that happened."

Walter whistled for a taxi, helped her into the backseat, closed the door, and blew her a parting kiss.

Deciding to walk a little instead of going straight home, he sauntered up Eighth Avenue, crossed Fifty-seventh Street and skirted Columbus Circle, reminiscing on the many languorous hours he and Eva had spent together before the ugly breakup.

She seemed all right this evening. No animosity. No anger that he could discern. Enough water over the dam, perhaps? Too bad it had ended so badly, he thought. She knew I had my problems in San Francisco. Fuckin' narcs thought they'd made the bust of their lives. Broadway star arrested! She could have bailed me out of the whole thing with all her money. Then she turns around and swears there's nobody else can do her fuckin' *Goodbye Dobbin* on Broadway except me—once out of the can, that is. She always thought she was a hot number. The more I fucked her, the more she wanted. Hell! What was I supposed to do? Come crawlin' back to Momma? I didn't let her down. She let me down.

Fifteen years ago Eva and Walter had traversed this route to his small flat on West Sixty-ninth Street. Walter always had the belittling feeling that Eva was getting a kick out of "slumming" on the West Side, stealing into his fourth-floor, three-room walk-up, reaching for his zipper before the door was closed and locked. She wanted it, all right. She was obsessed!

"I'm old enough to be your mother," she would say, as she knelt before him. "Does that bother you?"

She wasn't all that old then, but she was too old now.

He let himself into his apartment—personal tribute to his skyrocketing successes of the past six or seven years at the Met. The plaque on his bedroom door read: IL TENORE. Walter's king-size bed was on a platform in the center of the large room; so, in a prone position, he could still see the arches of the Metropolitan Opera in the plaza across the way. Eva Stein had never been inside this room. It would probably offend her taste. But it sure as hell wasn't slumming.

At exactly ten o'clock the buzzer sounded from downstairs. "Lady on the way up," the doorman announced. Walter peeled off his string tie with the turquoise tips, unbuttoned his western-style shirt to the navel, and swept the lady—Mimi Charron—off her feet, not depositing her until they had reached the couch.

THE GENERAL MANAGER

Peter Camden, along with his assistant, Lennie Kempenski, and Stanley, one of the stage managers, was trying to console the disconsolate Dorothy Costa, whose profuse tears were tracing crooked rivulets through her Aida makeup. The catcalls from the audience—specifically the standing-room areas— were sustained. The wretched soprano would not go before the curtain to take her bows. So Peter could do nothing but escort her back to her dressing room, listen to her wailing, and try to calm her hysteria. Also, he would have to convince her to finish the performance. There was one act to go.

"I should never have let you talk me into singing tonight. I'm hoarse as a dog," she croaked.

Lieutenant Pasing caught Peter, as he was holding the dressing-room door for the distraught soprano. "When you can break free for a minute, I'd like to talk to you," he said.

"Wait for me here. As soon as the fourth act begins, when Costa is back onstage, we can talk."

Lennie Kempenski rushed through the hallway to the stage on a dead run. "What do we do now, Mr. Camden?"

"I want a uniformed security guard placed at each standing-room area. If that mob continues this uproar, have them ousted. And Lennie, post a sign closing the standing room until further notice. That bunch has gone too far."

The last act having begun, Peter sat with Lieutenant Pasing on the couch in the artists' dressing-room area. They both looked tired.

157

"Walter Prince didn't arrive at Kennedy this evening, as planned," Pasing said.

"What? Hold on. Don't tell me we've got another . . ."

"No, no more violence. My man waited for Prince's flight. He didn't get off, so he checked two other planes arriving from San Francisco. No Prince. He called me. I questioned the doorman at Prince's apartment, right across Broadway. Prince arrived on Wednesday morning at six o'clock. He's been here since before Petrov was executed, and before Charron was poisoned."

Pasing smiled at the look of confusion on Peter's face. "I want to know why he came to New York earlier than expected. I want to know what he was doing all week. I want to know: Why the mystery?"

"I'm certain there's an explanation. All you have to do is ask him."

"Oh, I'll ask him all right, when I can find him. But here's a pertinent question for you, Mr. Camden: Who stands most to profit by the death of Charron and Petrov?"

"I don't know that. No one does."

"Another tenor, sir," Pasing said. "Eliminate the competition."

"That is too farfetched for belief!"

"Not so. I'm going to dissect Mr. Prince and Mr. Corsini before this is over. I don't believe either tenor can stand investigation. I'll see to Ludwig when he arrives."

With weary footsteps, Peter walked slowly across the backstage on the way to his office.

Act 3

Protegga il giusto cielo . . .
(May just heaven protect . . .)

—*Don Giovanni*,
     W. A. Mozart and Lorenzo da Ponte

Scene 1

THE INSPECTOR

SATURDAY, OCTOBER 31, NEW YORK, NEW YORK

The telephone jangling at this ungodly hour was nothing unusual. Seven o'clock on a Saturday morning was as good a
time as any for conversation. But Lieutenant Theodore Pasing
was in a mood akin to the ugly, gray dawn outside his Elmhurst,
Queens, apartment. He shuffled about in a black-and-gray-
striped robe, which might have been appropriate in a prison,
an unconscious choice befitting Pasing's common, everyday
mien. His meerschaum pipe, which he had already fired, was
perfuming the house with billowing Danish tobacco smoke
and softened his combative image.

"Answer it, Liz," he called to his wife. "I'm trying to get
the coffee to perk, and I haven't shaved yet."

"Liz" for Lissette, not Elizabeth, rolled onto her husband's
side of the bed and located the receiver.

"Pasing," she said, still half asleep. "For you," she called.

Pasing shuffled into the bedroom area. The apartment consisted of a large L-shaped room, which served as living room, dining room, and bedroom, with kitchen and bathroom separate. It was what one would call "utilitarian," but it had been home for Ted and Lissette Pasing since their move to the New York Police Department from the San Francisco Police Department in 1969.

"Pasing," he said into the receiver. "No, Mr. Camden, it's never too early for a civil servant. I'm at your service. In fact, I was going to call you when I got to the office. I've got something downtown I'd like you to see. And I've got some more questions. . . . What's that again? You want to tag along? . . . So happens, I was going to ask you to do just that. I can use your input. Can you meet me at the Tombs? Say about forty-five minutes?" Pasing smiled. "Of course you wouldn't know where the Tombs is. It's 100 Centre Street. Come by taxi or you'll never get there. Thanks, Mr. Camden."

He turned to his wife. "That was Peter Camden, the Lord High Commissioner over at the Met. He's anxious to get some answers. Two days I've been on this case and *he* wants results. He's used to getting *his* way, doing things *his* way. Now he's scared. Don't blame him, but it only makes it worse. He wants to come along on my investigation, probably to make sure I'm not too hard on his committee members and opera donors. But I can use him. He knows just about all there is to know about this opera business, it's singers, musicians, workers, everybody. And he wants to stop the destruction of his Gala. So do I."

"All you need is an amateur Sherlock Holmes hanging on to your coattails," Liz said.

"No, you know me better than that. I'll do the investigating and Camden will supply the footnotes, save me legwork."

"Could it be you're feeling a little helpless, rummaging around in the hallowed halls of opera? You'll have Mr. Camden to lean on, perhaps?"

162

"All I know is we have two bodies . . . no real clues and more than a handful of suspects. Look at what I've done here." Pasing held up a piece of yellow legal paper. "I made a chart of the people I think are involved in some way in these murders. Maybe it's a bit soon, but I've got to start someplace."

"Did I mention Sherlock Holmes?" she asked.

He did not take the bait. "Now, listen. We have a Gala. A concert to raise money for the opera house. We have a lot of tenors involved—big names—and we've got the planners and sponsors. One large happy family. Everybody knows everybody, works together. And somewhere in this family is a very rotten apple."

Pasing placed the piece of legal paper on the bedside table, so his wife could see it.

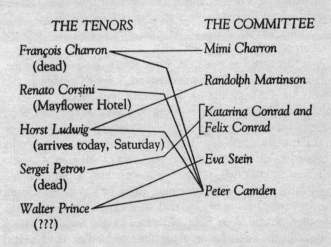

THE TENORS	THE COMMITTEE
François Charron (dead)	Mimi Charron
Renato Corsini (Mayflower Hotel)	Randolph Martinson
Horst Ludwig (arrives today, Saturday)	Katarina Conrad and Felix Conrad
Sergei Petrov (dead)	Eva Stein
Walter Prince (???)	Peter Camden

"You see, Liz, the tenors know or knew about each other, the committee members know each other and each has had personal dealings with at least one of the tenors on the list. François Charron was poisoned Thursday night at Mamma Guardino's restaurant with Mimi Charron, his former wife, a few feet away when it happened. Petrov is dead. Execution.

I know the chart indicates Katarina Conrad knew Petrov, but that's only because she was the only one who could communicate with him in Russian. She didn't have him killed, I'm pretty sure. She could know something, and she's as mysterious as hell. I ran a computer check on her yesterday that really got me going. Some past! Very interesting."

"O.K.," Liz said, interested now, "but these are just names. What if the killings are political or gang-related? They may have nothing to do with this Gala."

"Right. But I've got to start somewhere. I'm calling on those three ladies of the committee. Going this morning. Then I'm going to try to find Walter Prince. The last name on the list there. In my estimation, this Prince has the best motive, the best reason in the world to do away with Petrov and Charron. He's one of them. He's a tenor, but then Corsini and Ludwig are tenors, too. . . ." His voice trailed off.

She smiled at him. "Why do they always give you the tough ones?"

"Because I'm the best. But I can't do this one alone. There's too much I don't understand. I want Camden in this with me. He's got the inside information I need."

Ted Pasing, standing at the washbasin in the bathroom, used a bar of regular soap to lather his face, preparing to scrape off the night's stubble of beard with a disposable razor. As he hacked away, he continued to elaborate on his plan of attack: "I'm going after this Prince. The more I think about him, find out things about him, the more I think he's involved. Seems to be common knowledge that he's slept with most of the women on the West Side. Now he's having an affair with a singer in the opera house. Angelina Lombardini. And he had an affair with this committee member, Eva Stein. That's why I put that line on the chart between them.

"AAAeee!" he yelled, cutting short his saga. "Goddamn razor cut me."

"Are you all right?" Liz asked from the kitchen.

"Yes, but the thought just came to me. I've forgotten someone very important . . . Dr. Alberto Danieli."

Scene 2

THE DOCTOR

SATURDAY, OCTOBER 31, NEW YORK, NEW YORK

"The doctor will see you now." The nurse, primly attired in white uniform, hose, and thick rubber-soled shoes, gray hair under the white cap with a red cross as the only ornamentation, led Frederick Horne into treatment room 6. The room was one of many stretching along a corridor of Dr. Alberto Danieli's elaborate suite of offices on the ground floor at his Sutton Place South address.

Dr. Danieli's profession was the diagnosis and cure of diseases of the ear, nose, and throat, and he had been performing his chosen labors for over forty years.

"What seems to be the trouble, Freddie?" he asked.

"No voice," whispered Freddie Horne. "I can't sing and I've got to be in the Gala tomorrow night."

Dr. Danieli looked into Freddie's nose and ears, then probed above and below his larynx with the thumb and index finger of his right hand, holding his tongue, wrapped in gauze, between the left-hand thumb and index finger, his mirror avoiding the uvula to catch a glimpse of the infected vocal cords. He listened to a requested vocal *e* from the stricken bass-baritone, but there was no sound forthcoming, so he released his grip on the protruding tongue and sat back in his chair with a sigh.

"Looks bad," Dr. Danieli said. "*Male*—bad!" Another sigh. "Laryngitis. Also, a swelling of the left vocal cord. Could develop into a node. I don't say it will, but it could."

"Holy Christ!"

"You've been pushing your voice too hard." The pudgy fingers probed again the swollen glands in Freddie's throat.

"I have to, Dr. Danieli. I'm singing the heavy stuff now— Wagner and Strauss. There's no place for me in the *cantabile* roles anymore, with Plishka, Morris, and Raimondi still going strong. Not a hope in hell!" His voice was almost inaudible. "I've got to sing the Gala."

"I'm going to put you on the machines, and then you can pick up your prescriptions from the nurse on your way out. Try not to speak." The Toulouse-Lautrec figure in his physician's smock, a foot shorter than Horne, could project a commanding mien, his voice biting and rising in pitch and volume. "Mark the rehearsal and sing the Gala, if you must."

Dr. Danieli's machines were unproven and, among some of the more knowledgeable of the singing community, a source of ridicule and derision. One device had two circular discs that looked like antennae, which were placed on either side of the larynx and purportedly vibrated and massaged the vocal cords by means of sound waves. Most of the patients felt nothing and received no relief. Another machine had a large metal disc the size of a serving plate protruding from its side. The vibrations, as one pressed his or her chest against the throbbing monster for thirty minutes, were to dislodge mucus from the lungs. There was much coughing and spitting after the treatment, but most likely it was because of the prolonged, concentrated pressure against the chest. When the bill for the tiresome treatment arrived sometime around the first of the month, the coughing often recurred.

But Walter Prince, Angelina Lombardini, Francesca Zandonai, and many Broadway actors and singers swore by the machines, and Horne himself had been helped, so he went willingly.

"Can you speak with Eva Stein, doctor?" his nurse asked, catching him between rooms, as he went to another waiting patient.

"Yes, of course." He scuttled to an office to take the call. "Ah, my dear Eva," Dr. Danieli began. "Are you well?"

There was a long pause while she talked.

"I'll be at your apartment at seven o'clock this evening. Perhaps you will give an elderly friend a nice Cognac." He replaced the receiver on the cradle and resumed his rounds.

Scene 3

THE GENERAL MANAGER

SATURDAY, OCTOBER 31, NEW YORK, NEW YORK

Ascending the steps to the ominous building, Peter harbored a gnawing feeling of doom. The look of the building didn't help. The stern face of the uniformed security guard performing a body-check didn't help.

Peter produced his driver's license and Metropolitan Opera identification card with his picture before being buzzed, along with an accompanying policeman, through a door. He was led to an office without a window, consisting of a metal desk, two metal chairs, a metal filing case, and Lieutenant Pasing.

"You made it."

"I made it."

"Please sit down, Mr. Camden. Smoke, if you like." He

167

produced a cigar from a desk drawer. "I think you'll like this brand." His ever-present pipe was between his teeth.

"I feel the nasties coming on. It's a feeling I get in the pit of my stomach when I have to do something I don't care to do." He puffed several great clouds of smoke into the already airless room. "I'm not saying I've done some super sleuthing, but I've got to start pinpointing suspects or my rather impatient boss gets very impatient; and we have no case."

Peter nodded noncommittally.

"I'm going to show you something upstairs in a minute, but first let me lead up to it. I have a feeling Walter Prince is our man. I'm going to take him into custody. Today."

Peter felt electric bolts in his brain. "What? Are you mad? I've got a multi-million-dollar Gala tomorrow night. I can't do it without him. That would leave me only Corsini and Ludwig to carry the evening. Impossible!" He rose to thrust his face close to the lieutenant for emphasis. "If you arrest him, you're going to have to lock me up, too. I think the Met lawyers will have something to say about this."

"Sit back down and listen to me. Prince is the one most likely to profit from the death of tenors. He wants to be number one. I truly think he'd murder his own mother to secure his status. And he's got a past. Yes, he has a voice, but there's some doubt about his character."

"Nobody cares what he does in his personal life," Peter said. "He's a grown man. That's his business. As long as it doesn't reflect on the Met. He's a hero to his fans."

"You just said it. As long as it doesn't reflect on the Met. Does serving time behind bars for murdering a Met employee throw bad light on the Met?"

"You know it does. But we don't know if he's killed a cockroach. I can't believe he's a murderer."

"I'd count him out of your plans for tomorrow night and the next ninety-nine years, because he may be behind these killings. The other tenors are well known. Prince is not. He's an almost ran. I'd bet money, if I had any, he wants to be

number one. Has for a long time—sort of festering inside."
Pasing's broadside launched, he surged ahead. "We look for
reason, for motivation, for gain. Prince has them all. I'm not
saying he put the poison in Charron's glass. He wasn't there.
But I don't think it would take much to get a confession out
of his girl friend—Madame Mimi Charron."

"What in God's name are you talking about?"

"Mimi Charron and Walter Prince—shocks you, I know—
are a hot item. They have been for a long spell. She must
have hated that husband of hers at one time. It'll be in her
past. We'll find it. Is she so hung up on Prince she'd do
anything, even poison her former husband, to hang on to
him? Easiest thing in the world! She was the only one at
Mamma Guardino's with half a motive. Prince didn't have to
be anywhere near."

Peter felt his anger rising. "Not only was he not anywhere
near, he was three thousand miles away on Thursday night,
in San Francisco. And, if that's all you have—this farfetched
notion—please spare me and let me get back to my other
insoluble problems."

"Hold on. I'm far from finished. I could book you too,
Camden, to keep you here. You're in the big middle of this,
and you don't seem to know how serious it is." He stared at
Peter, a slight smile on his lips. "Your Walter Prince flew to
New York on Wednesday, arriving at six A.M. at Kennedy.
He couldn't get into his apartment because the superintendent
had changed one of the three locks on his door and had
forgotten to give a key to the doorman, since Prince wasn't
expected until Friday evening. Prince made a hell of a row.
So, eventually, they got the door open. Naturally, the doorman was specific as to arrival time and—most important—
that it was Walter Prince. The doorman was most cooperative.
He identified Mimi Charron as the lady who spent last night
with Prince. And, according to our doorman, Mimi has been
a frequent visitor to his apartment."

Peter tried to retain his sanity. He thought ahead to

tomorrow night. The ramifications of the imprisonment of Walter Prince were too awful to contemplate. One thing he knew, or hoped he knew: Walter Prince must not be found. He must sing the Gala. And if it took a kidnapping charge to protect the event, so be it. He would let the attorneys worry about the man across the metal desk. Now he had to find a way to get out of that office.

"I don't suppose you could concentrate on the killer of Sergei Petrov and leave Walter alone?"

"Not a chance. I'm convinced both the killings are connected. There's more, Camden. Come with me. I'm saving the best for last."

Pasing led Peter out the door into the hallway to be picked up again by the ever vigilant cameras. "We've got a story here like that one in *Murder on the Orient Express.* Remember that? Everybody was in on the murder. I think we have a lot of people in on these murders, too, masterminded by Walter Prince for his own ends."

If Peter had felt physically better, he would have laughed out loud. Was this man inept? Or was he truly talented at his job under this presumptuous, professorial mask?

Pasing guided Peter up one flight of stairs to a large room filled with computer equipment, tape machines, television monitors, and pieces of hardware Peter didn't recognize. Two men were engrossed in editing tape when Pasing interrupted. "Larry, this is Peter Camden. He's the general manager of the Metropolitan Opera. Give us a minute?"

"Absolutely, lieutenant. You want a run-up on that Interpol list we looked at last night?"

"Right. Just run Katarina Tomassy," Pasing said.

The fingers of the operator flashed over the keys. "There it is," he said. "Katarina Tomassy: Unavailable. Cease Investigation. Re: Fairfax, Virginia.

"You see that, Camden? God damn it!" Pasing growled. "Fairfax, Virginia, is CIA. Last night, we did a run-up. Katarina Tomassy was born in Budapest, educated in Moscow, disappeared from 1968 to 1973, and surfaced as an interpreter for an OPEC conference in Rotterdam. I suppose that's where she met Felix Conrad—at an oil meeting. Now, today, Larry pulls this up again. Nothing. Not a goddamn thing! Unavailable information. No information." Pasing's face reddened, as though he had been holding his breath.

Peter, too, was deeply concerned. This was a tack he had been pondering. Because of his knowledge of Katarina's affair with Randolph Martinson—her insistence on his conducting the Gala—he had begun to suspect the pair of some kind of complicity in Petrov's death.

"As soon as you told me of Petrov's execution," he said, "I began to think of who was closest to him. And, although it can only be random conjecture on my part, Katarina is the one possible link. I've been aware of an indiscretion—an affair with Randolph Martinson—which discolors the image I once had of her. But . . . I'm not judging her, lieutenant. I merely state a situation, as I know it. She's a wonderful woman, but Felix is one of my best friends. I'd hate to see him hurt, if you have to pry into Katarina's life."

"I knew you could help me," Pasing said, smiling. "Now you're beginning to think like a detective. Your head is full of information I have to have, if we're to solve these riddles. So far, the people I've met, since I came on the case, defy all imagination. To say the very least, they're complex. We have a hard job ahead of us, Camden. If Katarina Tomassy is involved as deeply as I think, with Randolph Martinson, then he joins her at the top of the list of suspects. Pretty soon it'll be a battalion."

The lack of air and the constant cloud of thick tobacco smoke was giving Peter a headache. He dropped heavily into a chair, pressing his fingertips to his temples. He wanted to escape through the nearest exit.

Pasing, pacing, spoke. "We've got an international incident here, even though the Russian consul is soft-pedaling it. It's not just the killing of a Russian tenor. We've got the

171

CIA beginning a cover-up. You know what that means, Camden? Your Katarina Tomassy-Conrad is already under observation. She could be a suspected spy. She could be a counteragent. She could be involved in politics in Washington. . . ."

"Or she could be rich enough to pull some strings to get her dossier off of the telecomputers," said Peter, angrily.

"Larry, give me the other record. The police record on Walter Prince."

Larry's hands flew. The computer whirred. Walter Prince's record flashed on the screen for Pasing and Peter to read.

1960   *Assault with a deadly weapon* (brass knuckles) served: Fort Worth, Texas—nine months

1961   *Abetting prostitution* served: Fort Worth, Texas—sixty days

1962   *Illegal drug use* served: Fort Worth, Texas—sixty days

1968   *Illegal drug use*: San Francisco—released on bail

1971   *Illegal drug use* served: Soledad—one year

Peter was too stunned to speak.

"Nobody can stand investigation, Camden. Nobody. Your tenor is my prime suspect. So face it!" Pasing knocked the ashes from his pipe and placed it, bowl up, in his outer breast pocket. He pulled a chair close to Peter's. "That was my bust in San Francisco in 'sixty-eight. I remember Prince. I had to rough him up a little. My squad raided a house on Dolores Street. We surprised a bunch of dancers and singers. I pulled this blondie off Prince—didn't know him from Adam then, of course. She was down on him, giving him head, when we hit the door. He came off the couch like a windmill, swinging at everything. He was stoned and roaring mad. I popped him a couple of times to slow him down so we could haul the

172

whole crowd downtown." Pasing looked hard into Peter's eyes, sensing the confusion, regretting the harsh revelation.

"How the hell did he get to be an opera singer?" Not waiting for an answer, he poked his index finger against Peter's chest. "Don't tell me," he barked. "He has one hell of a tenor voice."

"Yes, one hell of a tenor voice, lieutenant. And maybe— just maybe—he's reformed." Confused and frightened, Peter could stand it in the room no longer. "You'll have to excuse me. I've got my own work to do."

"Do your work. But don't forget we've got an appointment with Eva Stein at eleven o'clock. I'll meet you at her apartment building. Be there."

Peter rushed out of the room, vaguely aware of Pasing's sardonic grin behind him. With a twenty-dollar bill, Peter challenged the first taxi driver on rank to mercurial speed. "Lincoln Center, as fast as you can make it."

Scene 4

THE GENERAL MANAGER

SATURDAY, OCTOBER 31, NEW YORK, NEW YORK

Peter forced himself to focus his attention on Maestro Randolph Martinson, who sat opposite him.

"I never would have asked Ludwig in the first place," Martinson said with apparent resolution. "I know him well, Mr. Camden. He is a troublemaker, arrogant and unreliable. Today he has back pains. Earlier it was neck pains, dysentery,

173

hemorrhoids, the common cold—anything to keep from rehearsing. I could have predicted he'd arrive late and probably whistle his run-through. How did you manage to get him here? And for a benefit?"

"I'm glad you asked me how and not why," Peter answered, fixing Martinson with an unwavering stare through red-rimmed eyes. "We know the why. He's the best heldentenor in the business. The how I'll tell you, although it's my business." Peter was ashen this Saturday morning, the day before the Gala. He faced a day of unrelenting crises, and he knew it. He would rely on the tenacity of will that had served him thus far in a job whose complexity only he could comprehend.

"You had trouble with Ludwig when you called him in Munich. Felix Conrad had difficulty, too. And my secretary, Hilda, is never allowed more than a 'hello' and a 'goodbye.' " Across Peter's desk, Martinson fidgeted in his chair, anxious to leave for his eleven o'clock rehearsal.

"Ludwig wanted you to submit a résumé to him of your conducting engagements since the last time the two of you worked together. Isn't that true?" An affirmative nod from Martinson. "He doesn't think much of you as a person *or* as a conductor. Isn't that true?" Again, agreement. "You've handled yourself very well this week with the orchestra, and I appreciate your flexibility in altering the program and the schedules. I don't want to know too much about this enmity between you and Ludwig. I just want the Gala to happen, and there's one day to go. Take hold of your feelings. We've had all the surprises we can stand in the past three days." Peter opened the humidor on his desk, offering a cigar to Martinson, who declined with a shake of his full head of chalk-white hair. "Mind if I smoke?" Peter asked, not waiting for the nod, but continuing. "I'm the only general manager of the Metropolitan Opera who dares smoke cigars. I never smoke around the singers—only in this room or outside the building—for fear of being strung up by my thumbs in the middle of Lincoln

Center Plaza. It's the job, maestro. It makes for ulcers, high blood pressure, heart attacks—something like a conductor's job—so lung cancer from cigars and cigarettes doesn't seem that much worse." Peter settled back in his maroon leather chair and tried to let some of the stress and tension of the past days drain off. "Do you like conducting this orchestra?" he asked.

"Very cooperative," the maestro managed to say.

"The Gala should be wonderful exposure for you."

"I'm under the impression I'm more of a chattel, an accompanist for the tenors," he answered caustically.

"Not at all. This is a great opportunity for everyone involved."

"That remains to be seen, Mr. Camden."

Why don't I trust this man? Peter thought. It must be the eyes. He hasn't once looked directly at me. Do I want to help him? Does he know that I know of the feelings Jill had for him when they were together at the New England Conservatory? Or not? And he's obviously oblivious to the common knowledge about his affair with Katarina. Is he of the caliber to be a conductor at the Met? The Met is special. It's not the place for just anybody. Would he fit in? Is he somebody I could confide in, if necessary? I think not. I don't know him well enough. That's it. I have to know more.

"I talked to Ludwig last night," Peter said. Caught him at the Arabella House in Munich at midnight. I told him he had better get his high-powered ass on the plane this morning or there would be no more career, not in the USA, or the UK, or the BDR, or the USSR. Nowhere on this globe would there be a place for him to sing."

"You can do that, Mr. Camden?" Martinson asked, his voice incredulous—or sarcastic.

"I can do that. I told him, too, that his last appearance in New York was not acceptable. I mentioned Holstead's crack in the *Daily Mirror*, which said he was 'losing his top voice, if he had one to begin with.' I told him I thought he needed

175

new exposure to the New York public. And I told him his shit pop record, which gives him most of his income, was not helping his image in the opera world and could be banned anytime. That got him. He'll arrive today at noon on the Lufthansa flight from Munich. I'll have to pay an extra air fare for his bodyguard, Heinrich Gerstmann. I told him we'd have to limit him to *one* bodyguard because we don't take to faggot parades in New York. God, he's arrogant! If we didn't need him, I'd do us all a favor and drop him."

Martinson rose to leave for his rehearsal.

"You realize how important the Gala is to me." It was a statement, not a question, from Peter Camden.

Scene 5

THE MAESTRO

JULY 1962, CENTRAL CITY, COLORADO

Eight thousand feet up in the Rocky Mountains of Colorado does not seem the most likely locale for an opera house and a colony of singers. At that altitude breathing is more difficult, so singers must take extra breaths, causing conductors, composers, and musicians anguish. In such rarefied air high notes are not well supported and may crack. Yet there exists a seven-hundred-seat gem of a theater at the top of Main Street, a street as steep as a ski jump, in the picturesque, once bawdy, gold-mining town of Central City. And every year an opera festival is held.

The main street maintains about one hundred yards of

business on either side. On the right side, going downhill below the Opera House, is the Teller House Hotel, with its prime attraction—the "face on the barroom floor"—captured for posterity in legend and song. Also on the right side is the Gin Mill and the Golden Nugget, both aptly named for the two most important pursuits of the miners of the last century.

Two small restaurants are on the left side. The rest of the mountain is residential, served by a courthouse, firehouse, whorehouse and post office. Not a likely place for an opera festival, but there it was every July.

Randolph Martinson, a piano major at the University of Colorado, was spending the summer between his junior and senior years as rehearsal pianist for the Central City Opera. The job was highly desirable for a young pianist, particularly a budding opera conductor. The pay was $111 per week, with generous benefits.

The Saturday matinee had just finished. It was a bright, colorful production of *Don Pasquale*. The cast boasted stars of the New York City Opera Company and the audience boasted opera fans from as far away as Milan, Berlin, Sydney, and Buenos Aires, who had flown into Denver and motored the forty to fifty miles west into the mountains to attend the festival.

Randolph Martinson had been playing all the chorus rehearsals for the opera of that evening, *Madama Butterfly*, so he was being permitted to conduct the offstage chorus. He was nervous but exhilarated as he hurried ahead of the matinee crowd down the hill to the side door of the Gold Nugget. He had promised to play for two of the understudies, who practiced their vocal art by making some extra money singing opera and operetta selections for the patrons of the bar.

Frederick Horne, the understudy for the part of Pasquale, and Marietta Todd, the understudy for the part of Norina, were waiting for him. Horne, the bass, was a college student—twenty, tall with brown hair, a John Barrymore profile, and the rough, raw-boned hands of a farmer. Todd had strawberry-blond hair and a Miss America figure. She was about the same age as Horne. Randolph was twenty-one and in love with them both. Horne and Todd were that spring's Opera in America audition winners. Both had accepted contracts for the summer just to learn their respective roles and to be part of the Central City Festival. They hoped it was only a matter of time before they both would be singing at the Met.

The Gold Nugget was jammed. Marietta Todd, seated atop the tall, white enameled upright piano with nyloned legs crossed provocatively, entertained. With her sheer, pale green summer frock temptingly hitched to show just enough under-thigh, she tossed off the Leonard Bernstein song "Glitter and Be Gay" and then, before the applause from the crowd had faltered, launched into a favorite from *Naughty Marietta*.

Frederick walked to the piano, put his hand on Randolph's shoulder, and, when Marietta finished, sang "Le veau d'or" from *Faust*. The singers were both heartily applauded.

Frederick Horne, Marietta Todd, and Randolph Martinson carried the glow of that Saturday to bed with them that night—Marietta's bed—and on many nights through the remainder of that mountaintop July. The threesome. Randolph hated to go back to Boulder to start his senior year at the University of Colorado. He set his sights that summer on the Metropolitan Opera. On conducting opera. His destiny!

After graduating from the University of Colorado, Randolph flew directly to New York to find work conducting. There was none. "What experience?" the agents asked. Not much. There was a paucity of jobs for opera conductors, and fewer jobs for orchestra conductors. Randolph Martinson was stymied. Where was Frederick Horne? Unavailable. Where was Marietta Todd? Busy. Engaged.

Over the Gately Bar at Fifteenth Street and Seventh Avenue, Randolph found a room barely large enough to house a lumpy double bed. The grimy bathroom was down the hall, to be shared with two winos. He had a nosy Hungarian landlady who demanded her one hundred dollars per month in advance.

Randolph had lived well in the home of his parents, and Randolph's talent as a pianist had won him scholarships to pay his way at the university. But now his funds were perilously low and he was too proud to ask his parents for help again.

Randolph stood at the stage door of the New York City Opera on Fifty-sixth Street, making idle conversation, seeking a friendly face, suggesting one of the singers might need some outside coaching or a pianist for an audition. He put a notice on the City Opera bulletin board: "Randolph Martinson, Coach/Accompanist." And he added his Hungarian landlady's telephone number. He began to get jobs. Slowly. He played cheap. Something was better than nothing.

After playing for two singers auditioning for the New England Opera Company in Boston, the dean of the New England Conservatory of Music, who recognized his talent, tendered him a graduate fellowship at the conservatory, and Randolph was on his way.

WEDNESDAY, OCTOBER 28, NEW YORK, NEW YORK.

Randolph Martinson's past came flooding back to him as he lay cradling a cigarette in the fingers of one hand and the blond head of Katarina Tomassy-Conrad in the crook of his left elbow. In the radiance of afterlove, Randolph was relaxed and thoughtful. The anonymity of the Mayflower Hotel was infinitely more private and secure than Randolph's apartment.

"Were you happy with rehearsal?" he asked.

"I was thrilled with you both. Sergei was glorious."

"I think he's the best tenor in the Gala."

"And you're the perfect conductor for it, my sweet Randy. You belong in *that* pit in front of *that* orchestra. You've worked

179

so hard. You deserve it." Katarina took the cigarette from his hand and dragged on it.

"I've you to thank for this, my darling Katya. For my whole career, for that matter. Without you I'd still be coaching mediocre singers or touring the hinterlands with arrogant assholes or has-been divas."

Katya, only feigning levity, prodded him. "We both know who the asshole is, don't we?"

"Horst Ludwig, the number one, prime, *prima*, first-rate, first-class, A-one horse's ass!" They both roared. Then they became quiet.

"Why do you stay married to Felix?" Randolph whispered.

"My dear, sweet, naïve love, some things we must do in this life, which are not pleasant or right, in order to fulfill a greater purpose. If I were married to you I could not achieve my goals and I could not help you to achieve yours. Does that answer your question?"

"Clearly." Randolph kissed her full, sensuous mouth.

Scene 6

THE AUSTRIAN WOMAN

SATURDAY, OCTOBER 31, NEW YORK, NEW YORK

Again Eva Stein had spent a restless night, filled with depressing thoughts of Walter Prince and sympathetic thoughts of Peter Camden. She had spoken to Peter this morning before he left home. Jill had been there, and, according to Peter's guarded conversation, she was still condemnatory and unyielding. Peter, heartsick, had been unashamedly frightened for the tenors, for those connected with the Gala, and for himself. He promised he would have time to meet with her that afternoon and would attempt to collect himself for a day that would include a matinee performance of *Tannhäuser*, an evening performance of the *Barber of Seville*, Gala rehearsals, and two meetings with board members on internal problems.

The doorbell to her apartment rang. She was expecting a Lieutenant Theodore Pasing, who had made an appointment yesterday for eleven o'clock today; but, usually, the doorman called to request permission to send someone up. Not this time.

Eva descended the stairs from her upstairs bedroom to the living room. She started to chastise Tina, her maid and housekeeper, for not going to greet the caller, when she remembered she had given her the weekend to visit relatives in Philadelphia. She pushed aside the peephole cover, squinted, and opened the door.

"Peter!" she exclaimed. "You didn't tell me you were coming."

"I'm sorry. This has not been one of my better mornings. This has not been one of my better *weeks*." Peter kissed Eva on the cheek and stepped inside the apartment ahead of Lieutenant Pasing.

"Eva, this is Inspector Pasing of Homicide. He's investigating these murders. I asked him if I could tag along."

"Actually, I asked him, Mrs. Stein. I know a little about opera, but nothing about the business end. Mr. Camden seems to know everything and everybody."

"Indeed he does, inspector," Eva said, shaking his hand and guiding them into the living room. The two men sat on the couch under the Monet, Eva in a side chair opposite. "My maid is off, so I'll do the honors. May I offer you some coffee or tea? The coffee is instant." Pasing and Peter both requested coffee and waited in silence until Eva returned from the kitchen.

"Do you mind if I smoke?" the lieutenant asked.

"Not at all. My husband, Manny, smoked the brand of cigars there in the humidor. Peter likes them, too," she said, smiling.

Peter and the lieutenant lit up, the panatella for Peter, the meerschaum for Pasing.

Pasing ran his hand through his thinning, white hair, seeming to form his thoughts before beginning. "I'm not certain we should be questioning you, Mrs. Stein. And I apologize for the intrusion here this morning. We have to have information. Anything you might know that can help us."

"I'm grateful something's being done. I'll help in any way I can, but I'm afraid we know no more than you. We're dumbfounded. Shocked. I haven't slept since Thursday. I've asked my friend, Dr. Danieli, to come tonight to give me a sedative. I'm usually pretty strong—but this! . . ."

"Losing sleep gives a person plenty of time to think," Pasing said, draining his cup. "How well do you know Walter Prince?"

"Very well. We had drinks at the Plaza last evening, and dinner at Patsy's."

"What did you talk about?"

"We commiserated about the deaths of François Charron and Petrov. And I filled him in on the changes to be made in the Gala."

"Did he seem nervous?"

"Well, yes he did. But he had just gotten off a plane from San Francisco, rushing like crazy to make our appointment."

Eva watched Pasing and Peter exchange glances.

"You were very close to Walter Prince at one time, I believe."

"Yes, I loved him very much." She looked to Peter, but his eyes were on his coffee cup. "It took me a long time to get over him, if one ever does get over something so intense.

I've never really forgiven him for sabotaging one of my shows. He got himself in trouble with the police in San Francisco. There was nothing I could do. He's a great tenor. As for his rating as a considerate human being: unprincipled, feckless, and cruel."

"I would say those were my findings also," Pasing said.

"I think you're being too harsh," Peter said. "Walter Prince is capable of many things—of deceits, but not murder."

"No, of course, not murder," Eva said. "He's a very weak man."

"Did you know Sergei Petrov?" Pasing asked Eva.

"Only by reputation."

"Charron?"

"No."

"Are you Jewish, Mrs. Stein?"

"No, but what's that got to do with anything? My husband was. Half the people in New York City are." Her voice rose.

"Just a question. I'm groping. No problem. Ever hear the name David bar Ephraim?"

"No, I don't think so. It's an Israeli . . . a Jewish name."

"Right. And he's linked up in the fight against anti-Semitism."

"That's not an ignoble cause, lieutenant."

"These people are playing tough these days. The JDL, I mean. I just thought you might have met David bar Ephraim at some time or another. He backs some Broadway shows. Throws some money around."

"Then why don't you arrest him, if he's done something wrong?"

"He's never done anything wrong, Mrs. Stein. We have nothing on him except hearsay, and not much of that."

"What does David bar Ephraim have to do with the deaths of Petrov and Charron?" Eva asked.

"Only Petrov. The JDL claims the hit; I don't know why."

"Could it have been a mistake, or perhaps some kind of paranoia about the Russians?" Peter asked.

"No mistake," Pasing said quickly. He rose and walked to the door, matter of factly glancing left and right, and returned to the living room. "Do you speak Italian, Mrs. Stein?"

"Yes."

"I may need you to interpret for me later. Not one person at Mamma Guardino's speaks good English. How is that? And that son of hers. Wet spaghetti. What's his name? Oh, yes." He laughed. "Everybody calls him Sonny. I'll bet that place goes to the dogs when he takes over." He paused to stare at Eva. "I forgot. You weren't there when Charron died. You missed the crazies."

Pasing stood facing the painting over the couch, appreciation in his look. "Mrs. Stein, I compliment you on your Monet. I've seen it in books. I didn't know it existed in a private collection. I won't even ask if it is the original. I'm sure it wouldn't be here if it weren't."

Eva felt the mood lift, the air clear. "How clever of you to know that, lieutenant! Are you a collector?"

"Hardly. Not on a detective's salary. But I do know the difference between a Manet and a Monet, a Watteau and a David. My wife and I love art. We love to listen to opera, too. 'You're just like your dad,' she tells me. He collected Caruso records. I'm pretty sure the chief chose me for this job because he knows I like opera. Just can't afford to go."

"You find whoever killed Charron and Petrov, and you will sit in my box, gratis, for as long as I'm general manager," Peter said.

Pasing crossed to the windows overlooking Fifth Avenue, his back to Eva and Peter. "I've been thinking about the operas you're presenting at the Gala."

"Excerpts," Peter corrected. "Acts, or in some cases scenes."

"Right. Scenes," Pasing continued. "In *Tosca*, four people die—a murder, two executions, and a suicide. In one night. That's about on a par with the Twenty-second Precinct over by the Met. Then you have this friend of Romeo—Mercutio—shish-kebabed. Then Romeo slips one under the ribs of the killer, drinks some poison, and Juliet kills herself."

"A colorful way of putting it, lieutenant. But what are you getting at?" Eva asked, somewhat confused at the inspector's sense of the dramatic. His manner—pipe in hand—was that of a professor in front of his class.

"I'm trying to work something out in my mind." Pasing turned to face her, eyes searching. "And, please, let's not let anyone tell us that television and movies show more violence than you do. Every time I turn a page in my opera book, somebody dies. Is it art? There may be other names for it."

"Just one minute, lieutenant," Peter said. "I think you're pressing a little hard. Don't you?"

"It's not finished, Camden. By my calculations, somebody else is due to get killed. Maybe more."

"Impossible," Eva said. "Everyone's guarded now, aren't they?"

"As well as we can," Pasing answered, his voice full of menace.

With her eyes, Eva begged Peter for help. She forced the heels of her hands against her temples. Peter hurried to her side and put his arm around her shoulders.

"You have a headache?" Pasing asked.

"Yes, just beginning."

"I won't keep you. But one last question, please. I think somebody is playing with us. Somebody who knows opera from the inside out. Somebody close to us, with a warped mind and a lot of hate. Who is the most informed person you know?"

Eva spoke without thinking. "Why, Peter, of course."

Lieutenant Pasing laughed. "Let's go, Mr. Camden. We have some more questions to ask. Thank you, Mrs. Stein, for your time and your cooperation."

Scene 7

THE FRENCH WOMAN

SATURDAY, OCTOBER 31, NEW YORK, NEW YORK

Hysterical weeping came from behind a curtain that served to give a modicum of privacy to the small room in the rear of the Madison Avenue boutique known simply as Juliette. The wailing caused the customers to leave, so Mimi Charron's store manager locked the front door and put up the Closed sign, although they had just opened.

Mimi Charron had not slept the entire night. The warmth of love had cooled with the rising sun. It would rekindle, but not until she could be in the arms of Walter Prince again. Mimi had come to the boutique at the request of the New York Police Department. And she wept in the presence of a serious-looking man in a three-piece suit who was filling the cubicle with pipe smoke. Peter Camden stood, immobile, within earshot.

"We were married only a short time," she said.

"Did you hate François Charron?" Pasing asked.

She only cried harder.

"Try to get a hold on yourself. You've got a serious problem here. You see, you're the only person at Mamma Guardino's with any kind of reason to kill him."

"I've had little contact with François over the years. I did not kill him. I always loved his voice. I wanted him to sing on the Gala." She spoke through and around a handkerchief. "C'est horrible, n'est-ce pas? Horrible!"

"Why do you keep his name?"

"Because it is prettier than Dogereau. I am born Dogereau. It is an ugly name."

186

"Why didn't you stay in Paris?"

"I had a lover. A very strong love. I followed him here to New York." The tears were ebbing. "He is a tenor, too. Much different from François. He is big. A Texan. I worship him."

Pasing didn't need to ask who the tenor was.

In her pert, vivacious way, Mimi had made all the advances to the Texas tenor, and she had found this tall man more than willing. She was starving. He was food.

She remembered, too, the rebuff she had encountered when she turned up at his New York apartment one month after his Paris engagement ended. She forged ahead that night, asking him into the hallway, since the woman seated ever so seductively on the white couch in a state of semi-undress, was obviously ready to ignite, and extracted a promise that they would rendezvous on the Metropolitan Opera spring tour, which began the next day.

She followed him to Boston to hear his Cavaradossi in *Tosca* and made her way into his suite at the Copley Plaza Hotel. They made love in Atlanta, Memphis, and Dallas, Minneapolis, Detroit, and Cleveland.

The tour ended back in New York when the trees in Central Park were in bloom. But Mimi found her romance had wilted. He locked her out of his apartment and out of his life. They had gotten back together last summer. For how long? Unimportant. One night with Walter Prince was better than a hundred nights with anyone else. She was obsessed with her Texan.

Pasing broke her reverie. "Did François have any other women that you know of . . . aside from Jacquelyn de la Ville, I mean?"

"*Oui*, there was one. François always spoke of Madeleine Sauvet. I never saw her. It was a love from his youth. She was never out of his thoughts. He loved her very much, but he betrayed her. He was young. They were both young. I felt he would have done anything to have had her back when he had matured, but it was too late. He said she was Jewish, and that she had been a nonperson of the war. François was not a bad man. He was a weak man."

"Are you Jewish?"

"Yes."

"Was he?"

"No."

"Thank you, Miss Charron," Pasing said.

Not five minutes after the inspector left, Mimi Charron received a phone call.

"Oui, mon cher, c'est moi. . . . C'est formidable! Non, il n'est pas ici, maintenant. . . . Ce n'est pas possible . . . A bientôt." Mimi blew a kiss into the mouthpiece, threw a black fox fur jacket around her shoulders, and hurried down Madison Avenue.

Scene 8

THE HUNGARIAN WOMAN

SATURDAY, OCTOBER 31, NEW YORK, NEW YORK

Pasing had left the Plymouth in a loading zone. Although to all disinterested passersby the car was unmarked, to a traffic cop the NYPD license would tell the story.

"You must be aware of a pattern by now," Pasing said as they drove up Park Avenue. "Thirty-three years of policing and a degree in criminology and psychology tells me Walter

Prince is behind these killings with motivation, cause, and personal gain. I know it bothers you a lot, but try to look at it logically. He's heading for a fall in any case. He can't continue this Casanova scenario much longer without someone catching on to him—husband or brother. In a word, he's a congenital shit, Mr. Camden."

Pasing had called the husband of Katarina Tomassy-Conrad to suggest that the four of them meet as soon as possible to discuss the death of François Charron, since both Felix and Katarina had been at the restaurant. They were admitted by the doorman at the Sixty-ninth Street entrance and announced through the house phone. The inspector and Peter were greeted at the door by the couple Pasing had met only momentarily on Thursday night.

Pasing had heard that the theater world, television, and the movies were reserved for the beautiful people, but added as of that moment the world of opera. Katarina Conrad was strikingly beautiful, with long yellow tresses down the back of a long yellow dressing gown. Felix was handsome in a carefully groomed Brooks Brothers manner. And, thinking back, Mimi Charron was one of the most beautiful women he had ever met, regardless of her sorrowful façade.

They were ushered into a lavish salon, where Peter had been often. It looked like a room in a museum. It was at least sixty feet long, with a marble fireplace centered on one wall, a Bechstein grand piano at one end, and walls lined with paintings. Pasing recognized a Picasso. In one corner was a huge glass case, which, according to a brief explanation by the host, held the finest collection of Celtic art objects outside of Europe.

"I asked Mr. Camden to come along," Pasing announced. Wasting no time with idle conversation, he went on.

"Mrs. Conrad, have you ever been to Russia?" She's as cool as the Charron woman is hysterical; opposite side of the coin, he thought.

"I've been to Russia many times," she said.

"You contacted the Russian ministry and the State Department in Washington to obtain a visa for Sergei. You had no trouble at all doing that. Do you know people in politics, the Russians?"

"I'm the only one on the committee who speaks or understands Russian. I was the obvious candidate to do the job."

"Had you ever met Petrov?"

"No."

"What do you know about him?"

"She doesn't know any more than the rest of us," said Felix Conrad. "We know him from his records like everyone else in the United States. We were looking forward to this Gala, as a chance to hear him and allow other opera lovers to hear him. Why do you ask about Petrov? I thought we were going to try to explain Charron's death."

"I didn't come here to talk exclusively about Charron. Petrov was executed by the Jewish Defense League. A brutal killing. It took us a long time to get an identity. It was a warning, my friends. Someone is trying to call our attention to the fact that anti-Semitism still exists. The JDL does not kill at random, as some of our current terrorists do. No, they're saying that just below the surface of our democratic society Jews are being victimized—whether it be in politics, the arts, business. And they're going to continue to protect and police their own. You, Mr. and Mrs. Conrad, are in a position to know what is going on. Especially you, Mrs. Conrad, because you were the only one to talk to Sergei Petrov in New York City. What did he tell you?"

"He told her nothing!" Felix Conrad raised his voice. "It's a stupid question. We have no knowledge concerning this act. If Petrov was a Jew hater, it has nothing to do with us. And we certainly know less about Charron. My God, it was enough of a blow to us, seeing him lying there like a rag doll."

"He's right," Peter said. "This is getting out of hand."

Pasing considered. The computer readout had revealed Katarina Tomassy, the daughter of a Hungarian Communist, to be a high-level political suspect. It told her educational background and her recent professional accomplishments but left a five-year void. What had she done in those years? Pasing ached to know.

"I'm not here to bully you. The questions are pertinent. The answers must be valid. Do either of you know any of the other tenors in the Gala?"

"Only by reputation," Katarina said.

"Walter Prince?"

"No." The lie was obvious to Peter, who knew Walter Prince had been to their home on numerous occasions.

"Maybe you didn't know Petrov personally, but I'll wager someone you know knows him. Think about it. I've got time."

"I've told you all I know about Sergei Petrov," she said quietly. "A great tenor of the Bolshoi Opera. I'm sad to have known him for such a brief time. We have nothing more to say about this terrible deed."

Mr. and Mrs. Felix Conrad rose as one and walked across the museum to the entryway, signaling emphatically the end of the inquisition. Katarina's piercing gaze cut through Peter, condemning him for his lack of support. Lieutenant Pasing and Peter followed them.

"These two killings stink," Pasing said suddenly. "It's not over, and I think you're both involved. You've got motives. Not so simple, these motives, but they're there. I've got a pretty good history on you, Mrs. Conrad. I'll want you to explain what you were doing between 1968 and 1973. Let's not discuss it now. I'll get back to you."

Felix Conrad slammed the heavy door behind them.

Scene 9

THE GENERAL MANAGER

SATURDAY, OCTOBER 31, NEW YORK, NEW YORK

A throng of some two hundred standees had congregated in the lobby of the Met as Peter entered. The noise of the acrimonious deliberation threatened the continuance of the performance of *Tannhäuser* in the auditorium. The angry debate and discourse was over the declaration made on a display placard next to the box office: NO STANDING-ROOM TICKETS UNTIL FURTHER NOTICE. The sign had been placed there before the matinee performance at Peter's instruction.

"Ladies and gentlemen, please," Peter shouted above the bedlam. Some of the debate lessened. "I'm Peter Camden, the general manager of the Metropolitan." Silence. Peter continued in a more moderate tone: "I ordered the standing room closed until further notice because of the uncontrolled, disruptive display at the performance of *Aida* last evening. It cannot happen in the Metropolitan Opera House. I will not allow it. We are here to listen to great performances of the operatic masterworks in elegance and tranquillity. The Met is not a place for political rallies. After the Gala tomorrow night, I will meet with any spokesman you delegate to discuss a solution. There is nothing more I care to say or do now. So, please let me pass."

I don't think I can take any more crises, Peter thought, as Hilda entered his office, carrying a tray with a paper cup of orange juice, a cellophane-wrapped tuna-fish-on-whole-wheat-bread sandwich, and a cellophane-wrapped cardboard container of Jell-O. Under her arm was a clipboard.

"The canteen is jammed today," she said. "We have

192

chorus and extra chorus for the *Tannhäuser*. The orchestra, cast, dancers, ushers. I hope they have enough food stocked."

"Why don't we do smaller operas, Hilda? Tell you what. Let's do a Mozart cycle. Small casts and orchestra. Balance the budget and keep the canteen as it is."

In the few minutes Peter had been in his office, he had suffused the air with cigar smoke. And his countenance was the same dingy gray. He took the paper cup of orange juice to the bar niche, poured two fingers of vodka into it, and returned to devour his sandwich.

"You don't look too well," Hilda said.

"Correct. I'm not well. My stomach hurts. My mind hurts. And it's only the middle of the day. I've been with Lieutenant Pasing all morning. He's been bulldozing his way through the Gala committee, using the techniques he acquired on the narcotics and vice squad in San Francisco. Mimi Charron is in a state of hysteria over her former husband's death, aided by the lieutenant's driving interrogation. He has Felix Conrad ready to sue, if that's possible. Eva's home and sanity were invaded this morning. I'm next to the edge, so I'll just fortify." This last sentence an explanation as he downed the adulterated orange juice.

"Hilda, please write a note to Mimi Charron thanking her for agreeing to pay for shipping François' body back to Paris. The Met should take care of it under the circumstances, but I appreciate her offer and respect her feelings. I've been in touch with the Russian embassy with help from Katarina Conrad, and I've agreed that we'll handle the expenses for the return of Sergei Petrov to his family."

Peter was finding it increasingly difficult to speak. "Did you have anything to do with the seating arrangement for Charron's party? Or was that all Tony Garbatini's plan?" he asked.

"Tony did everything."

"Who sat nearest to François? Do you remember?"

"Yes. Mr. and Mrs. Conrad sat directly across the table from him."

Peter rose abruptly, turning his back on Hilda. She left, closing the door behind her.

His mind seemed suddenly acute, and he spoke to Pasing mentally. Lieutenant Pasing, I totally disapprove of your methods, and I think you are completely wrong. In my life I've never witnessed a greater affront. You coerced those people into deliberate lies. You knew the answers, and you made fools of them. How dishonest can you be? You've gained nothing of value. Under your civilized exterior, the face you showed to them is a Grand Inquisitor right out of *Don Carlos.* You said you needed my help. You could just as easily arrest me. I'm sure I'm as guilty as Walter Prince. What a stupid, far-fetched idea! I've got to hide Walter until the Gala, even if it means I go to jail. Think, damn it! What do I do now?

Peter replaced the vodka he had consumed, half filling the paper cup, and spoke aloud. "I don't mean to alarm you unnecessarily, Peter, but your Gala is not on yet. And I don't think, Mr. General Manager, you can count on Lieutenant Pasing to be of any real help, either by finding the killer or by just leaving you alone. You are going to have to do it yourself." His voice was strong. Stentorian.

At the wall cabinet to the right of his desk, Peter found the dossier on Horst Ludwig, who by now should have arrived at JFK from Munich. Turning to allow the light from the windows on the south side of the room to clearly illumine the words, he thought, Can I protect this man, too? Can I do it alone? Where do I start? He read:

Horst Ludwig
Debut—1973—Walther von Stolzing in *Die Meistersinger*

AGE GIVEN AT DEBUT: 33 (born 1940)
ROLES PERFORMED AT THE MET: Siegmund, Siegfried in

Götterdämmerung, Lohengrin, Parsifal, Walther von
Stolzing

REMARKS: Outstanding heldentenor. Belligerent to colleagues, especially conductors and stage directors.
Intolerant of American politics. Homosexual.

Who might want him dead? Peter asked himself. The
unfortunate answer: Any number of people.

Scene 10

THE GERMAN

DECEMBER 1964, MUNICH, GERMANY

Christmas Eve found Hans Schober, the director of one of
the three government-approved theatrical agencies in Munich, and his assistant in the agency, Monika Sonderling,
leaving the National Theater close to midnight. They had
just sat through the last act of *Carmen*, sung in German. The
performance had not had one redeeming moment.

"We're going someplace where we can get blind drunk,"
Hans mumbled to Monika. "I won't allow my psyche to be
dragged down any lower." He ambled down a narrow street
leading toward the Marienplatz, Monika following. "Thank
God I don't represent any of them. They're a disgrace to
the art."

They slushed through the snow past a couple hugging
each other against the cold. Hans stopped and sang a few bars

of "Stille Nacht, Heilige Nacht" just outside the church of Saint Michael of the Angels. And then, feeling numb, they stepped inside a *Nachtlocale* called Die Pflaume. There were two bars and a hundred or so small booths, clustered in helter-skelter fashion, benches, and stools. There was a small dance floor and a tiny bandstand. The din was ear-splitting.

Hans ordered two pint steins of Pschorrbräu as a spotlight came up on a young man costumed in black shirt and trousers with a red scarf knotted around his neck. His hair was the same white-blond color as Monika's, but twice as long. The group behind him played a few chords and he broke into "Volare." The crowd was with him. What had been bedlam became reverence. Then the entertainer put the microphone aside and went on to sing "Dein ist mein ganzes Herz" to an ovation.

"What a sound!" Hans shouted above the roar. "Am I hearing right? Is that heldentenor material or am I crazy?"

"Pure gold!" Monika exclaimed. "I'll find out his name and whether he has a manager. That's a young Siegmund-Siegfried, if I ever heard one."

His name was Horst Ludwig. Hans signed him to an exclusive management contract, and bookings fell upon Horst like rain. With well-timed publicity, a world concert tour, and a recording of Wagner arias, he became Germany's reigning heldentenor within three years.

Shortly after his return from his tour of the United States, he and Monika were married. She had announced she was pregnant. Their entire relationship had consisted of a flirtation, coy on her part, shallow on his until he invited her to go to the Traum disco just a few streets from Schober's agency.

Horst had little recollection of the night of shimmering, undulating colored lights, and bodies in the disco. Joints were passed from hand to mouth to hand again, and the music surged and ebbed. Horst was moving to the persistent beat, ensnared in the rhythm, tottering delicately on the rim of consciousness. He remembered the smiling face of Monika

196

Sonderling, moving, disappearing, returning to guide him through the labyrinth of night. There was one moment of nightmare, fractional lucidity, when he screamed her name: "Monika, wife of Satan!" and fell, spiraling, into a well of infinity.

Horst and Monika had a brief civil wedding at the *Rathaus* near the *Hofbräuhaus* where they had met. The wedding took thirty minutes and the honeymoon one night at the Hotel Vierjahreszeiten, close to the National Theater.

"You bitch!" he whispered over the rim of his beer stein, as they sat in the hotel bar.

Monika stared at him, confused, not certain of what she had heard.

"You trapped me, you bitch. You will not have that baby. It's not mine."

"It is yours. And you married me," Monika stuttered, ashamed, looking to see if any of the other people in the bar had heard Horst's accusation. "I didn't trap you. I love you."

"Donkey shit!"

"I'm going to the room, Horst. You stay here and vomit."

"You brood mare! Go to your bed by yourself. I'll never be drunk enough again to fuck you."

Monika waited in her room the entire night. Horst never came. The next morning she went back to her small apartment in Sankt Georgenstrasse, near Hans Schober's agency, and waited some more.

When Horst didn't arrive, Monika went back to work at the agency. Hans was in touch with Horst to confirm bookings, but he would not discuss the situation with Monika. She fought back her grief and prepared for the arrival of her baby— Horst's child.

Monika was in her seventh month, still working. There was no word from Horst, although she knew he was singing all over Germany. She felt she had to see him, plead with him to acknowledge and love this wonderful being growing within. He can't be that unfeeling, she thought.

The calendar on Hans Schober's desk read: "December 1, 1967. Meet Horst, Schloss Rosenburg, Starnbergersee, 1900." Monika decided she would be there, too.

It was called a castle, this thirty-room estate, but it had been built as a hunting lodge by the prince of Orléans some hundred years earlier. It was the same today as in the nineteenth century, except for one striking addition: there, directly in front of the large portal, dominating the lawn, was a swimming pool—empty except for dirty snow and leaves—built in the shape of a swastika. Monika's mouth fell open. She felt as if she would faint.

There were automobiles parked at odd angles on the lawn in the snow, on the gravel driveway, and further up on the main road, called Bergstrasse. Monika could see activity through the windows as she approached the front door. She did not have to knock. The door was open, despite the freezing weather. She went inside.

Monika knew practically everyone there. A man grasped her by the shoulders and lifted her off the floor to kiss her on the mouth, breath pungent from many steins of beer and Jägermeister schnapps. "*Liebchen,*" he roared. "*Willkommen.*" It was the resonant voice of a bass-baritone client of Hans Schober, Odin Herzog. She had always wondered where he lived, what his life style was. Now she knew. He lived like a prince in a vast hunting lodge, big enough to be called a *Schloss*, with a swastika-shaped swimming pool, a Nazi flag—new—draped over one entire wall, and a picture—all too familiar—of Adolf Hitler above the fireplace. Candles in wrought-iron candelabrums were placed in every corner of the entry room, dining room, and salon on the ground floor. There were black candles in sconces on every wall, generating eerie light.

Odin's lady friend, Heidelinde, was a singer also, but much younger than her helden bass-baritone lover. She, too, was a Schober artist.

Monika greeted a baritone from the Munich National

Theater who, along with his soprano wife, had become world-famous from recordings. A tenor on Schober's list, who sang the Wagner repertoire in second-line houses, brought her a beer and a line of conversation.

"Since when does your office book American singers first, above the regulars?" he asked. "I can understand if Horst Ludwig or young Kollo gets to sing the new Köln *Lohengrin*, but Edward Carmichael? Who did that? You or Herr Schober? That part belonged to me. That production was designed for me. If I don't get to Herr Schober first, tell him I won't stay with an agency that doesn't go by the rules. No outsiders."

Monika had no answer for him. She looked about the room. The party was moving upstairs.

The crowd proceeded to the third floor, where there was a meeting or party room that stretched the length of the hunting lodge. The open staircase became quite steep. Monika's legs, with the added weight of her pregnancy, were wobbly. She thought she might fall, so she held firmly to the banister.

Long tables lined the walls on all sides, and each was covered with food, beer, and wine. There was no particular seating arrangement. Monika sat between a bass from Bonn and a stage director from Augsburg who was also a business acquaintance. In the far corner, Hans Schober at his side, sat her heldentenor husband—stone drunk.

Horst was unable to see her, but Hans Schober did, crossed the room, kissed her on both cheeks, and explained. "I never would have asked you here, Monika. This is no place for you. Horst is in a bad way psychologically, and seeing you here won't help. Please go."

"I have to see my husband," she said. "I'm carrying his child, and I don't know if I can survive without some help, some sympathy or love from him. What kind of man is he?"

"Very well. I'll try to get you to him," Hans said.

He started to lead her through the crowd, when Odin Herzog entered, followed by two men—physical equals to the towering bass-baritone. Alone, she returned to her chair. Hans hurried back to Horst. All three wore brown shirts, black riding pants, black leather boots, and black armbands with the Nazi swastika emblazoned in red. Their left wrists were bound together by a black cord. As they reached the center of the room, they snapped to attention, heels cracking together like the discharge of a carbine, right arms jerked to a rigid salute.

"*Heil, Hitler!*"

Over one hundred people in the room rose to their feet. "*Heil Hitler!*" came the chorus. Monika could not stand. She pressed her hands over her stomach and forced herself not to scream. Hans pulled Horst to his feet and was holding his right hand aloft in the salute.

"God help me," Monika prayed aloud.

"In the name of the chancellor, we in this gathering pledge: Loyalty forever."

"Loyalty forever," repeated the still-standing throng.

"We will renew our strength through our solidarity."

The followers repeated the pledge.

"There will be no intruders: Jew, Turk, Arab, Negro, American, British, French—no nonbeliever."

". . . no nonbeliever."

"We will rise again," Odin roared.

". . . rise again."

And they sang—all those Mozartean, Wagnerian, Straussian voices—as one. They sang "Das Heimatland," and Monika saw tears flow from Odin's eyes.

"*Heil, Hitler,*" he shouted, frenzied, as the last notes ricocheted off the timbered walls.

Monika felt as if she were part of a silent movie. She saw Heidelinde Schneider, Odin's lady friend, approach her, screaming obscenities. She heard: "How dare you come here? You vile bitch!" Monika sensed her right arm being raised in the Nazi salute. A soprano, wife of the baritone from Munich's National Theater, seized her left arm and pulled her to her feet.

"*Heil, Hitler. Sieg, heil!*" she screamed. "Say it."

All around her others were staring. The bass from Bonn, the stage director from Augsburg. Monika wrenched her arm free and fled. She could not move fast enough in her condition. Heidelinde intercepted her, grasped her hair from behind, spun her around, and slapped her open hand across Monika's mouth. Completely off balance, she was hurled backward down the steep flight of stairs to the second floor below. Horst, with vacuous eyes, saw nothing from his slumped position in the corner.

Hans Schober carried the comatose Monika to his Mercedes and drove like a demon down one of Adolf Hitler's famed autobahns into the Grünewald section of Munich. There, at the Krankenhaus Sankt Ursula, Monika lost her child.

Broken mentally and physically, Monika lay in her hospital bed long past the time for her to leave. The first two weeks, Hans came every day to visit, then less frequently, and finally, after a month of her self-inflicted convalescence, not at all. Monika had not spoken a word since the accident.

A week after *Sylvesterabend*, January 8, 1968, Monika visited an attorney and sued Horst Ludwig for divorce. She received one-half million *Deutschemark*. Her attorney had no difficulty obtaining her settlement. "The information . . . to which you are privy is sufficient to secure anything you require," he assured her. "However, it would be my suggestion that you leave Germany. Go to America, perhaps. It is safe there. But go quickly."

Hans succeeded in building Horst Ludwig into a national idol. Horst was assured that he could sing in Germany in whatever opera he chose, whenever he wanted. Hans held back. He booked Horst everywhere but Bayreuth so Horst would be fully prepared when the time came.

It came. *Siegfried* in a new production in the season of 1973—July and August.

Strangely, in March 1973, an unforeseen pattern began in Horst's behavior. He was missing for days without any explanation to Hans. He asked to be released from all contracts until Bayreuth. Hans was disturbed. He blamed himself for the heavy schedule he had mapped for Horst. He blamed the *Fön*—the atmospheric pressure known to Munich, Salzburg, and many areas in close proximity to the Alps, which causes euphoria, memory lapse, heart attacks, and numerous forms of irregular behavior. He blamed everything except Horst. By May, Hans decided he had better keep closer tabs on Horst, discover the real reason for his behavior.

Hans waited at the National Theater until Horst finished the private coaching session for the role of Siegfried with the *répétiteur* Klaus Berman. He saw him leave by the stage entrance, so he followed, as quickly as he could without being seen.

Horst took a taxi in front of the Vierjahreszeiten Hotel. Hans took the next one. They raced north into the Schwabing district. The taxi ahead discharged Horst at the corner of Leopoldstrasse and Martiusstrasse. Hans himself was alighting when he saw Horst disappear into the apartment block on Martiusstrasse. He followed.

Hans disliked this mission, but he resigned himself to it. The elevator floor indicator read: 3. He waited five minutes before climbing the stairs to the third floor. If he was discovered, he had decided to confess that he was, in fact, spying. He did not bargain for, nor was he prepared for, what he discovered.

"*Gott in Himmel, Heinrich, Ich kann nicht. Lieber, Du bist zu gross!*" The familiar tenor voice came from the door opposite the stairwell, one of three doors on the floor.

"*Ach, Heinrich, nocheinmal. Ja, nocheinmal. Gott, oh, Gott!*" The tone was childlike, blubbering, unheroic.

There followed the most confusing mixture of animal grunting, sobs, and inhuman wails. Hans could envision the act of sodomy being performed on Siegfried. The love struggle continued.

"*Ich liebe dich!*" the heldentenor shrieked.

Hans walked down the stairs. The distance between them grew, but the sound in his ears did not diminish. It rang out in increasing cacophony, infamous. Hans trudged down Martiusstrasse, hands jammed into his coat pockets, head bent.

None of us can help you now, Horst. You are damned forever!

Scene 11

THE ISRAELI

SATURDAY, OCTOBER 31, NEW YORK, NEW YORK

"Target two has arrived," the guarded voice said over the wire. His rehearsal is on C-level stage at the Met at five o'clock. His hotel is the Pierre. Are you prepared? Did you give him the money?"

David bar Ephraim smiled, flipped open a datebook, jotted down the information. "This is the big one, isn't it?" he asked, not expecting an answer. "Yes, I've contacted the man, not one of us, but sympathetic. He has all kinds of motivation—as you said—a fanatic. Nothing to worry about. Read the papers, my darling." He hung up on the faint voice and put in a call to the Ansonia Hotel.

"I'd like to speak with Frederick Horne, if you please," he said.

Scene 12

THE GENERAL MANAGER

SATURDAY, OCTOBER 31, NEW YORK, NEW YORK

Hilda hurried to Peter as he entered the executive suite. "I'm glad you're back," she said.

"I was just checking around the house. I don't know what I'm looking for, but the atmosphere is really dreary. So's the performance."

"Horst Ludwig has arrived. The car met him at Kennedy, bringing him directly here for his rehearsal. Maestro Martinson has taken him to the greenroom to discuss the cuts and to run over the music with him. His traveling companion, Mr. Heinrich Gerstmann, is with them. And Walter Prince, who had a run-through of the *Cavalleria* with piano in the Orchestra Room at two o'clock, is waiting for you in your office."

"Would you get Eva Stein on your phone before I see Prince?"

Seated in Hilda's office with the door closed, Peter spoke to Eva.

"Sorry to disturb you, but we have to move fast. Can you hide Walter Prince in your apartment until after the Gala?"

"Why, yes . . . certainly. Why?"

"Because Lieutenant Pasing wants to arrest him. He thinks Walter's behind the killings. He thinks he's responsible, along with Mimi, for Charron's death. And he thinks Walter had something to do with Petrov, eliminating most of the big tenor competition for the Gala or anywhere else."

"That's the most preposterous thing I've ever heard! What kind of inspector is he?"

"Walter has the motivation, Pasing feels. And, since he's

204

in charge of this case, he assures me he can book Walter and cancel the Gala. Walter's the prime suspect, Eva, and I'm almost ready to cut my wrists."

"Then send him over to my apartment right away. He can have the guest bedroom downstairs. You, Peter, had better call the Met attorneys to get some kind of restraining order on Lieutenant Pasing until after the Gala. We've got to have Walter Prince, no matter what. Without him we'd have to cancel."

"God, Eva, I love you. You're the best support a man could want. Actually, I'd rather send Walter to a hotel, and come to you myself."

Eva laughed. "You charming man. You read my mind. But first things first. Have Billy the Kid get over here as fast as he can, even though we may all be in jail tomorrow for obstruction of justice. The Gala will go on."

Peter entered his office, where Walter Prince grasped his shoulders in lean, hard hands. "Boss, you look like hell! Last time I saw you you were just kinda frail-lookin'. But now you look like John the Baptist, just scrambled up outta the cistern."

"Hello, Walter. Welcome back to Happy Hollow. There's far too much insanity around here. Maybe some of your kind of humor can change the atmosphere." Peter flopped on the couch. "I'd like to chat with you and I'd like to offer you a drink, but you're in trouble and you probably don't even know how or why. There's an inspector assigned to the case. Name's Pasing. You don't know him, but he knows you. He ran you in, in some kind of drug bust in San Francisco in 1968. And when he found you were one of the participants in the same Gala as Charron and Petrov, he began to build a case with you as the number one suspect. He wants to arrest you, but without you there's no Gala. I've asked Eva to let you stay in her apartment until after the performance tomorrow night. I'll let the lawyers go to work on Lieutenant Pasing. I don't think he can close the doors on us. Also, he'd have a lot of people down on his neck, including one district judge, who just happens to be a board member."

Prince's face had gone pale. "Ho-ly shit! That's the most amaz—"

Peter cut him off. "If it'll make you feel any better, you're not alone. Pasing thinks you and Mimi Charron are in this together. Isn't that something?"

"Who the hell is Mimi Charron?" Walter asked. "Call Eva. Tell her I'm on my way."

He left. Peter flipped on the in-house speaker system as Tannhäuser dramatized his pilgrimage to Holy Rome. He lay back on the green velvet couch and closed his eyes, letting the music wash over him.

Scene 13

THE GERMAN

SATURDAY, OCTOBER 31, NEW YORK, NEW YORK

Murderous red. Blood. Blinding red. Hate, madness, frenzied red. Insanity. Vengeance. Loathing.

Freddie Horne lashed out with his weapon. The long, sharp, lethal barber's shears had magically leapt into his hand from the makeup tray on the table.

Checkerboard lights tore at his head. The shears—his holy sword, the spear of Wotan—slashed the cheek of the hairless sloth who stood in the way of his assault. The path clear, he thrust into the object of his hate, the pure-white hero. The blades penetrated, driven by superhuman force, into the neck at the base of the skull, to strike the brain. Hold firm your weapon, Hagen; the sword hilt is already covered with red. Red fire spewed from the hero's ear, eye, nose; bubbles came black from the sacred throat.

Only the finger holes of the scissors were visible at the base of Horst's skull.

In a move, the giant Heinrich Gerstmann had Freddie's head in the vise of his massive forearms and in slow motion forced him to his knees. With his own knee in Freddie's back, Heinrich twisted the singer's neck until it snapped with the crack of a bullwhip. Released, Freddie fell like a puppet when the strings are cut. He lay staring out of vacant eyes at the bloodied carpet. He had felt nothing. Freddie's mind had been dead before Heinrich reached him. Hate had killed it.

Heinrich Gerstmann, Horst's companion and lover, rushed from the tenor's dressing room as fast as his bulk would permit.

In the wig and makeup room across the corridor from the principal tenor's dressing room, Paolo Palmieri, the bearded head of the makeup department, was lighting a last Benson and Hedges. He tossed the gold-and-green box in the waste-basket, hoping he hadn't smoked the whole pack during that one afternoon—that one *Tannhäuser* performance. Sitting in the barber's chair, which served for special wig fittings—the perfect place for a nap between matinee and evening perfor-mances—he propped one foot on the makeup desk. He found the smoke irritating and removed his glasses to rub his eyes.

The artists' dressing-room area had just cleared with the departure of Marta Nader, the Elisabeth of the afternoon, followed admiringly by an entourage of friends and hangers-on. She does have class, Paolo mused. And I'll bet I'm the only one around here who knows her cunt hair doesn't match that famous shock of red-orange. He laughed out loud. She had often let her dressing gown fall open for him when he was supposed to be concentrating on her makeup.

Paolo was only half aware that he heard someone enter the S-8 dressing room. He caught a sibilant *s* from the one and only Freddie Horne, better known as Queen Elizabeth the Third. There had been some muffled conversation when the door closed. Paolo continued to take his break.

It was the only quiet time on Saturday. One half hour between the time the dressing rooms cleared and the arrival of the first of the evening's players. Tonight Enzo Baroni would be coming in early to allow Paolo sufficient time to fashion his masterpiece—the face of the singing teacher and cleverest con man in opera literature, Don Basilio.

Paolo was jolted out of his reverie by a cry of rage heard through the door to dressing room S-8. Then, before he could settle back in his chair, a commotion began. He went into the corridor to listen. The argument started at a high pitch, but amazingly, to Paolo, it crescendoed. Loud healthy operatic voices, trying to top each other. He recognized the resonant baritone of Horne, the tenor of Horst Ludwig.

The tenor said: "I don't want to hear any of your sad, pathetic tales. You can come to Munich, but the door is closed. I'm not about to stick my neck out for you, for old time's sake or any reason. You suck, faggot. Get out."

Paolo couldn't understand all of the argument, and part of the shouting was in German. But the shouts were obviously those of fury. Only at the moment of impact did Paolo sense the presence of anyone else in the corridor. Heinrich Gerstmann hurled him aside and wrenched open the door to the dressing room. Paolo, prone on the carpet, could not see inside the room, but the agonized hate, put into sound, shook him to his toes. Then there was nothing. Silence. Paolo rose to his knees, and, suddenly, the bald giant lurched from the room and rushed down the hallway toward the loading-dock exit.

Paolo rose to his feet, made his way to the house phone on an end table just inches away from the dressing-room door, and dialed the switchboard.

"Doris, get Camden down to the artists' dressing-room area right now. Emergency. Dressing room S-8."

Paolo waited for the general manager, who came with a security guard in his wake.

"My God in heaven!" Peter Camden said. "Not again."

Paolo entered the room to stand beside his boss. The hair on his neck prickled. Breath escaped his mouth in a rasp as he tried to speak and swallow at the same time. His consciousness was shattered. It was horror in a cinematic display—unimaginable in real life. Paolo's knees went to rubber. He reeled into the hallway, hands over his eyes, closing out the sight of death. His boss stood, staring at the barbarity.

Peter backed away from the hideous sight, out the door, reaching for the house phone. Controlling the panic in his voice, he told Doris of the horror, asking her to alert security, the police—and, if possible, to find Lieutenant Pasing and bring him to the dressing room.

Two security guards were first on the scene. In minutes, two New York City policemen were there as well. Ten minutes later, Lieutenant Pasing arrived. He had stationed himself in the Grand Foyer to watch the departure of the matinee audience. His men were looking for Walter Prince. No Prince. No Mimi Charron. No nothing. Again he had been at the wrong place at the wrong time. It was not at all like him. He hated to admit he was confused. Impotent.

Pasing sent a police photographer on his way to the lab, dispatched Heinrich Gerstmann, who had been found by two NYPD cops sitting on a bench in adjacent Damrosch Park, head in hands, to the Tombs. He sent the two corpses by way of the Roosevelt Hospital ambulance service to the morgue across town at Bellevue. He cleared the area of stagehands, commanded the door to S-8 to be locked. The lieutenant heard Paolo's story, writing it down in a looseleaf pocket-sized notebook.

"Oh, Mr. Camden!" said Doris, having deserted the switchboard to more closely view the activity. "That huge man, the one with no hair—Maestro Martinson spoke to him. They spoke German. I think he was an acquaintance of Horst Ludwig. His name was Gerstmann. He was waiting for the rehearsal of *Götterdämmerung* to be over. I wouldn't let him go back here to the dressing rooms, but Maestro said it was perfectly all right, and the guard buzzed him through the door. I guess now it wasn't all right, but they were all friends."

"They're all friends, for sure. Now two more of the friends are dead. Just one big happy family," Pasing said, following Peter Camden, who was fleeing through the black-and-yellow-striped double door leading to the stage.

The third-act *Tannhäuser* set, depicting the valley of Wartburg in medieval Europe, had been struck and stored on C-level. The house of Dr. Bartolo in Seville, with the fountain in front and Rosina's tiny wrought-iron balcony jutting above it, had been erected for the evening performance of the *Barber of Seville*. Peter hurried across the set on the way to his office.

Pasing addressed his retreating figure. "Talk to me a second." Peter, caught in midstride, was in front of the mock fountain. He sat down on it with a thump. Pasing sat beside him. They stared straight ahead at the closed curtain.

"Is this the drop that cracks the crystal? Or the straw that breaks the camel's back?" Peter asked.

"Both. The Gala has to be canceled," Pasing said, not trying to soften the announcement. "If you go on, there will be another dead tenor tomorrow."

"Perhaps all of them."

"No. Corsini has to be protected from Walter Prince."

"You don't mean that!" Peter blurted out, incredulous. "After what just happened? Walter had nothing to do with that. That's another kind of insanity." Peter tried to rise. Pasing grasped his arm, detaining him.

"Where is he?"

"I don't know."

"I think you do, but I'm not going to press you just now. This madness can't be allowed to continue. I don't want to see any more dead bodies. It's a plan to stop your Gala, so stop it before you're very, very sorry."

Peter didn't speak. He stared.

Pasing rose to go. "My men at the Mayflower Hotel are on an around-the-clock surveillance of Corsini. He's been in his room all day, had one visitor. Dr. Alberto Danieli came to see him twice." He stared at Peter. "Prince had Charron killed. Don't hide him."

Scene 14

THE GENERAL MANAGER

SATURDAY, OCTOBER 31, NEW YORK, NEW YORK

Peter eased onto his office couch, holding a full glass of Scotch. His soul was sick. His aching eyelids screwed tightly closed, blocking out all but the hateful scene he had just witnessed. It was burned onto the retina of his mind—never to fade or lose color. He thought: I knew this was bound to happen. If I had trusted my instincts, my perception, I could surely have prevented those two from ever being alone. It was there in the pattern. Freddie Horne was programmed to kill Horst Ludwig, just as Hagen killed Siegfried with a cowardly stab in the back. They had just finished rehearsing that very scene on C-level. Who could plan such a thing?

Peter took a long pull on his drink, feeling the burning all the way down.

Petrov had been executed . . . like Cavaradossi. And Charron had been poisoned . . . like Roméo. Then Ludwig was stabbed . . . like Siegfried, Peter reasoned.

Oh, God! I could have stopped them. I waited too long.

The intercom phone buzzed. "Yes, Lennie?" he said, trying to calm his senses along with his voice. "Please tell the gentleman at the *Times* that the Gala will certainly happen . . . tomorrow night, as planned. Tell him I am in an important meeting, but that everything is under control and, that as morose as we feel here at the Met over the horror of the past week, the show must go on. And then go home, Lennie."

"Christ in heaven!" Peter said aloud to his now empty tumbler. "Why don't you have another drink before you throw up all your pomposity and your self-pity?" He went to the bar and refilled his glass.

"O.K., what are the options? What are the alternatives? Number one: I'll see Pasing in hell before I'll cancel my Gala. But what are the ramifications? Walter Prince, who is a patent liar, has all but slammed the door of his jail cell. I don't know what I can do for him after the Gala. Perhaps the attorneys can fend off Pasing until Monday—especially, if Walter can't be found until he sings. And, if Pasing is correct, Walter has implicated Mimi. God, what a mess!"

Peter lifted the telephone receiver from the desk console, dialed Eva Stein's number.

"May I speak with Mrs. Stein?" Peter asked of the man who answered the phone. "Ah, Doctor Danieli, it's good to talk with you again. She's asleep? Oh, you gave her a sedative. Is she all right? . . . Thank God! Yes, I know you were with Renato yesterday and today . . . I see . . . You're sure the sore throat isn't serious? . . . I know he canceled his final rehearsal. You were the Corsini family doctor in Spoleto? That's very interesting . . . Then you know him well . . . His father, too, of course . . . and our Francesca Zandonai? You *do* have a personal interest in this Gala. Yes, I'm sure he'll be in glorious voice tomorrow night. Please, doctor, a favor . . . Could you make certain Renato gets to the theater tomorrow? I'll send a car for you both. Thank you for everything. With you helping, I won't worry . . . Please tell Mrs. Stein I called . . . Rest is what we all need. *Si, ci vediamo!* . . . Oh, Doctor Danieli. Did Walter Prince get there all right? . . . What? . . . He hasn't arrived? . . . Did he call? My God!" Peter hung up.

Scene 15

THE AUSTRIAN WOMAN

SATURDAY, OCTOBER 31, NEW YORK, NEW YORK

Dr. Alberto Danieli replaced the receiver in its cradle on Eva Stein's desk, and returned to the wing chair facing it. Eva placed a bell of Cognac in his hand, dropped in a twist of lemon, and sat opposite him. The desk lamp was the only illumination in the study.

"*Grazie, Alberto.* I have nothing more to say to Peter Camden. And I can't abide his whining."

"It's almost over, Margarita. François is dead."

"And Sergei Petrov."

"You didn't know Petrov. François was personal."

"They are all personal," Eva said. "Petrov knew my sister

213

Eugenia, sang with her at the Bolshoi. Then he destroyed her career and her life. For what? For his own career. There was a brief mention in a Moscow newspaper of drugs being discovered in Eugenia Mischetsky's dressing room. The Bolshoi released her, and she disappeared. I have tried for years to find out something, anything. Then a tenor here in New York, who got out of Russia, assured me it was Sergei Petrov who found the drugs. With other inquiries, I discovered Petrov had secured his future at the Bolshoi by helping the party keep Jews and other undesirables out of the opera."

"*Cara Margarita*, you have suffered so much pain. And you have given so much love." The dwarflike doctor crossed to take Eva's hand, pressed her fingers to his lips. "I remember, as if it were yesterday, when you came to Spoleto, into Gian Carlo's life. You made him content. He loved you very much."

"And I loved him. He was so good to me, so kind. Then Renato killed him. It tore my heart out."

"I know, *cara Margarita*. I know."

"You're my oldest, my only true friend, Alberto. How I cherish our friendship."

"You'll always be like a daughter to me. Always Margarita. Never Eva Stein."

"I've taken many names. Before I was Margarita I was Madeleine Sauvet, a poor, beaten little girl. For a brief time I had a chance for a life, for love. But I gave myself for nothing. My love was betrayed by a naïve boy, who threw me away because he thought I was a Jew, and a soiled woman. François, like Petrov, deserved to die. He had been allowed to live with his dishonor long enough."

The phone rang. Eva signaled Dr. Danieli to answer. He said, "Hello." And he listened. He hung up.

"Horst Ludwig is dead."

"Monika Sonderling is revenged! He killed my child. He killed me. At long last, the monster is dead. I, Monika Sonderling, am revenged!"

Dr. Danieli crossed himself, returned to his chair, and stared at the floor.

Eva's eyes were cold, her tone modulated and reserved. "Tomorrow night will be the end. The whole world will watch my final justice. Walter Prince will die at the hands of his lover's husband. Onstage, in full view, Alfio di Giulio will carve out his heart. Walter Prince above all. It is rustic chivalry, you reprehensible bastard!"

Eva refilled Dr. Danieli's empty glass as if nothing she had said had affected her emotionally.

"Peter Camden believes this Gala to be his invention. How wrong he is. It is mine. It has been since the beginning."

"What about Renato?" Dr. Danieli asked.

"He dies, even as he lives. Every day he suffers the guilt of his father's death. He'll go mad. Or take his own life, as Otello does. Let him sing and go home to Spoleto to the scene of all his infamy."

Dr. Danieli finished his Cognac and rose to leave.

"I'd better give you your injection now. I have to go home. I've decided to go away soon."

"Back to Spoleto?"

"Farther."

He filled a syringe from a bottle in his case, located a vein in Eva's forearm, and injected the liquid. He placed a cotton ball over the barely visible aperture, packed and closed his case. "That should get you through tomorrow night," he said.

"*Grazie mille, Alberto. Addio.*"

Scene 16

THE GENERAL MANAGER

SATURDAY, OCTOBER 31, NEW YORK, NEW YORK

The first act of the *Barber of Seville* had just concluded. Peter turned off the house speaker. He was well into his pint bottle of Scotch. Hilda and Lennie and the rest of the office staff had gone home, leaving him officially "on duty" in case of an emergency. "What emergency?" he asked in halfhearted, half-sober jocularity. Peter was seriously contemplating one of the couches as a receptacle for his aching body and head, when the door was pushed open.

"I won't come in, Peter," a voice said. "I have to tell you something, but you mustn't reveal my identity."

The outer-office area of the executive suite was pitch-black, and the presence of someone in that darkness made the gooseflesh rise all over his body. He squinted into the void.

"Neither Felix nor I had anything to do with Petrov's death. You must believe that, Peter."

"Come in, Katarina. There's no one else here."

"No. Felix and I have guests in our box this evening. I must get back. He doesn't know I'm here."

"Do you have something to do with the government, the CIA, as Lieutenant Pasing suggests?"

"Yes, Peter, I do. But that's not why I came."

"Whatever you want to confide in me stops here. Trust me."

"I didn't recognize it in time, and I should have told you yesterday, but I saw who killed François Charron. It was the doctor. The one who looks like Toulouse-Lautrec."

"My God in heaven!" he groaned. "Danieli!" But Katarina had gone.

216

I believe you, Katarina, Peter thought. And I believe Walter Prince and Mimi are innocent. And I believe my alcohol-influenced brain is beginning to work again. You are blind. Right in front of your eyes is the answer. How simple! How clear! The elusive Russian connection! Process of elimination?

Peter made his way to the elevator, which would take him to B-level and the Met's archives, the knowledge that he was on to something hurrying his pace. "Total eclipse," he mumbled to himself. "No sun, no moon. All dark amidst the blaze of noon." Samson was blinded by a woman. Oedipus blinded himself for a woman. Always a woman.

The sliding door of the elevator at B-level revealed two locked doors. Peter inserted a master key in the lock, which turned easily and allowed him entrance into opera history. The L-shaped room with the costumes belonging to Caruso and Scotti, Martinelli and Tibbett, Ponselle, Bori, Pons, and Albanese was to the left. The files with personal contracts and private letters, the shelves of books and memorabilia, were to the right. The archives, the creation of Mrs. John DeWitt Peltz, was today the domain of Robert Tuggle, who wore a shortish beard and moustache to go with his dedicated, authoritative mien.

Peter went straight to the shelves behind Tuggle's desk, not about to unlock any file or drawer marked PERSONAL or PRIVATE. Standing at the shelves, he opened the book furthest to the left on the top shelf, not bothering to look at its title or author. He was probing for one name: Mischetsky. *Victor Book of Operas*. Nothing. *Covent Garden Royal Opera Annals*. Nothing. *Opera in Concert in New York*. Nothing. On and on he delved. Index to the m's. There were dozens of books, with and without pictures, cataloguing the performances of opera at the Met and elsewhere since Peri invented the art form some three centuries ago.

He found it! Eugenia Mischetsky: pages 17, 37, 71, 72, 107. The book was the *Annals of the Bolshoi*—Moscow, 1950–

1975, translated for English-speaking opera lovers by Katarina Tomassy-Conrad. It was a relatively new book, similar to Francis Robinson's painstakingly prepared histories of the Met. On page 107, Peter looked at a picture of Eugenia Mischetsky, costumed as the tragic Lisa in Tchaikovsky's *Pique Dame*. She could have been the twin sister of Eva instead of her junior by seven or eight years. She was in the ardent embrace of Ghermann, her soldier lover in the opera. Peter recognized immediately the operatic lover holding Eugenia Mischetsky-Stein. The Ghermann was Sergei Petrov. Peter closed the book, his heart pounding a hole in his chest. He practically ran back to his office.

Barging through his office door, he ran headlong into Jill, who was standing in the middle of the room awaiting his return. He took her in his arms, holding her, as if she might vanish. Impulsively, he kissed her forehead, her cheeks, her neck, her lips. He could not let her go. He needed her warmth, her compassion. He needed Jill more than he ever had.

"Well, that's some kind of a greeting. The real Peter Camden has come back. Do that again," Jill said, laughing.

"Jill, Jill. What a fool I've been. What an absolute, senseless fool. I'm so glad you're here."

"I couldn't stay away. God, what you must be going through! Oh, my darling, what terrible catastrophes! I want to help, to be beside you. I don't know how you've made it through these last two days."

"Is that all it's been? Two days since the maelstrom began?"

Peter was not yet ready to reveal his findings even to Jill.

"This I promise you," he said. "Eva Stein is no longer a part of my life. That is the past, an unfortunate mistake. I love you, and only you, and ask . . . that you try to forgive me."

Jill kissed him warmly, lovingly, held him close. "I'll work on it," she said.

Scene 17

THE GENERAL MANAGER

SATURDAY, OCTOBER 31, NEW YORK, NEW YORK

It was midnight. Jill sat at one end of the couch in Peter's study, a glass of Cognac in one hand, a cigarette in the other, and her feet in Peter's lap. Both had on pale green terrycloth robes, and both were slightly flushed from making love.

"Do you know," Jill said, "I don't think we really have to talk to justify our love, or to prove anything. What we just proved is that what we had is better now. Maybe it took a psychic jolt to bring us to our senses."

"I love you, Jill. I should be on my knees, begging forgiveness," Peter said.

"Nonsense! You haven't lost me. And I'm not going to give you up."

The phone rang. "I'd better take it. I left a message for Pasing. It's probably he." Peter picked up on the fourth ring, and listened.

"Yes, I can get over there," he said. "Probably in half an hour. Downstairs in the lobby. . . . No, lieutenant, I can't tell you my source. I'll be there."

In the bedroom, Jill had already found a pair of corduroy slacks, a sweater, and an old leather jacket for Peter. He dressed quickly, keeping his eyes on Jill, who lounged provocatively on the bed, her auburn hair spread out over the pillow, and her long shapely legs crossed, showing alabaster thigh. Peter wanted her badly. He smiled. She knew what he wanted to say before he said it.

"I'll be back as soon as I can. We're meeting at Danieli's apartment."

"I'll be waiting," Jill said.

A cold rain was slicing down. Peter raced across to the north side of Seventy-second Street. Fortunately, a yellow cab was cruising by. He hailed it, giving the 47 Sutton Place South address. At his destination Pasing and another man were waiting inside the revolving glass door.

"Camden, this is Sergeant Reynolds. He's been looking for Walter Prince all day. No luck, so I asked him to come over here with me." Peter and the sergeant shook hands. The doorman came hurrying across the lobby.

"I knocked on his door," the doorman said. "There's no answer, but Dr. Danieli's Labrador is yowling something fierce."

"I think you'd better let us in that apartment now."

"Yes, lieutenant. I have the key right here."

The doorman led them to the back elevator of the East River tower. They rode up to the twenty-first floor, and the doorman let them into the apartment. In a glance, Peter's eyes took in the living room: Windows to the East River. White grand piano—Chickering (redone)—backed by an ornate bookcase with a glass front containing black leather-bound opera scores. Two facing white couches and oval white coffee table on curlicue gold-antiqued legs. Several white chairs in conversational arrangement. Paintings lined the walls. And a thick white carpet, running wall-to-wall in the living room and stretching to all the rooms.

Only someone with a dark-stained side would strive so diligently to live in so pure an environment, Peter thought.

"In here, Camden," said Pasing, having found the master bedroom.

Peter stood at the foot of the bed next to a whimpering, white Labrador. Dr. Alberto Danieli lay in ashen repose, dressed in a white pajama top, his hands folded across his stomach, over a spotless white sheet. On the nightstand was a white telephone, a syringe, and a typewritten note:

Protegga il giusto cielo,
Il zelo del mio cor.
Per te, con grande amore,
Mia figlia, Margarita.

Alberto

"Would you translate that for us?" Pasing asked, handing the note to Peter.

Peter read: " 'May just heaven protect the zeal of my heart. For you, with great love, my daughter, Margarita.' And it's signed Alberto." Peter paused, searching his mind for meaning. Who is Margarita? he asked himself. What does this have to do with Charron? For whom did Alberto give his soul and his life?

"What's it mean?" Pasing asked.

"I wish I knew. It's from *Don Giovanni*, a quote. It's called the 'Vengeance Trio.' Donna Anna, Donna Elvira, and Don Ottavio pray for justice for the killing of Donna Anna's father by Giovanni."

"Do you know any of these people?" Pasing asked. The lieutenant had dispatched the doorman and the sergeant to call for help, and he was standing at a large table covered with framed photos of all sizes.

"Yes, I know many. They are obviously his clients and friends. Here's Renato Corsini, Zandonai, Lombardini, Poggi, Pobbe, Cioni, Colzani, et cetera. And here is our Walter Prince."

Peter handed the photo of Prince to Pasing, who held it in both hands as if he had unearthed a precious relic on an archaeological dig. It was an ordinary publicity head-shot, as were almost all of the photos on the table. Almost! Peter's gaze held. Quickly turning to see if the inspector had witnessed his discovery, but certain he was too preoccupied with the knowledge that Prince was a client of the doctor, and thus

221

even more suspect, he placed himself between the photo table and the lieutenant.

He leaned closer. The photo was not a professional shot. It was a black-and-white eight-by-five snapshot, picturing a white-haired man flanked by an easily recognizable young Renato Corsini and a well-proportioned equally young woman with fair hair, standing on the steps of a church or a cathedral.

The inscription, in a constricted, self-conscious hand, read: *Mia Famiglia—Renato, Signor Gian Carlo, and Margarita. Spoleto 1956.*

Peter slipped the small photo, frame and all, inside his leather jacket and started for the door. "I'm leaving, lieutenant, if you don't need me anymore. I've had about all I can take."

"Right. I'll be busy here for a while. If you talk to Prince, tell him not to leave town."

Dr. Alberto Danieli was a complex man, Peter noted. His was the fathomless love of father for daughter, whether tied together by blood or not, that enabled him to poison François Charron for Margarita. To him it was justified paternal sacrifice. It was still not clear to Peter why Margarita wanted François Charron dead, but what was vividly clear was that the Margarita in the picture—fair hair or not—was Eva Stein.

Finale

Un bacio, un bacio ancora, un altro bacio!
(A kiss, again a kiss, another kiss!)

—*Otello*
    Giuseppe Verdi and Arrigo Boito

Gala

Sunday Evening, November 1, 8:00–11:00

Conductor: *Randolph Martinson*
Director: *Jonathan Jeffries*
Lighting: *Gil Wexford*

I

LARGO   G. F. HÄNDEL

II
A Tribute. *Peter Camden*

III
OVERTURE to *TANNHÄUSER*   RICHARD WAGNER

IV
TOSCA (Act III)   GIACOMO PUCCINI

Tosca . . *Angelina Lombardini*
Mario Cavaradossi . . *Walter Prince*

INTERMISSION

V
OTELLO (Act IV)   GIUSEPPE VERDI
Otello . . *Renato Corsini*
Desdemona . . *Francesca Zandonai*
Emilia . . *Shirley Love*
Iago . . *Sherrill Milnes*
Lodovico . . *Paul Plishka*
Cassio . . *William Lewis*
Montano . . *John Darrencamp*

INTERMISSION

225

CAVALLERIA RUSTICANA   PIETRO MASCAGNI

(Intermezzo and Finale)
Turiddu . . *Walter Prince*
Alfio . . *Richard Clark*
Mamma Lucia . . *Batyah ben David*
Lola . . *Ariel Bybee*

Gala

The setting sun lost its battle with the heavy cloud cover, presaging weather for the *Gala* analogous to the existing mood backstage at the Met and in Peter Camden's office. Peter stared from his office window into the settling shadows of Damrosch Park below him, the scaly bandshell looking like the dorsal fin of a sea monster cleaving the dark waves of trees. Behind him in the room, Lieutenant Pasing occupied his desk, perusing the dossiers of Walter Prince and Renato Corsini. His dormant meerschaum and exanimate expression clearly indicated his own disheartenment.

"I can't shake it, no matter how hard I try," Pasing said, breaking a long silence. "The killing should be over. The JDL claims Petrov. Danieli poisoned Charron—if your source is correct. Ludwig and Horne are dead, and we've got Heinrich Gerstmann behind bars. The commissioner is perfectly satisfied with the outcome. I can't keep Prince from singing, but

I still think he's behind this. I've got a gnawing inside of me that won't quit."

"That makes two of us," Peter said. And for different reasons, he thought. Dr. Danieli killed himself, closing the door on a wealth of information. I told Pasing that the doctor had poisoned Charron, but is that really the truth? I have only Katarina Tomassy-Conrad's word. Now it doesn't matter. There will be no need for proof. My God, what a dunce I am! I could have prevented Danieli's suicide if I had followed up on the information. I can't let it happen again. And I don't dare reveal to Pasing my discovery. For the moment, Eva Stein is my secret. I have to wait, anticipate her next move. If Pasing knew she was the Margarita in the photo, he would begin to piece her story together, as I have, and probably scare her off. In which case, she would go free, because he doesn't have a shred of evidence to suspect her—let alone convict her.

"You found Walter Prince," Pasing said. "Where was he?"

"I didn't find him. He called me at home this morning. He spent the night at the Westbury Hotel. Mimi Charron's with him."

Pasing growled, "Well, that's safety in numbers. I'm not happy with that, Camden. It's obstruction of justice. Did you tell him I'm looking for him?"

"Of course, but that didn't help his anxiety. He's certain he's next. I don't know how to assure him he isn't in danger."

"Did you tell him we have the answer to the Charron killing?"

"Yes. But he says he's got other worries. I'm not sure what he meant."

"You can bet I'll keep an eye on him tonight."

The knock on the door preceded Jill's arrival with their two daughters, Janet and Jackie. Dressed in a black-and-white, strapless Bill Blass original, Jill brightened the atmosphere

227

considerably. The evening gown was two years old, but had been worn only once or twice before. With her red hair worn long to the shoulders, and a sapphire necklace at her throat to match her eyes, she was ravishing. Peter was proud of her. Pasing stood and was introduced to Janet and Jackie, who had arrived home at noon from Bosford and regaled Peter with prep-school gossip and lore until he left for the Met at four o'clock.

"Give me five minutes to get into my tails, and we'll face the music," Peter said, retiring to an anterior dressing room down the hall to change into his formal attire for the evening, which was to begin with a pre-opera dinner on the Grand Tier at six o'clock. There would be supper and dancing at midnight.

Peter had asked his personnel to start final preparations for the Gala at two o'clock, so rehearsal-department and in-house staff had made certain the myriad tasks leading to the performance were accomplished. Stagehands and artists would be arriving now. Peter gauged that the *Tosca* Act III set, having been used in some thirty or forty performances and rehearsals, would require less than half an hour to assemble. He was proud of the precision with which opera was produced at the Met. When in motion, it was a smoothly functioning machine, unlike most European houses—especially in Italy and France—and challenged only by the San Francisco Opera.

On the Grand Tier, the "show must go on" atmosphere was palpable—there was no wake here. Elbow to elbow, the rich and the very rich shouldered their way to and from the open bar.

The security guards had given up trying to watch for unwanted guests. All that glittered this evening at the Met was twenty-one-carat and up. Every great dress designer was represented, and every East Side beauty salon. Celebrities from all areas of the arts and show business were much in evidence. The security people were busy watching them.

Danny Kaye, in velvet tux, was seen with his beautiful wife on his arm. Tony Randall, opera aficionado extraordinare, was talking opera with José Ferrer. Zinka Milanov, Licia Albanese, Bidù Sayão, and Rose Bampton, four fabulous divas, were seated at the same table. And Sir Rudolf Bing entered amid applause, kissed each proferred hand, and, ignoring place cards, seated himself at the main banquet-sized table in the far northeast corner of the Grand Tier next to Jill. He sat in William Rockefeller's assigned seat. Schuyler Chapin, another distinguished former general manager of the Met, who took the helm after the untimely death of Goeran Gentele, and piloted the Metropolitan vessel through rough waters, beamed his way through the throng with his equally popular wife, Betty, on his arm. They sat next to Bing.

Peter Camden, standing beside Jill, praised the board of directors, the cast, the crew—who were naturally not present—and the committee for the Gala. Mimi Charron and Katarina and Felix Conrad were seated at the table directly across from Peter. Randolph Martinson and Eva Stein were not present.

The famous Chagall murals looking down on the multitude seemed more striking than ever, the colors more vivid. Peter knew that Sir Rudolf Bing felt that these murals were his proudest legacy to the Met; it had been his idea to engage his friend to commit his superlative talent to their creation.

But Peter could not concentrate on or enjoy the festivities. With all the noise and frivolity, Peter thought, it's as if the horror of the past days never happened. In all conversations, reference to the heinous acts was never made. The Gala went on.

"Darling," Peter said to Jill, "I'm going to have to miss the dinner. I have to meet Pasing backstage. We've got a lot to do before the performance. Please do the honors here, and I'll meet you and the girls in the box."

Jill nodded her assent and kissed him on the cheek. He

rose, shook hands with Sir Rudolf, Schuyler Chapin, and Felix Conrad, and made his way out of the throng to the orchestra level and backstage.

The soprano Angelina Lombardini, holding the receiver, listened to the shielded, secretive voice: "Where's your husband?"

"I don't know," the soprano said.

"*Dov' è vostro marito?*" the voice insisted.

"*Milano, naturalmente. A casa in Milano.*" Angelina knew nothing. She presumed her husband had gone back to Milan. She was too frightened to think otherwise.

The caller rang off without further questions.

On an ordinary evening, Walter Prince would get to the theater early, unannounced, to do his prep, which consisted of a good fifteen or twenty minutes of vocalises on the second floor out of earshot of other artists. Part of this was courtesy, part privacy. Then the makeup and costume, and, with dressing room cleared, a quiet review of the score to refresh his memory.

Tonight was different. Camden had ordered an historical happening. Photographers would record it. Thousands of eyes would remember it accurately and inaccurately for decades, perhaps centuries.

Wearing white tie and tails, emerging from a burgundy Mercedes, Walter was ushered into the artists' area, where at least twenty flashbulbs ruined his vision. He was led, literally blinded, to his dressing room. Fortunately, he had found his voice in the shower an hour ago. Walter quickly donned his familiar Cavaradossi trousers, jacket, and Wellington boots, designed for him and stored upstairs for use when needed. He noticed the label with his name sewn inside the coat collar, and remembered his debut as Narraboth in *Salome*, in a production brought over from the old Met, when he had been wrapped into an oversized, musty, decades-old tunic that held a label indicating it had belonged to the great Tamagno. Then there were the high platform boots, that debut night, which read "Svanholm" on the soles and increased Walter's height from six feet two to six feet six. Svanholm had been a short man, and the boots were made especially for him.

Wonder what tenor will inherit my boots? he thought. That's immortality!

Peter Camden poked his head through the open door. "Give 'em hell," he said, wringing Walter's hand in his strong, congenial manner. "We're all grateful to you for stepping in this way for Petrov. We'll all toast you afterwards." He closed the door.

The mention of Petrov's name made Walter's stomach turn over. Jesus Christ! he thought. All I need is to be reminded what a sittin' duck I am.

Walter tried a pianissimo phrase of the aria "E lucevan le stelle" and then crossed to Angelina Lombardini's dressing room. He pushed her door open.

"Come in," Angelina called. "Oh, it's you." She kissed him on the mouth. "Why didn't you fly back with me from San Francisco?"

"You know damn well why! Where the hell is that maniac husband of yours?"

"He disappeared, Walter. He probably went home to Milan. Don't worry," she purred. "Some woman called me today, asking where he was. She sounded anxious."

"What? Who was she?" Again his insides churned. He shrugged it off.

"I don't know. She hung up before I could ask. But, Walter," Angelina said coaxingly, pressing herself against him. "Just sing and tonight I will come to you. Why don't you love me?"

"I do, diva," he said, as he locked both his hands behind her and squeezed her pelvis hard against his. She emitted a piping squeal and pulled away.

"*Piu tardi*, for sure. Now we sing, *si?*"

"Now we sing, diva."

Behind the stage manager's desk on stage right, Peter Camden waited to go before the great golden curtain to welcome the Gala audience and to ask them to stand while the orchestra played Händel's "Largo" in memory of the three tenors and one bass-baritone who had died that week. Peter was in turmoil. He stood with his handkerchief pressed to his eyes, as much to shut out the light as to absorb the perspiration. A cloud of doom hung over the Metropolitan Opera.

Peter saw Lieutenant Pasing, observing the No Smoking sign, chewing on the stem of his meerschaum.

"O.K., Mr. Camden." It was the cue from one of the stage managers, Chris. Chris would call all the curtain and light cues. Stanley, the other stage manager, would second him by making certain the singers, supers, and chorus were on the spot on time, every time. They were an efficient pair.

Peter stepped before the curtain. There was applause. He spoke solemnly: "Let us bow our heads in silent prayer for the immortal souls of those who have departed from us this past week, as Maestro Martinson leads the orchestra in Händel's 'Largo.' It was another tenor—gone from us now, who made the melody of the 'Largo' known to all of us in song—Enrico Caruso. The tenor voice. May it ever inspire us, thrill us with its clarion ring."

The Gala had begun.

The Metropolitan Opera Orchestra played the inspiring overture to *Tannhäuser*, and then, after a few minutes' pause, began the beautiful opening of the third act of *Tosca*. The curtain went up on the Castel Sant'Angelo rising above the river Tiber in nineteenth-century Rome. Walter Prince, as the Bonapartist Cavaradossi, awaiting his execution, writes a farewell letter to his beloved Floria Tosca.

Walter sang the aria better than he had ever sung it. He concentrated on revealing the pain and despair of the lonely painter at the end of his life. There was no self-pity, only resignation and love. The applause and cheers at the end of the aria helped to allay his apprehension of the audience's feeling toward him. They had forgotten that Petrov was supposed to have sung.

The act went smoothly. Angelina, supreme, soared on the high B-flat before her leap from the parapet following his execution. The house erupted around them as he took her hand, leading her before the curtain to accept the thunderous accolades. Angelina threw her arms around Walter and kissed him to shouts of *"Bravi!"* and *"Bis!"*

Peter breathed more easily. He had checked every musket the firing squad used in the mock execution and commanded a surly stagehand to add two extra mattresses for Angelina to land on when she leapt to her death.

Eva, whose party had occupied the parterre box next to that of the general manager, flew into Walter's dressing room, looking beautiful in a tight-fitting, floor-length black silk sheath, more radiant than he had ever seen her.

"Walter, I'm so proud of you. It's such a success. Everyone loves it. God, Walter, such excitement!" She kissed him on both cheeks. "I was so worried about you when you didn't show up at my apartment last night. Where did you go?"

"Thought I'd hole up in a hotel. Camden's seein' ghosts. Ain't gonna be no more killin'. That's over," he said, forcing the false bravura.

"I know. No more tragedy. Just happiness. O.K.?"

"O.K.," he said.

"This is going to be a night we'll never forget," Eva said, exiting, then turned back to him to say, "I'm going to watch the *Otello* scene from the wings. Want to join me?"

233

"Good idea. I promise I won't be jealous of Corsini. Not tonight. I'll change my costume, get a cup of coffee, and meet you there."

Renato's hand over her mouth strangled her cry. He held it there and kicked shut her dressing-room door. "I got your card." He spoke in quiet, controlled Italian. "You slut. You've gone too far."

"What card?" She gasped, pulling his hand away. "I don't know what you're talking about." She trembled with the initial fear brought on by his sudden appearance, the hideous contour of hate in his face. "You're out of your mind. I didn't want to see you, sing with you, any more than you did with me. I loved you once. But not now."

Renato forced her slowly to her chair and positioned himself above her. This is not right, she thought. I'm not Desdemona. I'm not his wife, his love. But Otello's hands are on my throat. It is my suffocation. She had no breath left to form a scream.

"You sent the card. I don't believe . . ."

A rap on the door saved her. She wanted to shout her salvation. "Come in," she said, amazingly controlled, pushing her assailant aside. Renato made space between them. "Oh, Peter, darling, I'm happy you're here. Our star is just beginning to get the opening-night jitters. I'm trying to assure him he'll be fabulous."

"I wanted to wish you *toi, toi, toi,* and see if you needed anything, Francesca."

"You're an angel. I adore you, but I've a few things to do before I go on that stage. Maybe you could take charge of Renato. After all, he's the real star of the evening."

Renato Corsini, his temper blacker than the makeup he wore as the Moor, made his way backstage to await his cue.

Seeing Corsini's intensity, Peter decided he was already into the role, and postponed conversation with him until after the act. He acknowledged Lieutenant Pasing, who was still stationed stage right behind the stage manager's desk, making Stan and Chris nervous with his questions. Peter felt better having him nearby.

Peter had checked to make sure Otello's suicidal sword had a blunt edge and a cover of thick adhesive tape. His eyes never left Corsini. He had taken onto himself the awesome task of preventing another death.

Fear began to take the place of the inner prodding. Be calm, Peter told himself. Think! I'm desperately afraid for Renato and for Walter. If the mind that fashioned this scenario—most surely Eva's—functions according to pattern, Otello will take his own life, and Turiddu—the part played by Walter Prince—will die by stabbing. Renato will be forced to commit suicide, and a cuckolded husband will seek sweet revenge on Walter Prince, driving a knife into his heart. Eva is the scorned woman. And Mimi has no husband, so Angelina is the Lola, whose husband will destroy Turiddu—Walter Prince. God help me, Peter prayed.

Francesca Zandonai opened the fourth act of *Otello* with the "Willow Song." Her singing was ethereal, a miracle of sound. She poured forth an arching lyric line that had the audience breathless. Her innocence shone through the gloomy half-light of the castle bedchamber. Her subsequent prayer brought tears to the eyes of many in the audience.

Renato crossed himself, whispered, "Hail, Mary, full of grace. The Lord is with Thee. Blessed art Thou among women and blessed is the fruit of Thy womb, Jesus," and entered the set. There was a shudder throughout the audience. The commanding presence of the Otello, surrounded by the mystique of the personal life of the tenor, generated a ghostly chill. He sang. He questioned Desdemona, his intensity building, his blind jealousy driving him to the inevitable act, the maddened destruction of the one precious life-object he cherished.

The act, brutal, stifling the very air that had given her life, had once lifted her voice, and their spirits, in joyous song. In love. He crushed her with the hands that once had caressed her tender beauty—pale, innocent beauty. Hands that had loved her.

"Niun mi tema," Otello began, despair rising in his throat, as he held his sword before his eyes, guilt like a hangman's rope encircling his neck. "Do not fear me."

Renato's dark, sonorous sound filled the auditorium with glory, tearing at each heart, causing the body to thrill and the eyes to mist. Otello, Moor of Venice, ill-fated warrior. Strong in war, but humbled by man's vile, inhuman jealousy.

As his sword hand moved, he saw her. There, in the light spill from the stage. In the wing stage left. Margarita Secchi! It was surely her. Renato's legs would hardly support him. Otello fell. With the strength left to him, he kissed the lips of his beloved wife, Desdemona. But Margarita was still there, her eyes piercing him, accusing him. *"Un bacio, un altro bacio . . ."*

Every person fortunate enough to be present was on his feet. Men shouted themselves hoarse. They would not stop, could not stop. The applause came like a rainstorm each time Renato took his bows, the decibel level at each call mounting. One of the greatest tenor voices of the century had sung his greatest performance.

Renato, unsmiling, looked as if he would fall. He searched the wing stage left. Margarita had vanished. But the face of Gian Carlo loomed in his vision. The guilt of Otello was still there. It was his own. He could not much longer bear the violent pain gouging his consciousness. The madness was burgeoning.

"Help me, someone," he begged, once inside his dressing room. "O Mary, Mother of God, help me. His face is in front of me. Do something. Go away, Gian Carlo. You are dead! Leave me! Both of you. She was there, too. Margarita Secchi was there, too. Right there on the stage." He was raving. "O my Lord, I have sinned; but I beg forgiveness. *Help me!*" he cried, the tears coursing down his cheeks.

Peter, on his knees beside the prostrate tenor, was the only one who knew what he was talking about. He had seen the photo of Renato, his father, and Eva. Yes, Margarita Secchi had been there, standing next to Walter Prince, watching with well-concealed abhorrence from the wings. Peter thanked God: Renato was still alive. He had escaped.

Standing in the wings with Eva, Walter was too affected to speak. He knew, throughout the scene, that he was witnessing the most touching performance he would ever see. In the relatively short time Renato Corsini was onstage, he had traversed the entire spectrum of emotion, from pain to violence. From tenderness to hate. A never-to-be-forgotten portrayal. Eva had gone back to her guests. Walter remained standing there long after the curtain calls were over.

Peter and Franco, the dresser, helped Renato out of his costume and makeup and out a side door, where his chauffeur was instructed to drive him to the Mayflower. Shaking, but in control, Peter went to his office to join Jill and have a strong Scotch on the rocks. He told Jill that, after intermission, he would hear the *Cavalleria* from backstage. Peter knew now what to look for. Renato Corsini had survived the scene, certainly not in good shape, but physically unharmed.

Lennie Kempenski didn't bother to knock, slamming the door back against the wall. "Mr. Camden," he blurted out. "They caught some man backstage, says he's Angelina Lombardini's husband. One of the security guards tried to get this di Giulio to leave, and he pulled a knife on him. The guard caught him from behind, took the knife away. Lieutenant Pasing's got di Giulio now in dressing room thirty-six, grilling the shit out of him—oh sorry, Mrs. Camden." He sat down on one of the couches, winded.

Peter smiled. "Thank you, Lennie. You've just given me a gift. Come, darling, we'd better get back to our box. The finale is about to begin."

Entering his box, Peter saw that Katarina, Felix, and Mimi were chatting animatedly in the box to Peter's right, obviously caught up in the enthusiasm of the moment. He interrupted, telling them of the news of Alfio di Giulio's arrest. Then, when Eva returned to her box, he leaned over the railing to speak to her.

"Security caught Angelina Lombardini's husband backstage," he told her. "Seems he didn't want to leave the area, and pulled a knife. Pasing has him in custody. I thought you'd like to know. What a night!"

The houselights dimmed, so Peter was not certain what Eva's expression revealed. She didn't answer him, but merely focused her attention on the stage.

God help me, I'm right, he thought, keeping an eye on Eva's silhouette, as the first notes from the orchestra broke the silence. It was the Intermezzo from Mascagni's *Cavalleria Rusticana*, the final segment of the Gala. He waited for Eva to move.

The Intermezzo over, the church emptied of villagers, homeward-bound after the Easter services.

Eva hadn't stirred. She stared at the stage. You're going to have to do it yourself, Eva, Peter said to himself. That's the lover who walked out on you. The others were long in the past. This is the one who hurt you the most. It shows all over you. Make your move.

Walter, as the small-town "dandy" Turiddu, steps onto a table, offering wine and camaraderie to all present in the piazza of the little Sicilian village that Easter Sunday morning. His bright tenor, pealing forth like the bells of the *duomo* behind him, lights up the sky with its sound. He sets a foot firmly on the table, leans back, and looses a high C right on the button, clear and ringing, as the audience across the footlights joins the townspeople onstage in vociferous praise.

What are you waiting for? Peter thought.

The scene continues with the entrance of his girl friend Lola's husband, Alfio, a mule driver, and the inevitable confrontation. Turiddu, spurred on by the wine to foolhardy bravura, and insulted by Alfio's refusal to join them in a glass of wine, challenges Alfio to a knife duel by biting him on the ear, the ultimate Sicilian condescension.

Not much time, Eva. Follow your scenario.

Alfio spits out his acceptance and goes to prepare to fight Turiddu in a field outside of town. Turiddu takes a further pull on the wine flask and calls to Mamma Lucia to help him. There is no turning back at this point or he would be termed the worst sort of coward. He must accept his fate. Win or lose. The wine has made him dizzy, and he turns his thoughts to Santuzza, the girl he had wronged, who carried his child. "Help me, Mamma," he begs: *"Voi dovrete fare."*

As if a veil had been lifted that had obscured his vision, Peter saw the scenario in vivid detail. You've succeeded, Eva, in insulting my intelligence. You've used me in your game, a pitiful dupe. How ingenious to let me think I was responsible for the planning of the Gala. This is an age of great tenors: Pavarotti, Domingo, Vickers, Kraus, Carreras. Why did we choose these five? I was blinded by you. It was you who devised the plan to convene five tenors who in different ways had entered your life, brutalized you, and fled, causing you mortal anguish. Somehow while I feel sorry for you, I can't possibly condone your need for revenge. Is it some kind of wild justice you seek? Well, Eva, the Gala was certainly a glorious opportunity for you.

Centering on Sergei Petrov's well-known anti-Semitism, Eva no doubt had made contact with the JDL, Peter was certain. Perhaps she had funded them, and surely she had provided information and motivation for his execution—he was a political stain that had to be removed. Then more important to her, if my assumptions are correct, Petrov's death avenged the destruction of her sister Eugenia's opera career in Russia. There can be no other explanation for these bizarre coincidences, Peter thought. What did Petrov do to Eugenia Mischetsky?

Why did you have Dr. Danieli poison François Charron? When and where did your paths cross? Since you kept your *other* identity secret, who are you? Margarita Secchi? If so, then how do you plan to kill Renato Corsini? There is no doubt that the white-haired man in the photo was Renato's father. Were you the father's lover, his mistress, his wife? In his note Dr. Danieli had written: "May just heaven protect the zeal of my heart." What sort of unholy collusion did the two of you concoct? Are you the head of a political cell, Eva? No, this has to be your own private vendetta. Danieli killed because he thought of you as a daughter. He wrote in the note: *"Mia figlia."* He must have loved you greatly, and shared your pain. But weren't you clever, having me to your apartment last Thursday evening. You were nowhere near Charron when he died, or were you? I was only with you until about 9:30.

Peter's mind was whirling. But like a child's puzzle, the large pieces were falling together. The exterior, public Eva Stein is specious in the extreme, Peter thought. She sits there: beautiful, contained, ultra-elegant, yet her entire being is underpinned with deceit. She was capable of finding those vulnerable spots in the personality and pride of Freddie Horne in order to prod him into destroying the arrogant Horst Ludwig. I'd swear she bought him, assuring him he would be acting in self-defense. And Freddie was not beyond seeking psychic reward. He would have been easily coerced into bringing down the god-hero, his onetime lover. Was the killing of Ludwig for political reasons, too, as in Petrov's case? Was Horst Ludwig anti-Semitic? Was Charron? Are all these murders because of anti-Semitism? Hatred? In my estimation, the answer is yes!

God knows I've been stupid up to this point, but the next few minutes have to prove me right. What's going on in that convoluted brain of yours? You didn't flinch when I told you Angelina Lombardini's husband had been apprehended backstage. He can no longer carry out your crime. You're truly mad, Eva. Only a revenge-crazed mind would sanction the next step, and you're the only one who knows what it is. *You* have to take the assassin's place. *You* have to plunge the knife into Walter Prince's heart. Isn't that right, Eva? He *has* to die, as he lived: the small-town dandy, who used you and dropped you. Is that enough to kill for? Is it all part of your monstrous scheme? The time has come, Eva. You'll have to end it yourself.

Eva slipped out the door of the parterre box. Peter counted to twenty-five and followed. He didn't see which direction she took, but he knew she must go onto stage left in order to intercept Walter as he exited the set. Peter hurried around the outer corridor, past the reception area. Eva was nowhere to be seen. Eva didn't know the staging of this opera. Peter did.

"Ch'io le avea giurato." Walter was nearing the last few phrases of the aria, and then would run off stage left, ostensibly to die at the hand of Alfio, who waited in the garden.

"Oh God, God," Eva groaned, as she ran back of the stage manager's desk. I'm on the wrong side of the stage! her mind screamed. He can't exit in this direction. How can I get there in time? He must not live. More than all the others, the bastard must die. Soul killer! Monster! I can do it. I have to do it myself. Now! Let the world know his villainy.

She was crying from frustration. He was there across an uncrossable chasm. Sixty feet away. Too far.

She made her way around the back of the scenery, searching for a weapon, anything. On the properties table, probably placed there by the Cassio or the Montano after the *Otello*, lay a sharp pointed dagger. She grasped it to her breast and ran.

She tripped over a thin steel cable, falling, tearing her black silk sheath and the skin of her knees. Her expostulation of air elicited a sharp "Quiet!" from Stanley at his board. She stumbled through the labyrinth of black velour curtain legs that masked the backstage working area from the audience. A nightmare forest. She thought she might be able to cross behind the stage *duomo*. Her pulse was pounding in her temples.

"Oh my God!" The scenery took up every foot of space right up to the steel fire door that separated the playing area downstage from the deep upstage scenery dock. At that moment, access to the stage-right dock was blocked off. She tried the sliding door through the fire curtain, but it was too heavy for her. She screamed to a stagehand to help her. He was about to refuse entry until he saw her panic. He jerked it open. The rear scenery dock was clear. Eva ran as fast as she could, her heart pumping wildly, to the identical door stage left. Walter was just rising to a glorious B-flat. *"S'io non tornassi, fate da madre a Santa."* She could hear him onstage. Thank God the opposite fire door was open. She plunged headlong into the mob of choristers in the wings stage left, fighting her way through the darkness.

"Un bacio, mamma. Addio." Walter was on the final A-flat, and had begun his exit, running toward stage left, when Peter saw Eva, light from the stage glinting off the blade of the dagger held before her. He had placed himself in the shadows ten feet from the latticework archway through which Walter would leave the set. At the exact second Eva threw herself at the onrushing tenor, Peter lunged, deflecting Eva's arm in a downward motion.

The knife lodged in Walter's thigh. Eva and Walter

242

sprawled on the floor from the jarring collision. Eva, recovering, pulled the knife free, and like a wounded animal scrambled to refuge, dragging her injured left leg and brandishing the knife in her right hand. Peter made an effort to stop her, but she swung the blade, missing his face by inches.

The stage was blocked with choristers, the curtain about to fall. Stagehands jammed the exit to the stage door. A wounded Walter Prince, blood seeping through his fingers, as he held his thigh, was between Eva and the dressing-room exit.

Eva dragged herself up what appeared to be the only escape route open to her—the metal stairs to the electricians' grid. Waving the knife wildly, she pulled herself heavily from rung to rung, higher and higher. Peter, keeping a distance, climbed after her. At the third landing, she glared down at Peter, eyes burning like a treed panther.

"You too, you bastard," she screamed. "You're just like the others. You used me, threw me away like garbage. You deserve to die like the rest." She lifted the knife, as if to fling it, then swung out onto the last access ladder, climbing higher to the iron grid, which stretched across the entire proscenium of the stage. Peter approached as far as he thought safe, concentrating on Eva's terrified eyes. She's mad, he thought.

"It's all right, Margarita," he said, as soothingly as possible. "It's all over, dear. Come down now."

"No," she wailed. "Margarita Secchi is dead. Monika Sonderling is dead. Madeleine Sauvet is dead. *They* killed them. *Ich heisse Eva. Nur Eva. Verstehen Sie?* Die, you bastards. Die, as you killed my baby. Die, as you destroyed my life . . . and the love I gave you."

With a keen like a dying animal, she halted on the grid, holding the dagger aloft.

"Hold it right there," boomed the authoritative voice of Lieutenant Pasing, who had climbed to the stage-right side of the grid. Peter, who was moving too, saw Pasing's snub-nosed .45 drawn and pointed directly at Eva.

243

"Don't shoot her," Peter screamed.

At the sound of Peter's voice, an electrician behind Lieutenant Pasing leaned out from the grid and swiveled a high-powered klieg light to bathe Eva in white-hot illumination. Blinded, confused, off-balance, she stumbled to a halt, spun toward Peter, reaching to him for help . . . and she was gone. Tumbling helplessly over the low railing, she plunged four stories to her death—down stage center.

The chorus was standing, as if in an Egyptian frieze, around the broken body. Stricken, Peter, followed by Lieutenant Pasing, slowly retraced his steps down the metal ladder from the electricians' grid to stage level. Every step he took toward her drove a stiletto of pain into his heart. What hopeless tragedy! What grief! The chorus and stagehands in their real-life immobility looked to Peter like the final tableau of any one of many operas. A thoughtful chorister removed his coat and placed it over the bloodied head and shoulders of Eva's body. Peter was thankful for that.

A stagehand had used his belt as a makeshift tourniquet around Walter's upper thigh to stop the bleeding. Another had cut away the costume trouser to douse the wound with antiseptic and bandage it as best he could. Was it fear or fatigue or anger that gave Walter's face a gray-green pallor the light makeup couldn't hide?

"Is that bitch dead?" Walter asked, seeing Peter clear the last step of the electricians' stairs. "She tried to kill me! You saved my life."

Peter winced, paused, and spoke to Artie, a stage boss, who was standing near Walter. "Better see he gets to Roosevelt Hospital to have him checked out. His limo's just outside the stage door."

Pasing was already standing by the body, as the stage managers, Chris and Stanley, quietly dispersed the chorus to their dressing rooms. It was a strangely noiseless exodus.

Peter joined Pasing.

"It's over, lieutenant," Peter said. "Here lies your killer. She's not dangerous now. Her personal phantom died with her. She suffered. All the pain, all the betrayal, all the devastating loss of hope, she bore alone. She couldn't help herself. Her despair was too great."

"Why didn't you tell me it was Eva Stein?" Pasing asked.

"Because I never wanted to believe she was capable of such madness. I couldn't . . . not until the end."

"That's obstruction of justice, Camden."

"You asked me to help you. That made me part and parcel of the investigation. I'm inexperienced, but I don't think we had a case against Eva Stein."

"You're right there. We could have never gotten her to court."

Extending his hand, Peter said, "Justice *has* been done, inspector. Eva was sentenced to a lifetime in hell. Is there a higher price to pay?"

Peter knelt beside her and wept.

Postlude

WIRE STORY

MONDAY, NOVEMBER 23

TENOR DEAD IN ITALY

Renato Corsini, internationally renowned tenor, fell to his death from an ancient viaduct, spanning a three-hundred-foot-deep chasm, leading into the Umbrian city of Spoleto, Italy, yesterday. The son of Italy's foremost automobile tsar, Gian Carlo Corsini, sang his last performance at the highly successful Metropolitan Opera Gala on November 1.

Corsini made his debut at the Metropolitan Opera, after successes throughout the world, at the age of thirty-four, as Otello—a role that would be associated with his name for his entire career. Other roles at the Met were Radames, Manrico, Pollione, and the Calaf.

He was unmarried. There are no living relatives.

Mystery surrounds the accident, since it was from that same promontory that Renato Corsini's father fell to his death twenty-five years ago.